D0208647

LT. PAVEL CHEKOV AND JOHN C. KIRK FACED THE FIRING SQUAD . . .

The Nazi SS man smiled into Chekov's face, his jaw jutting outward in a cocky grin. "Do you have any final words?" asked the SS man.

Chekov smiled, inwardly pleased at his composure during what were undoubtedly his last moments on earth. "Your Führer is going to kill himself, and your precious Reich is going to stand as a symbol of all that's vile," he said evenly.

The Nazi shoved them against the wall and stepped away. Chekov took his place next to Kirk as the American muttered, "Don't worry."

"No?"

"No." Kirk showed the hint of a smile. "I'm working on a plan."

Chekov looked at the firing squad before them, raising their rifles and taking dead aim.

"I can't wait to hear it . . ."

Look for STAR TREK Fiction from Pocket Books

Star Trek: The Original Series

Star Trek: The Next Generation

STAR TREK®

HOME IS THE HUNTER

DANA KRAMER-ROLLS

POCKET BOOKS

New York   London   Toronto   Sydney   Tokyo   Singapore

This book is a work of fiction. Names, characters, places and incidents are either the product of the author's imagination or are used fictitiously. Any resemblance to actual events or locales or persons, living or dead, is entirely coincidental.

The plot and background details of *Home Is the Hunter* are solely the author's interpretation of the universe of STAR TREK and vary in some respects from the universe as created by Gene Roddenberry.

An *Original* Publication of POCKET BOOKS

 POCKET BOOKS, a division of Simon & Schuster 1230 Avenue of the Americas, New York, NY 10020

Copyright © 1990 by Paramount Pictures. All Rights Reserved.

 STAR TREK is a Registered Trademark of Paramount Pictures.

This book is published by Pocket Books, a division of Simon & Schuster, under exclusive license from Paramount Pictures.

All rights reserved, including the right to reproduce this book or portions thereof in any form whatsoever. For information address Pocket Books, 1230 Avenue of the Americas, New York, NY 10020

ISBN: 0-671-66662-2

First Pocket Books printing December 1990

10 9 8 7 6 5 4 3 2 1

POCKET and colophon are registered trademarks of Simon & Schuster.

Printed in the U.S.A.

HOME IS THE HUNTER

Historian's Note

This adventure takes place shortly after the events chronicled in *Star Trek: The Motion Picture*.

Chapter One

SULU AWOKE in the middle of a battle.

He awoke, but didn't open his eyes at first. His mind told him, quite logically, that he could not possibly be where he thought he was. *I'm not really in a battle. I'm not awake yet, I'm still dreaming.*

A clang again, steel on steel, and the kind of shout that demanded attention. Even if this were a dream, he had to see it. Opening his eyes, he peered through the coarse grass and spat out a mouthful of grit.

Yes, ahead there were about a dozen men, or at least there were a lot of waving arms and swinging weapons. *I'm dreaming all right,* Sulu thought, not daring to believe his eyes. Whatever this dream was, it was a good one. "Ballet of death" was an overused phrase, and yet it fit these samurai in the midst of pitched battle.

Sulu leapt to his feet and discovered he was wearing laminar armor. So much the better. He reached for his *katana,* with the assurance of a dreamer that it would be there. It was. He ran, or rather waddled, with the ungainly speed armored men had known for the history of warfare, slashing, cutting, screaming at

1

whatever moved. But he was still too far from the center of the fighting to do much more than lop off some branches of offending trees. He called out a challenge to the nearest soldiers—and in the finest classical Japanese. Yes, this was a super-fine dream. When he woke up, he promised himself to really learn the language of his forebears.

The exertion left him giddy, his thoughts moving like thick mud. He was also sweating and breathless as he took stock of the fight. The adage "fight smart" had been drilled into him too well for him to go tumbling off like this, even in a fantasy battle, although he was beginning to notice that this fantasy was pretty gritty. The cold suspicion that this wasn't a dream flirted with his consciousness, but he told himself that was impossible.

A small column of samurai still held the road some yards ahead. A palanquin sat in the road, defended by four women slashing with *naginatas*. Then the noblewoman stepped from behind the curtains, a small sword in her hands, joining her personal maids in the final assault. The soldiers were fast giving ground to the attackers, who seemed more like a mob of brigands than anything else.

Sulu shook his head. This couldn't be real. It had to be a dream. Besides, a lady was in trouble, he concluded. Sulu belted out his best *kei* and ran hell-bent at the attackers, his sword slashing across a man's chest. The man cried out as he went down, and the warmth of the splattered blood stopped Sulu.

And a warning screamed in Sulu's mind: *It's no dream! You just cut down a human being as if he were kindling!*

Sulu stepped back, reality versus fantasy smashing against his brain. It was real. It couldn't be real. He had been . . . where? Not here. Fleeting recollections of the *Enterprise*, and then there had been a flash . . .

There was an empty space in his mind that he could almost feel, as if it were a physical block.

He was alerted by the furious screams of the others attacking him. The first man was still writhing on the ground. Sulu took a defensive stance and knew he was in trouble. He couldn't kill. He wouldn't . . . except they were clearly not hampered by such constrictions.

The movements came to him as if he'd always known them, and yet he overrode the compulsion to take men's lives. Instead every blow was carefully aimed at an extremity—to disable rather than kill.

He slashed to his right, cutting down a man who was blindsiding him, while blocking a blow from the left with his *sia*, or scabbard. With a fluid motion he supported the back of the razor-sharp blade of his sword, blocking a blow from the front, then stabbed another man behind him as he spun the sword around to dispatch still another who raced at him. The blood sprayed from the blade in a haze of red. Too deep, he'd cut too deep. *My God, my God . . .*

He blocked the downward slash of a *naginata* wielded by one of the brigands, sliding down its long wooden haft and disengaging to cut the legs out from his next opponent. It took on an unreal slow motion, each cut and parry by the numbers, a mindless and deadly dance. Very soon he stood alone, the pile of moaning bodies surrounding him.

He found his voice and cried out, "What's happening? What am I doing here? Who are you? Tell me! Now!"

And then, as if on cue, each of his opponents suddenly trembled and died. Just like that.

He spun in place, confused, not understanding. Then he saw their faces, framed in a rictus of death, and he understood. Poison. Possibly concealed under their tongues, or secreted on their person. Death was an acceptable, even preferred, substitute for capture.

His mind struggled to comprehend.

Shaking, he turned back to the palanquin, his head bowed in pain and shock. Sulu forced himself to look up. One man stood protecting the lady, surrounded by his own share of defeated enemy. Two of her maids were still alive, and perhaps a half dozen of the soldiers from the column.

Sulu bowed to the man—although it was his body, not his mind, that seemed to be in charge.

The man barked out, "Who are you?"

"Suru," he said, and frowned. He wondered why he couldn't pronounce his name correctly, but of course in Japanese there is no "letter l," and he was speaking Japanese. "Heihachiro, my lord," he replied, smiling to himself as he gave the name of "Starfleet's Commanding Admiral," Heihachiro Nogura.

A voice like the tinkling of bells said to him, "I am the Lady Oneko. You have served me well." The woman stood, both fragile as a reed and strong as a sword blade, almost disdainfully ignoring the blood that clung to her silken outer robe. Sulu caught his breath at her beauty. She was an ancient painting come to life, all the more glorious for the exotic, almost jarring perfection of her white-powdered face and red lips.

He noted that she was only a girl, a child-woman probably not yet out of her teens. Her ivory face and almond eyes were framed in demure beauty by a cascade of black hair, artfully draped over her shoulders, where it flowed back to be caught up in a ribbon. She wore an outer silk kimono of peach lined with bloodred, and the layers of her other robes peeked out at her throat like a field of brilliantly colored wildflowers. She was carefully wrapping the now sheathed small sword in a bag of silk brocade. When she was done, she tucked it, cocooned in its innocence, back into the belt of her robes.

She looked up, barely brushing his eyes with hers. Sulu felt as if he had been hit in the gut with a phaser stun. The feeling was not rational, or logical, but it was there. She returned to her palanquin.

A tall gray-haired man, handsome by any standard, strode to his side. "I am Watanenabe Sadayo. 'Suru,' eh? 'The one who tries.' But I think that the word 'suru' is also a pickpocket. Hmm," he said, scanning Sulu up and down. "You will return to the castle with me. The lord will wish to reward you. Take a horse from these brigands and follow me."

Sulu stood there, trying to digest what was happening. Should he just stay where he was? And do what? Wait for more brigands to show up? Perhaps he wouldn't be as lucky the next time.

"Why are you standing there?" came the no-nonsense demand. "Is there something wrong with the offered hospitality and reward of my lord?"

Sulu realized that if he inadvertently challenged someone's honor, there was going to be swordplay . . . and someone would die.

Which—if this was a dream—was immaterial.

But it wasn't. God help him, he was becoming more and more convinced of that.

Sulu bowed quickly. "Of course not. Your hospitality is most gracious."

"Then let us go quickly to the castle before we're accosted again," said Sadayo.

"What castle? Who is the lord?" Sulu asked, trying to shake the image of the woman which was still burned into his mind's eye.

"Fushimi Castle. Torii Mototada-domo," the leader said, swinging up to the saddle.

Wow, Sulu thought, *Torii Mototada*. Sulu had some favorites among the great samurai of history. His mother had quieted his restless childhood spirit with the stories of Benkei and Yoshitsune, and the fortunes

5

of the House of Minamoto. As a teenager he had discovered the intricate military politics of Hideyoshi and Tokugawa. And *bushi,* the warrior code of the samurai.

He rode on for hours, his thighs cramping from the unfamiliar activity. Nevertheless, he rode tall and proud as they traveled along the great Tokaido Road to meet with people from history that had died centuries ago.

What in hell am I doing here? he thought.

Chapter Two

Centuries Later . . .

KIRK HAD LOST MEN BEFORE, heaven knew. Losing men was nothing new for him. He'd lost men, women, and children. He'd seen planets struck down by invaders or forces of feast or famine. He'd seen worlds destroyed, suns collapsing on themselves, and starships swallowed by monstrosities huge beyond comprehension.

Death and destruction, so much death. Enough to overshadow all the good that he had done, and hopefully, would continue to do. But no matter how much he faced death, he would never acknowledge that death was a better man than he. Even though death would win, and continue to win, and—sooner or later—triumph over James T. Kirk. It was a matter of honor. Or perhaps just bull-headed stubbornness— as Dr. McCoy had said more than once.

He placed a hand on the unmoving, lifeless body of Lieutenant Garrovick, which lay in a small room adjacent to sickbay. Kirk winced at the ugly wounds studding the lieutenant's face and upper torso. His clothes were torn, and even though his face was lifeless, his final expression was one of chagrin and pain.

Damn, but losing a crewman was hard, even after all this time. Especially a crewman with whom he had a history, such as Garrovick, whose father had once been Kirk's commanding officer—another man Kirk had watched die.

"Bastards," he murmured. "Klingon bastards."

There was a soft footfall next to him, but Kirk didn't turn. He didn't need to.

"Never gets easier, does it, Jim?" the doctor asked.

Kirk let out a slow sigh. "The day it gets easier is the day I go behind a desk for good, Bones."

McCoy raised a bemused eyebrow. "Why? You think you can then calmly and coldly give orders that send other people to their potential deaths? Not you, Jim. You always feel that you can't order someone to do something that you wouldn't do yourself. That's why you always lead landing parties."

Kirk looked down at Garrovick once more. "Out of some misguided feeling of honor?"

"No. You lead landing parties because you're a damned fool who thinks he's going to live forever."

"Oh." Kirk's lips thinned. "Thank you for clarifying that."

"No problem. Jim, total faith in one's own immortality—that's the province of the young."

Kirk shook his head and eyed the dead man. "A lot of good it did Garrovick."

He turned and left sickbay. McCoy hesitated a moment, trying to decide whether his captain was in a mood to talk or to be left alone. McCoy was still unclear about the details of what in the world had gone wrong on the surface of Cragon V, which spun gracefully, and deceptively, peacefully below them. He knew that five men had gone down, and now four men had come back . . . except now three of the four who had returned had vanished to somewhere in the past.

He decided that remaining in ignorance wasn't going to do him a damned bit of good . . . perhaps about as much good as it was going to do Kirk, who was eating himself up over all of this.

McCoy knew that a short distance away sat a Klingon battle cruiser, staring at the *Enterprise,* as helpless and as frustrated as the *Enterprise* herself.

And sitting in sickbay staring at the walls wasn't going to help. McCoy walked out, stopping only to pick up a flask of Romulan ale.

He entered Kirk's quarters and stopped dead still as Kirk aimed a phaser at him. He sputtered a moment and then got out, "Good lord, Jim . . . have my bills been that high?"

Kirk did not so much as crack a smile. Instead he aimed the phaser just to McCoy's left and squeezed the trigger.

Nothing happened. Not so much as a faint whine of energy.

"Out of power?" asked McCoy, trying to appear nonplussed.

"Out of frustration," replied Kirk. He tossed the phaser onto a nearby couch. "They're all like that. Every phaser on the damned ship. And our ship's phaser banks, and the photon torpedoes. All thanks to that blasted Weyland. I've got a man lying dead in sickbay, the individual responsible sitting contentedly in his ship kilometers away . . . and I can't do anything except . . ."

"Drink?" offered McCoy.

He kept the label of the Romulan ale away from Kirk so that he wouldn't have to tolerate the captain's half-hearted protests. He poured Kirk a swig, which the captain promptly tossed back. It hit his system the way Romulan ale always did, and he gagged slightly. Kirk, graciously, didn't say anything.

"So what happened?" asked McCoy.

Kirk made a slight, dismissive wave. "You don't want to know."

"No, of course not," said McCoy reasonably. "I just came here to watch you act cranky and frustrated." The doctor's expression turned serious. "Besides, Jim, you think you're the only one with responsibilities? You lost a man. Well, I lost a patient. This situation is as much my business as it is yours."

Kirk regarded McCoy a moment, fingers steepled. "For someone who had to be practically dragged, kicking and screaming, back into Starfleet, it's good to know you haven't lost your ability to annoy your commanding officer."

"It's a knack."

Kirk nodded. Then he leaned forward and said, "All right. Here's what happened . . ."

In many ways, Cragon V reminded Kirk of Organia. A world where the people were hardworking and simple. The technology was, by Earth standards, blindingly primitive. Also, like Organia, Cragon V was of interest both to the Federation and the Klingons. Rather than having strategic importance like Organia, Cragon had an abundance of minerals that were of value both to the Federation and the Empire.

There were several other significant differences. First and foremost: Organians were not what they appeared to be. But the people of Cragon were exactly what they appeared to be: simple and easily influenced.

In the case of Organia, as well as other planets subsequently contested under the Organian Peace Treaty, the Klingons and the Federation had shown up at roughly the same time. Not so with Cragon, unfortunately. In this case, the Federation had been caught flatfooted. Previous mining surveys had been improperly carried out, and the Klingons were sharp enough to slip into the gap and show up on the planet several months before the Federation caught wind of it.

Kirk disliked many things, and high on that list was the idea of being one step behind the Klingons on anything of importance—especially when the lives of an innocent people were at stake.

Kirk stopped momentarily as the landing party drew up short to wait for him. He took a deep breath, the fresh air of Cragon tingling in his lungs. As much as he loved the *Enterprise,* and as carefully as the air inside the starship was treated to simulate a real environment, it still was not the same as standing on a genuine planet, breathing in fresh air.

Chekov stepped up to his silent captain, concerned. As security chief, it was his job to be concerned. "Is there a problem, Keptin?" he asked.

"No. No problem."

Lieutenant Garrovick smiled. "The captain has his own way of doing things, and tends to set his own schedule."

Kirk glanced slyly at the lieutenant. Most subordinate officers tended to walk on eggshells with Kirk, but not Garrovick, who had served with Kirk before. In fact, Garrovick had seen Kirk when the captain was probably at his lowest point emotionally, dealing with his guilt over his failure to respond to a threat, a bloodsucking cloud. It had been with the help of then-ensign Garrovick that Kirk had been able to finally destroy the creature.

Garrovick had received Kirk's highest recommendations and had been briskly promoted. Now, when Kirk's return to the *Enterprise* had been announced, Garrovick had requested transfer to the starship that had been his first deep-space assignment. Kirk had cheerfully welcomed him aboard, and Garrovick had been made Chekov's right-hand man.

In that position, Garrovick qualified as a member of the landing party for the Cragon expedition. Montgomery Scott had been selected for his engineering expertise and his ability to assess firsthand the technological state of Cragon—and, most importantly, whether the Klingons had seriously affected the status quo of the planet. Sulu was there too, since he had once been assigned—early in his career—to a three-month observation of a planet remarkably similar to Cragon. Chekov and Garrovick were there to provide security support. Kirk would have liked to bring a platoon, but attention to the Prime Directive meant trying not to come stomping through people's backyards with a veritable army. It would give the wrong impression of the Federation, since that type of force was not what the Federation was all about.

A pity, Kirk had thought glumly, that the Klingons felt no similar constraint.

"Quite right, Mr. Garrovick," the captain said briskly. "A schedule that we have to keep. Let's press on, gentlemen."

"The castle is just ahead, Keptin," Chekov informed him, stepping carefully through the underbrush.

"Good," said Kirk, carefully picking a bramble from his uniform.

Scotty was muttering under his breath. "What the devil is the good of transporter technology if it drops us off in the middle of nowhere?"

Kirk didn't bother to answer. Scotty knew the answer perfectly well—with less developed societies, the Federation felt it was best not to openly display advanced technology.

The castle was indeed ahead, perched high atop a steep hill. Scotty's breathing was labored and he thumped his stomach. "Glory, I'm out of shape. Only one thing for it."

"Exercise?" suggested Sulu. "You could take up running, or perhaps fencing . . ."

"Exercise, Mr. Sulu?" Scotty looked at him with exaggerated disdain. "I'm talking shore leave. Some time away."

"This from the man who used to turn down shore leave so he could read technical journals," Kirk said, brushing leaves out of his hair. He stopped to kick mud off his boots against a tree.

"I know how he feels," said Sulu. "I could use some heavy duty R and R myself."

"Maybe a week on a pleasure planet?" Chekov asked wistfully.

"No, home. I really want to go home for a while."

"San Francisco?" Scotty asked.

"No, I mean a real home. Japan, the way it was a few hundred years ago." Sulu's eyes glistened. "Yes, someplace where a man could really believe in living and dying for his king and country. Sometimes I almost envy the Romulans, and the Klingons, too. Their life is simple."

Scotty was about to chide Sulu for his rather militaristic outlook at life. But then he thought of the claymore that hung on the wall of his cabin. As much as he pooh-poohed Sulu for his fencing and romantic pretensions, Scott's heart swelled with pride at the long tradition of the Scots soldiers, a simple world of right and wrong.

"Yes," Chekov said thoughtfully, "a week in my homeland, sitting in a dacha with a glass of vodka, and a pretty girl, and the sound of balalaika music . . ." But what he saw in his mind was the last Pan-Soviet May Day Parade he had attended. And the strains of his national anthem hummed in his mind. How much his nation had endured, and how proud he was.

If they were lesser officers, Kirk would have reminded them that they should be on their toes. But he knew that their easy familiarity and chat was not distracting one iota from their attention to their duty and to their surroundings. Nevertheless, as they climbed up the steep hill that led to the castle where the ruler of Cragon was ostensibly in residence, Kirk felt constrained to say something.

"Careful, gentlemen," he said with humor. "You should always be wary of what you wish for. You may get it."

Chapter Three

Scotland, 1746

SCOTT WOKE UP with a galactic headache, and a peculiar chill to his hindquarters. He reached down and felt a bare hairy leg. That woke him, and he sat up, the contents of his brain pan lurching around like thick coolant.

"Ach," he groaned, covering his eyes protectively with one hand, his other propping him up on the very muddy ground. The chill wind was making his sinuses ache, and the light was bright enough to make his eyes throb. The thing that was supposed to be his brain was trying to figure out why the deck of a starship was wet, bumpy, and gritty, but two thoughts were one and a half too many in his current state, and he got back to the mystery of the hairy leg.

He opened one eye tentatively and looked around, the apparent cloud cover doing little to mitigate the glare of a planetary sun.

"What in heaven's name!" the engineer muttered, trying to take in the scene and analyze his position. He reached for his communicator, but found himself groping the fabric of a coarse shirt. *Well, at least I'm not stark naked.*

Exploring further, he reached a mass of even coarser wool gathered around his middle.

"Well, I'll be damned," he muttered, struggling to his feet, making a jaw-clenching, tooth-gritting effort to ignore the waves of coolant sloshing in his head. The folds of the gray and muddy-brown garment fell down to his knees, at least relieving the chill from the most tender part of his lower half. It was, no doubt, a great kilt, the old and traditional version of the neat, pleated small kilt that Scott had affected as part of his dress uniform. What he had draped over him now was little more than a blanket held in place by a heavy leather belt and a leather thong that tied the long loose end up around his shoulders. All in all, it was a primitive arrangement of haberdashery, at best.

Now . . . what the hell was he doing wearing it?

He searched his memory, his beautiful memory that enabled him to recall, at any given moment, any bit of detail he needed to maintain and repair the most complex vehicle in the galaxy. It was very disconcerting to find a hole in that selfsame memory.

He racked his brains. There had been a planet . . . and then a failed mission, and a fight . . . and they'd returned to the ship . . . But how did he get here?

He knocked on the side of his head as if to wake up memories that were sleeping in there. Nothing stirred.

He looked around with a deliberateness meant to calm the rising panic. He was about a hundred yards from a primitive two-story building—an inn, from the look of it. The creak of the sign about the door drew Scott's attention. A crude painting adorned the rough board, of a woman in a mob cap, bodice, and long petticoats, hanging from a gallows. In case the message wasn't clear, the words *The Hanged Woman* were crudely lettered below.

"Now there's a cheery thought," Scotty muttered, suppressing a chill that rippled up his spine, one not due to the cold. A wind with a hint of snow was blowing, sending the folds of the kilt flapping around his loins, the loose end snapping like a flag. He was alone without communications, on a planet heaven only knew where. "Oh, Montgomery," Scott said aloud, trying to hold on to his voice as a stanchion of reality, "this has got to be a dream." But his eyes were open, and he knew he was not going to wake up on the bridge of the *Enterprise*.

He walked, or rather wobbled, up the road to the door of The Hanged Woman, but his legs gave out just short of his goal and he collapsed again onto the road, his face splashing into a rain-filled pothole. He dragged himself forward enough to keep from drowning. Part of his brain was telling him that he had better move before he started to shake from shock and hypothermia, while the other part was telling him it didn't really care.

The upstairs window creaked open. Scott ignored it until the chill, smelly splash of a bucket of slops hit him squarely in the back. That finally did it. Pain or no pain, he was on his feet and scrabbling for cover against any further assault to his health and dignity.

"Argh," he growled. It could have been worse, he conjectured, as he examined the offal that tumbled off him and identified the bits as dinner scraps and scrub water, not the contents of a chamber pot.

"Hey, you! Move on!" Scott looked up to see a chunky woman with weather-raw red cheeks leaning out over the window ledge. She still held the basin in her massive muscular arms, which stuck out from rolled-up sleeves, testifying to a life of hard work.

"Who are you?" Scott shouted back, his burr becoming thicker by the moment. "What am I doing here?!"

"Screaming like a fool idiot," she shouted back. "I'll not have the likes of ye here. Be off or I'll fetch the master and he'll have a lead ball whizzing through your thick head in no time."

Scotty drew a breath to argue the point, but it seemed useless, and, even though the sun was getting higher—which meant he had a full day ahead of him—it was also getting colder. The sooner he got under way, the sooner he could find shelter before he froze. The problem of where he was, and why, would have to wait.

It was snowing hard before he was even out of sight of the inn. The engineer's feet, which were bare, were swelling and roughly the color of beets, except he couldn't even feel them for the numbing cold. And the wet wool that he wore was doing more harm than good in keeping the bitter wind from his body. It was The Hanged Woman, or death from exposure.

He chugged back up the road, his breath vaporizing before him in little dense puffs, his feet dragging painfully, leaving a long wavy track in the new-fallen snow.

There was a stable across the yard from the main house, and a screen of bushes, probably some ornamental hedgerow, which gave the grim inn some summer beauty as it marched untidily up to the stable wall. Using the cover, he slipped in unseen.

And not a moment too soon. Through a crack in the rough stable wall, Scotty watched a slender boy in his mid-teens come out of the rear door of the inn carrying a pair of empty wooden buckets. Scott half prayed, "Please don't come here. Please. Go away."

The boy went to the well in the middle of the yard and dropped the bucket with a splash, then turned the crank to bring the water up with a noisy creak. He did this until the two pails were full, and then, his chore done, returned to the house. Scotty let out his breath.

The warm manure smell of the barn swept over him

with a kind of nostalgic friendliness which belied the fact that he had spent most of his adult years in a relatively sterile and scentless starship. A horse neighed in the nearest stall, stomping with impatience, hoping perhaps for a run on spring grass which was not yet grown.

A rickety ladder led up to the hay loft, but negotiating the ladder was more than Mr. Scott had counted on with aching freezing toes, and it was two stumbling false starts until the sheer fear of being caught gave him the energy to make his way painfully up and into the loft. It was deserted except for a small pigeon coop.

He crawled to the far wall, buried himself in a soft pile of straw, and fell asleep to the gentle cooing of the birds.

It was dark but for the beams of moonlight, silver and cold stripes in the darkness, when Scott moaned awake, trying to remember something very important. What was it, now? The headache was back. Oh, yes, he thought, with a clammy shudder. He was somewhere . . . somewhere a lot like northern England or the Scots Lowlands, but as they were a long time ago.

He thought back to his ship, but there still was no clue to what had brought him to this place.

Scotty crawled across the loft to the ladder. He was stiff and achy from the cramped lumpy bed of old grass. His lips were parched and his mouth dry. The horse was gone from the stall below. The barn was still and empty. He slipped down the ladder, trying to be quiet, wincing when he missed the last step and clattered to the ground. He winced even more when he pushed the door open with a loud creak.

The well was too noisy to draw water, but luckily one of the buckets was still outside, covered only by a thin crust of ice. Food was next. Scotty tried the kitchen door, but it was bolted shut. The noise woke up the dog again. He was about to give up and make do when he noticed that the window was unlatched. Scotty's stomach growled loudly enough to wake the dead; or the dog, at least. He decided he would risk it.

Scott found the door to the pantry by following his nose, which led him to the overwhelming scent of hams and sausage which hung tantalizingly overhead and out of reach, along with sweet braids of onions.

A soft footfall behind him suddenly alerted him.

Scotty turned just in time to see the barrel end of a rifle swing toward him, and then it smashed into the side of his head.

He staggered back, his head spinning, and reached for his phaser, which of course wasn't there.

There was a roar in the darkness, a loud curse, and then another shout from a boy. Maybe the boy from before, he thought.

Then Scott was struck in the head again, a wave of nausea overwhelming him. He wretched and staggered forward. He felt blood trickling down his face, and his hands were suddenly closing on the front of somebody's clothes.

"Let go of me!" shouted Scott's attacker, and the engineer shoved him as hard as he could. Scotty heard a crashing of furniture and then staggered for the window.

Everything was spinning around, and he lurched drunkenly and smashed his poor head a third time against the edge of the window. He fell forward and out, landing face first in the dirt, his headache nearly overwhelming him.

He staggered back to the barn and pulled the door shut behind him. A boy's voice cried out, "I saw him! Plain as day! Tall fellow he was, with red hair and a beard! Ran down the road!"

Scotty was utterly confused and utterly sick. He couldn't put two words together in his head, and it was nothing short of a miracle that he managed to climb into the loft to hide. And there, consciousness fled.

Chapter Four

Centuries Later . . .

IN ORBIT AROUND CRAGON—a planet which, in future years, would be uttered as a curse by Klingons, along with the name of Organia and the home planet of tribbles—the bridge and instruments of the Klingon battle cruiser were under attack.

The attacker was Commander Kral. He was entitled, since after all it was his ship.

Relatively young for a Klingon commander, his age did not deter Kral from venting a rage worthy of the most experienced. At that moment he was smashing both of his massive, armored fists into the weapons console. "Useless!" he howled. "All the weaponry at my fingertips, rendered useless by that thrice damned Weyland! May he die with festering boils!"

Behind Kral, First Officer Kbrex stood with impassive calm, his hands draped behind his back. "Festering boils, Commander," he intoned.

"May the Bloating Sickness force his entrails oozing from every bodily orifice!"

"Every orifice, as you say, Commander."

His tone was silky, deferential, and entirely too . . . what? Kral glanced at his first officer with suspicion and then suddenly turned on him and snapped, "What could I have done to avoid this calamity, eh, Kbrex? What step should I have taken? What plans should I have made?"

Kbrex never blinked. His face was absolutely unreadable. "No Klingon is psychic, Commander," he said quietly. "In some situations, there is simply no one to blame."

Kral considered that a moment, then nodded brusquely and left the bridge, leaving the smoldering ruins of the weapons console in his wake.

Kbrex watched him go, then turned to the chief engineer. When he spoke now, the carefully controlled deference was no longer in evidence. Instead there was a sharp cunning and a modulated energy. "Get to work repairing that immediately," he said. "You never know when we may need it."

Kirk stared at the empty glass in his hand. He had been relating the events on Cragon to McCoy, but now his voice had trailed off as he remembered his eerily prophetic words to his men.

"Be careful what you wish for," Kirk said, shaking his head. "You may get it. Lord, Bones . . . if I'd only known."

"Was there any way you could have, Jim? Was there any warning?"

Kirk tried to come up with something.

"I don't know, Bones. I just . . . don't know. Perhaps I should have known when I met Weyland. But there was no way . . ." He looked to McCoy for an answer the doctor could not provide. "Was there?"

Garrovick, who had taken point, suddenly put up a hand. "Hold it," he said, and pointed just ahead of them. "There. You see it?"

At first Kirk didn't, but then he did see it, hidden by

a trick of the light. A trip wire, rigged just ahead of them.

"Anyone care to take a guess as to what that's connected to?" asked Kirk dryly.

"Some nasty little piece of work," Scotty commented.

"And I think we can surmise the folks who set it. Look there." Kirk pointed to a tree that was next to the wire. Carved into it, unobtrusively, was an unmistakable letter of the Klingon alphabet. "They've been through here, all right. Watch the trees for more warning symbols, gentlemen. If they have left themselves guides, we can make use of them, too."

Chekov glanced around, feeling as if every shadow was now hiding a potential enemy. "Why did they set it, Keptin?"

"One or both of two reasons." Kirk ticked them off on his hand. "First, they may have wanted to demonstrate to the inhabitants of Cragon V how one goes about setting lethal booby traps for an enemy—which implies that the Klingons have been stirring up civil unrest while they were here. The second is that the Klingons anticipated unwanted visitors of their own."

"Namely us," said Garrovick.

"Namely us," agreed Kirk. "Eyes all around, gentlemen. I'd prefer that we all get back in one piece. I have a standing bet with Admiral Nogura that leading landing parties is going to get me killed someday, and I'd hate to have to pay him off."

The *Enterprise* crew stepped gingerly over the deadly trip wire and proceeded. Some minutes later, and without further incident, they were in view of the castle.

Garrovick knocked on the main door after Chekov indicated that he should take the point. The door opened a fraction and a massive guard filled it. The men of the *Enterprise* immediately noticed that several of his weapons were Klingon issue. It did not look promising.

"We wish to see your leader," said Kirk. "We are from far away, and we understand that he resides here."

"We do not have a leader," replied the soldier. "We have a god."

"A god," said Kirk slowly.

Scotty closed his eyes for a moment and sighed. *Lord, please let it not be a supercomputer.*

"Yes," the soldier reaffirmed. "The immortal Weyland."

"I see. And is the immortal Weyland, uhm . . . available?"

Slowly the guard nodded. "He had been absent for a time . . . shortly before the coming of the T'lingons."

Kirk tensed at the word. Though the pronunciation was rough, the meaning was clear.

The guard continued, "But he has returned of late, and is in great rage regarding the advent of the T'lingons . . ."

"As well he should be," said Kirk briskly.

". . . as well as the coming of the Federation."

Kirk paused a moment, and the other members of the landing party looked at him. "We . . . just got here. How did immortal Weyland know of our presence?"

"Immortal Weyland knows everything," replied the guard.

"I . . . see."

"You do not believe."

"I'm willing to be convinced," said Kirk smoothly.

"You will be." He stepped back and the door opened wide.

The Federation party was led in through a cobblestone courtyard. There were people everywhere, in doorways, behind wagons, crowded behind each other, eyeing the strangers from a safe distance. Chekov smiled at a little girl, who was peeking around her mother's apron, her chubby little fists digging tightly onto the woman's stiffly embroidered skirts. The hard glare of a man with a grizzled beard and a large smithy's hammer melted Chekov's attempt at good humor.

Sulu fell into the easy cadence of the guard. He eyed the men with unsuppressed envy. Those were *real* warriors! Like the samurai of his ancient heritage. And not growling, vicious animals like the Klingons, but just proud men who served their people bravely. He squared his shoulders a fraction and straightened his back a bit as he strode into the unknown.

They were led into a fair-sized building, a dingy keep with algae-glistening walls. Dim, weak shafts of light filtered down from the high narrow windows. Torches were stuck in holes in the masonry, their smoke-blackened trails snaking up the walls toward the drafty window slits. Scott noted the simple engineering solution, although he was less than impressed by what he had seen so far.

They were led outdoors again, this time to an inner courtyard. The sound of metal ringing on metal ceased as they marched out into the square. A small group of young soldiers armed with heavy, short wooden swords and round wooden shields rimmed with iron bands had stopped their practice to gawk at the strangers. An old toothless soldier with one eye gave the newcomers a practiced once-over and then shouted at his charges to resume the drill.

In the center of the inner court was the round tower of the inner keep. The doors were a full ten feet tall, and made of bronze. The surface of the great bronze doors was covered with intricate scenes of warfare and pageantry. It took four men to swing them open.

Kirk blinked a few times to accustom his eyes to the

dim interior light. He could hardly hold his usual poker face as the room came into view. It was primitive, all right, but as beautiful as a great ancient cathedral. The audience chamber, which comprised the entire ground floor of the central keep, was huge, topped with a high-beamed ceiling. And what beams! Wood from some huge native tree, not rough-hewn, but polished and carved in an intricate interlace of dream beasts which were painted in wildly garish colors.

A ring of men armed with spears parted, revealing a man whose flowing white beard seemed out of place on his almost youthful face. His massive jeweled crown had the soft glow of pure gold. Kirk's gaze was not riveted on the artistry or display, but by the king's piercing blue eyes. He squinted to break the bond of that blinding stare.

"I am Weyland, and I rule here."

Kirk did not doubt it. Scotty bowed formally, using the kind reserved for the ceremonial king who still sat a British throne on Earth. Sulu bowed also, just a little short of how he imagined one would honor the similarly democratic Emperor of Japan. Even Chekov dropped his head in courtesy. Kirk and Garrovick remained as they were.

"Sir," Kirk began, "we are here to offer you the aid of the United Federation of Planets."

"I do not want you here. Why do you invade my home?"

"Sir, we did not invade," Kirk protested. "The Klingons, the other strangers, are very dangerous people. They have enslaved many people like yours, and we are here to offer you aid in protecting yourself . . ."

"I do not require your help."

"Please, sir, if I could merely explain the magnitude of the danger," Kirk said.

"I do not require your help," the "god" repeated. "You may leave."

"But, sir, you dunna understand—" Scott protested.

Weyland waved him to silence, an amused smile on his lips. "I imagine that all of this is my fault." Weyland actually seemed regretful. "My presence was required elsewhere, and so I had to leave my people for a time. It was an ill fortune that brought you and the Klingons to my planet during my absence. But make no mistake . . ."

"Captain Kirk," Kirk quickly prompted.

"Yes, Captain Kirk. Make no mistake that this planet is mine. The people are mine. And now that you are here—you, too, are mine."

Kirk raised a bemused eyebrow at that. "Really."

"Yes. You see differences between yourselves and your opponents. I, however, do not. However," and he sat back expansively, "I am a reasonable god. The Klingons will doubtless be showing up shortly. They can have their futile effort to convince me or threaten me, and you may join them. Then, Captain, you will be cordially invited once more to depart, where you may blast each other to hell and back for all that it matters to me. But I will tolerate no further interference with my people . . . and be warned—if any hardship or injury should be inflicted on any of my subjects, from the greatest of them to the most humble, then you shall pay dearly for it." He settled back in his throne. "You shall all pay dearly."

"You have my word of honor that we'll protect your people, sir," said Kirk.

"Right there, Bones," said Kirk, staring down at the Romulan ale in his glass. "When Weyland said that to me, I should have sensed that Weyland was more than he appeared to be. But I was confident in my precious superiority, and now my men have paid the price for it."

"There was no way you could have known, Jim." McCoy tried to sound soothing.

"I could have remembered from past mistakes. I was fooled by the Organians. Scotty has a favorite saying: 'Fool me once, shame on you. Fool me twice, shame on me.' Shame on me, Bones. Shame on me for sitting here, trying to figure out what I should have done, instead of what I should be doing."

"There's nothing we can do right now, Jim. We've explored all our options."

"Then we'll explore some new ones." He punched the intercom. "Kirk to bridge."

"Bridge, Spock here."

"Mr. Spock, conference room. We're going to try and figure a way out of this mess."

"Yes sir," said Spock briskly.

Kirk looked up at McCoy. "Fool me twice," he said softly. "Bones . . . you think Scotty is all right? Scotty, and Sulu, and Chekov?"

"I think, Jim, as insane as it may sound—that's already been decided, don't you think?"

Kirk nodded slowly. "Good point, Doctor. Good point."

Chapter Five

Somewhen in Russia . . .

WHEN CHEKOV AWOKE, it was to the sound of someone speaking in angry German. Then he heard someone else reply in German . . . except there was a faint tinge of a Russian accent.

He rolled over onto his back to see a charcoal-gray sky. There was dirt beneath him, rather than the solidity of the *Enterprise.*

Chekov sat up slowly as the angry voices from nearby became louder. He was only partially paying attention to them. His main mental exercise, at the moment, was trying to pull together his fractured memory.

He was . . . what? He had been on the planet Cragon. That much he remembered. With Kirk and Sulu and Scotty and Garrovick. And there had been —he rubbed his forehead—some sort of problem. Images flashed through his mind. Klingons and a blast of heat and light, and some sort of being seated on a throne. Then they'd returned to the *Enterprise . . .*

Dead. Someone was dead. Two someones were dead. Was he one of them? he wondered. He didn't think so . . .

Something had confronted them, and he—

"Pathetic!"

It was the pure German voice that was saying it. Chekov looked down at himself.

His crisp Starfleet uniform was gone. Small loss. He'd hated the gray anyway.

But it had been replaced by . . .

He stared at his body as if it belonged to someone else. It was some sort of stiff uniform. It was . . .

"German?" said Chekov to himself in utter mystification. "I'm a German?" But even as he spoke, his voice was still in the unmistakable Russian accent that had led to such easily-jibed words as "Keptin."

He was a Russian. In a German uniform—the type worn during World War II.

"Impossible," he muttered.

Slowly he staggered to his feet, and realized that he was cradling a helmet in his hands. Reflexively he put it on his head. Across his lap was a rifle of some sort. He examined it as if staring at an alien artifact.

He heard a whinnying sound nearby and looked off to his right. His eyes widened. He couldn't remember the last time he'd seen so much as a single horse, yet now here was a large number of them inside of some sort of pen—what was it called—a corral.

He glanced down at his arm. There was a swastika on it.

"You! Soldier!"

He felt himself going ashen as he turned slowly.

Not too far away from him there were three more men dressed in the same uniform he wore . . . but two of them were being held at gunpoint by the third. The one holding the gun said again, "Come here, soldier!" in the pure-sounding German that identified him as the more belligerent of the speakers Chekov had heard before.

Nazis. He was within spitting distance—appropriately—of Nazis.

And there, on the horizon line, was a war-torn city that Chekov had seen in much happier days. It was Stalingrad. He was in World War II Stalingrad.

"Are you deaf?" demanded the German soldier, his gaze never wavering from the two men who were apparently now prisoners, though they both wore German uniforms as well.

Chekov's feet were moving even though he was sure he had forgotten to tell them to do so. He trotted over to the soldier and nodded briskly.

"Go to the commander," the soldier said sharply. "Inform him that I have captured two Russians in a pathetic attempt to sneak onto the base by passing themselves off as Germans."

Chekov's mouth moved but nothing came out.

He knew it wasn't a dream, because he knew for a fact he dreamt in black and white. Back in his academy days—*forward* in his academy days?—he'd participated in a dream research project and had actually seen his own dream images. He'd done it to be near this gorgeous young technician on the research team. She'd had a figure that was—

"Are you daydreaming now?!" said the soldier, apparently on the verge of apoplexy.

Well, yes, he was. His mind was wandering because it was still having trouble coping with his situation, and somehow anything seemed better than dwelling on the inherent insanity of where and when he was.

As if addressing an idiot, the German said, "Get . . . the . . . commander."

Chekov looked into the eyes of the two Russians, whose hands were now in back of their heads, fingers interlaced. They were staring at him with smoldering intensity and a look of hopelessness that shook Chekov from his confusion. He still didn't understand, but that wasn't going to stop him from taking appropriate action.

The German soldier was now eyeing him with suspicion. Chekov saw that, ever so subtly, the soldier was ready to swing his rifle around at the slightest odd move on his part. Chekov dug into his memory to come up with the appropriate gesture, and he snapped his heels together and brought his hand up at an angle, palm down.

He turned briskly and walked in the direction of the corral.

"The commander's office is the other way!" came the angry shout, and then there was a rifle crack as a bullet winged just over Chekov's left shoulder.

Chekov leaped forward and yanked open the door of the corral, discharging his rifle just over the horses' heads.

The panicked animals whinnied and brayed, then charged forward.

Chekov rolled on his back to get out of the way as the horses pounded past him.

The thought suddenly flashed through his mind that this might not be one of his most brilliant ideas. Though he could not, of course, have simply shot the German. First, there were Prime Directive considerations. Secondly, he was not a cold-blooded killer. So he had chosen, instead, to do something that seemed —at the time—more neutral; namely, letting the horses out and having the chips fall where they may.

The problem was, Chekov knew, he was still playing with fire. Sure, shooting the soldier could screw up history—presuming he was really in the past and not suffering from some sort of induced hallucination. But having the soldier get trampled to death because of his actions was not a much better solution.

Fortunately, he saw that the German soldier had leaped out of the way and was now running like mad, shouting in his native tongue for help. The two

Russians-as-Germans were on the other side of the pounding river of horse flesh that had sprung up, Moseslike, to separate them from their attacker.

Chekov ran toward the Russian soldiers, swinging his rifle around to get it out of the way.

One of them turned, saw him coming, and brought his rifle up. Before Chekov could react, the man fired.

The shot glanced off Chekov's helmet and he went down, his head ringing.

There was something definitely inappropriate about this welcome, he thought, facedown in the dirt. His mind was scrambled and he heard shouting and anger all around him. His thought process became muddled. Still only barely coping with where he was, he stopped coping altogether and decided that he was on vacation in Stalingrad, and this whole thing was some sort of a living reenactment of a time from long ago in his country's past.

He was hauled to his feet, and found himself looking into the smoldering eyes of the German soldier.

Chekov smiled lopsidedly. "The costumes are wery nice," he said in bedraggled English.

The German slugged him in the face, and Chekov, mercifully, slipped into unconsciousness.

Chapter Six

COMMANDER KRAL SAT UP immediately when he heard the knock at his door. His fingers moved reflexively toward a weapon and then slowed, reasoning that an assassin would not take the time to announce himself.

"What do you want?"

The door hissed open and in it stood Vladra, from down in the science lab. She was regarding Kral with careful assessment, and he realized that she herself was wondering whether he had drawn on her. For one fleeting moment Kral was pleased that he had not. And then he wondered why he was pleased.

Vladra was a quite striking Klingon woman, actually a hair taller than Kral. He found her intriguing. There seemed to be a smoldering interest in her eyes that she was virtually daring him to ignite.

She appeared to consider her words carefully. "Commander. I want you to know that . . ."

Her voice trailed off. Such hesitations were inappropriate for a Klingon, and he was about to chide her for that but something stopped him. "What is it?" His voice was actually surprisingly soft this time.

She cleared her throat. "How does one determine," she asked, "upon which side one should be if there would seem to be a potential . . . change in command?"

He raised an eyebrow. "Is this a warning, Vladra?" he said slowly.

Kral was all too aware of how necessary proper phrasing was. It was considered a serious breach of etiquette to warn one's commander if an overthrow were in the works. Klingon commanders were supposed to be able to watch their own backs, else they deserved a knife in it. For committing such an act, Vladra was risking her own life. Kral would have been perfectly in line for disciplining her—fatally—for the implied insult that he could not take care of himself. But . . .

Kral's eyes narrowed. "You should make such choices based on your own desires and goals, I would think. Do you not agree?"

She nodded slowly, her eyes flashing.

"You pose, of course, a hypothetical situation," he said carefully.

"Of course," was the neutral reply.

There was silence for a moment, and then Vladra, in a carefully controlled voice, said, "If I learn specifics . . . so that I can make a more . . . interesting hypothetical decision . . . then I shall be certain to inform you, sir. Just so that it will stimulate our . . . hypothetical discussion."

"Yes, of course. I always consider such theoretical discussions most intriguing."

She inclined her head briefly, turned on her heel and left.

Kral stalked his cabin like a caged tiger. He had left the bridge because he had not wanted his frustration at his helplessness to boil over in front of his men, as it indeed already once had.

He kicked over a chair. "Damn it, I *earned* the promotion!" he screamed at himself. "The rank and the honorific, I earned it all!" He had distinguished himself in glorious combat, combat that had entitled him to name the ship that was now sitting helplessly above Cragon V. The glorious *Talon's Blood,* his ship. His ship, his frustration.

He glanced in the mirror, furious at his own features. His brow ridge still didn't have the knobbiness that came with age, and his forehead still shone with youthful glimmer. The sash of his new rank was heavy and not yet broken in. He still habitually tugged at it in an endless attempt to adjust it.

A command of his own, and now he wondered if he could keep it. He knew that even at the best of times, and with the loyalty of officers, the life expectancy of a young commander proving his spurs was short. These were not the best of times.

"Baahhh!" he grunted, throwing pieces of his body armor crashing across his cabin. He locked his agonizer in the small wall safe over his bunk. He was about to do the same with his disrupter, but he stared at it, giving it a little toss in his hand, enjoying the familiar weight and feel. He tucked it under his pillow and threw himself on the bed. Nothing would be gained by his fretting over the problem like a woman awaiting childbirth. Better to sleep on it. He let his mind reach out to the purity of the Naked Stars, and he drifted off to sleep. And just before he surrendered to the blissful, albeit temporary escape of slumber, his mind spun back to hours earlier on Cragon V, when he had come face to face with that creature from deep within the bowels of Klingon hell, Weyland . . .

Commander Kral pulled in a deep breath, barreled out his chest impressively, and approached the castle wherein—he had been informed by nervous townspeople—the great god Weyland had returned and wished to see him.

Kral was getting damned sick of this planet. His first mission in command of the *Ghargh* and what did he draw? A trip to some piddling planet—mineral rich, to be sure, but piddling—to supervise the aligning of its people with the Klingon empire. It had its amusements, to be certain. The natives had been quick and eager learners, and had come to revere the Klingons almost as all-knowing gods. A number of the Cragon natives had developed a bloodthirstiness that virtually rivaled Klingon berserkers.

For all of this, however, the natives still insisted that before the Klingons could be allowed to begin mining operations, they had to have permission from the great god Weyland, and unfortunately, Weyland was busy elsewhere. So the frustrated Klingons had been forced to cool their heels while indulging in the simple joy of teaching eager people how to fight.

Kral frequently, and quite vocally, longed for the days before the Organian treaty. The days when Klingons could just storm in and take what they wanted, when they wanted it. Now everything had to be nice and tidy. It was humiliating. By Kahless, the next thing you knew, the Klingons would wind up allies of those weak Federation types, as the Organians had claimed. He hoped he would be long dead before such a time.

Finally, finally, finally, Kral received word that this Weyland person had returned. The so-called god had doubtless been in some other place on the planet, practicing his god routine on other gullible savages. Well, fine. Kral would play the game and be done with this. Still, for all his disdain of the savage inhabitants of Cragon, he had a grudging professional admiration for the loyalty and efficiency of the local guard who watched Kral walk by. They smelled like warriors.

The boys in the practice yard on the inner keep stopped their ferocious spear thrusts against hay bales and sneaked wide-eyed looks at the Klingon, until a crusty old man with a patch over one eye bellowed them back to their task.

Kral studied the huge metal doors leading to the inner sanctum of this god, which was filled with strong men who were used to discipline. To befriend this god meant that a minimal Klingon presence could control a rich world in an important sector. Kral knew that accomplishing that would bring him much honor and power.

Kral hooked his thumbs onto his belt, swaggering a little as he strode into the audience chamber, allowing the heavy open-front coat to swing out impressively. His eyes quickly adjusted to the inside light. It was a testament to his will and training that he didn't falter as he took in the primitive magnificence of the huge room. He formally saluted the old man who sat in the rich, jewel-covered throne.

Weyland looked into Kral's eyes. Kral looked down. Not since he was a child had he felt so naked in the presence of a . . . a superior. He forced himself to return the stare, but his knees felt like water. And the most damning thing was that he knew Kbrex, his first officer, was standing right behind him and taking in the situation, sensing his commander's weakness. Hell take him!

"I am Weyland, and I rule here. You have taken as your own men who are mine. I am furious that, in my absence, you have endeavored to supersede my authority. You must leave this place. You *will* leave this place."

Kral snorted out his breath. Before he could reach his sidearm, the guards had a dozen spears pressed into his neck. Half a hundred more pinned the two huge Klingon security guards to the ground, while

Kbrex struggled in their grip as well. He grunted, "Commander! You must do something, now! This is intolerable!"

Like get myself killed? thought Kral. *You'd like that, wouldn't you, Kbrex?*

In an endless moment, Kral relaxed his hand, and, at a nod from the ruler, the warriors lowered their spear points. As insane as it seemed, Kral actually felt disappointed in the guards. He himself had trained them, shown them how to wield spears and honed their aggressiveness to a fighting edge. And now this Weyland came in and immediately turned them against him, with a word. Turned the skills he'd provided them against *him!*

"Now that we understand each other," the god said with disarming mildness, "you may speak if you feel a need to."

Kral swallowed hard. "I represent a great people, greater than you can imagine." The words comforted him, and as he felt the surge of their power, his uneasiness faded. "We are warriors. You are warriors. We do understand each other, Great Lord. The others, the Federation, they are weak. They also wish to ally themselves with you. But the Federation will offer you little. They will treat you as children. They will hold back the gifts of their worlds. We have already demonstrated our willingness to make you—"

"Over into the Klingon image!"

Kral spun the moment he heard the voice, and even before he saw the owner, he had a fairly clear idea of what he would see.

"Your timing, Federation man, is most irritating," he said to the men in the Starfleet uniforms who had entered with one of Weyland's guards on either side.

But Kbrex drew in a startled breath. "Kirk," he snarled. "James Kirk."

Kral did a double-take. This man, standing in the forefront of the Starfleet men, his arms folded and eyes blazing, was the formidable Captain Kirk? "So you are Kirk," said Kral. "You are somewhat less impressive than I would have imagined."

There was a snickering chortle from the other Klingons, which was quickly cut off when Kirk shot back, "Then you are as unimaginative as I would have suspected."

They glared at each other for a long moment, and then Weyland said briskly, "I see little difference between the Klingons and the Federation. You both wish to use my world for your own ends, and posture that you are motivated by concern for my people."

"Great Weyland, I assure you—" began Kirk.

But Weyland waved him off. "I am not interested in your assurances. And I am not interested in you. Leave. Now."

Kral bellowed, "We can make your home a cinder. How dare you, you primitive little worm . . ." His fists balled until his nails drove into his palms as he fought for a modicum of control. He continued with a bravado which he didn't feel once he looked at the old king. "I will forgive this outrage, for I admire courage and you have great courage. The Klingon empire still holds out its hand to you. But take heed, King Weyland, I will not hold out this offer again."

Kral spun on his heel and strode out, his heart pounding as he waited for the guards to fall on him, but they let him and his two men pass. The boys had left the practice yard. The guard was gone, but Kral saw a telltale glint of metal here and there. It was quite clear that the only path out was the one they had been escorted in.

They went through the front gates, the forest just ahead. There really was no reason at this point not to beam up, but something within Kral wouldn't let him go. He hated to just retreat in the face of defeat, and his mind was racing to try and find some sort of alternative. Some kind of plan.

A small boy stepped in the path of the Klingons. Kral looked down at him, bubbling with fury and humiliation. The child was scruffy-looking, even for one of these useless inhabitants, with dirty black hair and a vacuous look.

"Are you leaving?" he asked.

"What business is it of yours, you little fool," he snapped.

And from behind him he heard another of those blasted Starfleet men. "Ya dinna have to be so hard on the boy."

Kral turned to see the idiots directly behind him. "Blast you! This is all your fault, Kirk!"

Another of them, a shorter one, said, "If you think the keptin had anything to do with—"

"Enough, Chekov," said Kirk, never taking his eyes off the Klingons.

The small boy was tugging on Kral's sash. "I thought you were going to teach us how to kill. That's what you promised."

Kral looked down at the lad in surprise, and then up at Kirk, who was no longer trying to hide his anger. "Look at what you've done to these people," snapped the captain. "No wonder Weyland wants nothing to do with us. Look what you've done to his people in the short time you've been here."

Kbrex muttered under his breath, "He insults us with impunity. I can't believe it."

If Kbrex had taken dead aim with a phaser to Kral's head, he could not have scored a more direct hit. Incensed with seeing months of work go down the drain, Kral unloaded his fury on the closest target.

He yanked out his blaster and fired it directly at Kirk.

But as fast as he was, the Starfleet security guards were even faster, interposing themselves in front of Kirk, knocking him aside and returning fire with their own phasers. The Klingons immediately ducked for cover, firing their blasters as the Federation men sought cover as well.

Within seconds the air was filled with the sounds of weapons fire. Kbrex crouched next to Kral and said sharply, "You wisely defended our honor, Commander."

"Shut up!" snapped Kral, firing blindly around the rock that was his shelter.

Kbrex pulled something from his belt. Kral glanced at it and actually smiled. A plasma grenade. "Hurry," muttered Kral. "The Starfleet men will doubtlessly return to their ship within moments."

"They have no honor," said Kbrex, activating the grenade and hurling it. Above his head, phaser bolts flew, and he couldn't risk a glance to see how accurate the throw had been.

Then the Klingons heard a shout of alarm, but not of fear. Something was wrong, and Kral risked a glance around the rock.

What he saw stunned him.

The small boy who had spoken to him was standing barely a meter away from where the Federation men were crouched behind sheltering rocks and trees. He was holding the plasma grenade, turning it over and staring at it as if he'd found a new toy. His face was wide with a grin.

The grenade only had a five-second timer on it.

Kral immediately stood, and then a Federation man leaped from hiding. He heard Kirk's alarmed shout of

"Garrovick! What are you doing?!" Clearly, Kirk hadn't seen the grenade.

The one called Garrovick leaped at the boy and grabbed at the grenade. His fingers brushed against it, and the boy yanked it away with surprising stubbornness.

"Mine!" shouted the enraged boy, which would be the last word the boy ever uttered. He clasped the grenade to his small chest.

With a shout of panicked rage, Garrovick lunged forward, his fingers grasping at the grenade.

It went off.

A burst of light and heat surrounded the two of them, the stench of death and burned meat permeating the air. Kral looked away from the intensity of the light, looked into his soul and was distressed at the blackness he saw in there. Roaring in his ears was the sound of the grenade, the sound deafening, yet failing to drown out the brief scream of the one called Garrovick or the hopeless, desperate shout of Kirk. The child had apparently had no time to scream.

He looked back at the site of the destruction. Of the boy there was the barest remains of ashes. The grenade had vented the majority of its fury on the child who had been smothering it.

Garrovick lay on the ground, smoldering, unmoving. Kral could see even from where he was that the Federation man was dead.

"Commander," grated Kbrex. He shook Kral's shoulder. "Commander. Let's leave, immediately."

"Yes. Yes, you're right," said Kral, his mind still a fog. How the devil had it all fallen apart so quickly? What could have gone so horribly wrong in such a short period of time? Even as thoughts tumbled through his head, he had his communicator open and was alerting his ship.

He heard an infuriated shout from Kirk, a snarled challenge, and then the hum of the Klingon transporter drowned it all out.

The death of a child, he thought as the planet vanished around him. Where was the honor in that?

Chapter Seven

Japan, 1600

WHEN SULU HAD HEARD tales of feudal Japan, or conjured up images in his mind, somehow they had a gloss over them. A purity of image, with no real taste of reality to it.

There was more than enough reality surrounding him now, that was for sure.

They had passed groveling farmers, who looked up at him with a startling pathos. Sulu tried not to be affected by the scene, for he could sense the eyes of the gray-haired Sadayo on him. The noble samurai clearly had suspicions about him.

Would the formidable Sadayo, and the other soldiers, have been able to handle the brigands? Sulu kept telling himself that the answer was yes. To believe otherwise was too chilling, because that would mean he had already changed things.

He was smack in the middle of a Prime Directive nightmare. Did he cause the death of those men? No. No, he was certain he hadn't. Their death was written. They would have died in the attack. Or . . . what if the woman had? What if she was supposed to have died, and Sulu had saved her when she wasn't supposed to be saved?

Could he have caused someone, in the farflung future, to vanish? Or created someone who wasn't supposed to exist? Perhaps dozens of someones, or thousands. His mind whirled with the possibilities. What the devil was he supposed to do? Should he have just stood by and let her die—presuming that he had fully realized, at the time, that he was not caught in a dream. He was afraid to take a step, make any sort of move.

No. He couldn't have let her die. He was just going to have to follow his instincts, and trust them to guide him through.

They had entered the great, sprawling city of Kyoto. Not modern Kyoto, to be sure, but a disconcertingly primitive city of shops and temples and small houses, crowding each other onto crooked side streets. When Sulu had visited Kyoto—*his* Kyoto—he had occasionally wondered what it would be like to visit the city in all its feudal glory.

Somehow it had seemed a lot less grubby in his imaginings. And it had smelled a lot better.

Soon they passed the middle-class section and were riding through a district of elegant private homes which were the reward of lesser nobles and loyal retainers, and houses once owned by most of the major clans—where wives, daughters, and young sons were held in perpetual hostage to ensure loyalty to the current ruler in the endless power struggle that was Japanese history. But the capital had been moved to Edo, and the hostages, and the culture which they practiced to pass the endless days, had moved there also.

Toward mid-afternoon they wound their way past a network of wet and dry moats and over a number of bridges to the gate of a huge castle. Sulu looked up with wonder. Looming up was a smooth-walled mountain of stone. Above, in sharp contrast to the massive fortification at the base, were the living quarters, white walls and red-tile roofs stacked with pagodalike grace. Each roof line displayed support beams carved with fantastic animals, rendered with such skill they seemed to want to leap to life.

Moments later they were in the great courtyard, and Sulu and the others had dismounted.

"Follow me," Sadayo said.

They marched to a formal reception hall. Sadayo knelt outside the screen and announced himself and Sulu. They were admitted and both bowed to the ground. "Lord," Sadayo said, "the Lady Oneko's party was attacked by bandits. She is safe. This man, Suru Heihachiro, came to our aid."

Sulu's breath caught.

It was Torii Mototada.

He regarded Sulu with unrestrained interest, as if trying to see what was inside Sulu's head. Inwardly, Sulu trembled. This man was absolutely legendary. To be in front of him was to share in the legend.

Torii Mototada, the man who was a legend. A man who was larger than life.

He was shorter than Sulu.

Somehow Sulu had always envisioned him being a giant among men, not half a head shorter than himself. He stifled an impulse to laugh, and then the impulse quickly dissipated. Mototada did not need height. He had a staggering presence born of character and breeding.

"Would you serve me?" Lord Torii Mototada asked.

This was not a question asked lightly.

Instinct. What was his instinct telling him to say?

If he refused, that might engender questions—uncomfortable questions that Sulu couldn't answer. And he was still feeling disoriented enough that he didn't want to try and lie. For that matter, to refuse might even be an insult to honor.

Honor was a concept that Sulu understood intellectually, and of course it was part of his upbringing. But it wasn't the suffocating presence that hung over him here.

Honor.

It would indeed be an honor to serve Mototada. To be part of a legend. There was something almost comforting about it. Cast adrift in a sea of time, here was a life preserver being tossed to him.

"Yes, lord," Sulu answered, bowing formally.

"I, Torii Mototada, shall give you the gift of a new name. You shall now be Okiri Heihachiro, Big Cut Heihachiro. You shall have a hundred koku income, and you shall be a retainer in my service, and you shall be in my bodyguard. Do you accept?"

"Ha," Sulu snapped in the clipped warrior pronunciation for the word for yes, "I am most grateful for the great honor you bestow. I shall look to you for guidance, that I may serve you worthily."

It was then he decided that he was probably losing his mind.

Chapter Eight

Scotland, 1746

SCOTTY MOANED, clutching at his head.

"Hush!"

He rolled over and peered with bleary eyes at a face that took a few moments to snap into focus. It was the young man he'd seen . . .

He'd seen . . .

When?

Scotty frowned, trying to remember . . . trying to piece together the events of the recent . . . what? Days? Years? What?

"Don't raise such a ruckus," the boy cautioned him. "You'll alert the soldiers. Or the master."

"Oh . . . I see . . . That's clear enough," Scotty said, even though it wasn't.

"I'll get you some clothes," hissed the boy. "You'll need them. A kilted highlander is not welcome in these parts. Who the devil are you, anyway?"

Scotty touched the dried blood on his face. "I'm—" His voice caught and he frowned, trying to pull it out.

"You're a Scotsman, obviously," the boy said with impatience.

"Scott! I'm . . . Montgomery Scott." He sat up and

the world spun around him. He reached down to brace himself. "Montgomery Scott," he said again, as if taking refuge in the one thing he was sure of.

"Where did you come from? How did you get here?"

"I . . ." He frowned. Images that made no sense flashed before him. "I don't know. I dinna ken how I got here." He looked at the boy hopefully. "Do you?"

The boy looked taken aback. "You must know."

"I did. I . . ." He shook his head, the simple motion being enough to make him hurt all the more. "But I don't. I . . ."

"Look, enough for this later. I've got to go now."

Scotty lay back, staring at the ceiling as the boy scampered down the ladder with the agility of a monkey.

Scott.

Montgomery Scott.

And he was a . . .

He sought the word. Machines. He was good with machines, he remembered. And he could . . .

Could what?

About an hour later the boy dragged up a bundle and held it out to Scotty. "Here you go," he said.

The bundle consisted of a pair of knee breeches of coarse wool, a clean white linen shirt, as well as underlinen, stockings, and a pair of shoes—which fit after some addition of a little straw at the toe—a vest, a coat, and tricorn hat.

Scott dressed, rolled up the soiled wool kilt and oversized shift called a *leine* and hid them in the hay.

"Thank you, lad. Now perhaps you'll tell me why you stole from your master to help a stranger?"

The boy's eyes narrowed. "I did not steal. They were left by a lodger. And the innkeeper is not my master. I've only just been hired here. And as to why, I have my reasons," he answered with an implied challenge. He added somewhat scornfully, "I saw you last night, and that *was* stealing!"

Scotty shrugged. He was not in condition to argue. He barely remembered last night.

The boy couldn't have been more than fourteen or fifteen, but he had a kind of adult toughness.

"Well, I'll not argue with my good luck," Scott returned evenly. "Tell me, boy, you mentioned soldiers. What soldiers?"

"Well . . . they're not actually here yet," admitted the boy. "But they're coming. Fat Billy's boys are coming to stay. They have been chasing the prince's men all the way up from near London town, I hear. Frankly . . . I think Prince Charles is going to need a miracle."

And suddenly it clicked into Scott's mind.

"That's it," he whispered.

"What?" said the boy.

"I remember," Scott said with growing excitement. "I was trying to remember what I could do. What my skills are. And I just remembered . . . my reputation."

"What reputation?"

And Scotty smiled in satisfaction. "I'm a Miracle Worker," he said confidently.

Chapter Nine

Stalingrad, 1942

CHEKOV WAS SITTING next to Sulu, Scotty, and Kirk, and they were all laughing over this bizarre vacation that Chekov had had.

Chekov saw himself, smiling and bleeding, and telling his friends in avid and enthused detail about what he'd just been through.

The Battle of Stalingrad had been Russian determination at its absolute best. Stalingrad, a sprawling but narrow band of civilization and industry, lay hugging the west shore of the great river. Farther to the west, the Don, the other great river, had been crossed and the German Sixth Army now sought to control the city. Once Stalingrad fell, the Germans hoped to cross the Volga and press their attack to the heart of the Soviet Union.

Whatever strategic value there might have been in capturing Stalingrad had been long forgotten, however, in the battle of egos. Hitler was determined to level the city, and Stalin wanted it held at all costs. And the costs to both sides were already staggering.

The Russian people had put up a resistance that Berlin still wouldn't believe—fighting house to house, hand to hand, holding the city with a tenuous toehold.

And every bullet, every shoe, every pound of grain, every replacement soldier, had to be barged across the Volga under the constant and devastating fire of German mortar and the low-level strafing by the Stukkas and Ju-88s which bombed incessantly despite the antiaircraft guns on both shores of the river. Many men and women didn't survive the trip to the west shore.

Chekov had been about to tell his shipmates more. About the famous statue of the Stone Crocodile. About Stalin, for whom the city was named. Except there was a rat crawling across his face.

He sat up with a cry of revulsion. There was an alarmed squeal as he batted at his face, sending the rodent tumbling off and onto the nearby filthy floor of the cell.

The smiling images of his friends slipped away, and the true confusing horror of his real-life situation slammed home to him. He backward-crabbed across the floor until he banged into a wall.

It was dark in the cell, his eyes not yet adjusted to the one dim bulb overhead. Chekov stammered, again in English, "Vere am I? Vat is happening? How did I get here?"

There was a low laugh from within the darkness of the cell.

"Well, now isn't that convenient."

Chekov squinted. "Am I still in Stalingrad?" He was still hoping that somehow Sulu would suddenly come leaping out, laughing and telling his old friend that the entire business was an elaborate gag.

"Nope," said the voice, decidedly American, and even oddly familiar. "Chicago. Don't you realize where you are? This is Wrigley Field."

Chekov looked around. "I think you are kidding."

"And I think," said the voice, "that you krauts must think I'm a total idiot."

Kraut. Chekov's first instinct was to think the reference was to something put on a hot dog. Then he realized. "I'm not a kraut—a German. I'm a Russian. My name is Chekov."

"Oh yeah? Loved *Uncle Vanya*. Look, what do you people take me for? Guy comes in here, conveniently speaking English. You think that after the beatings, the wires . . . everything you people have tried, that now you can trick me into spilling everything by putting a spy in here with me. No chance."

"No chance," said Chekov vacantly, still looking around. It was still dark as hell. There was an unpleasant stench to the cell, and in every shadow vermin of some sort lurked.

Out of habit he reached for his communicator. None was there, of course.

"Scotty," he said softly, "beam me the hell out of here."

"Name's not Scotty, pal," said the other prisoner. "You want the name? You want the rank? You want the serial number? That's all you're going to get. If you don't get tired of hearing it, I don't get tired of saying it." The American sounded bitter and tired. He had the air of someone who had made peace with the fact that he was going to die, and was only awaiting the answer of "when" with a sort of disassociated interest.

And then Chekov's eyes widened as the man intoned, "My name is John C. Kirk. Lieutenant. United States Army Air Corps, serial number 0–159466. And that, my friend, is all you're going to hear out of me."

Chapter Ten

IT HAD BEEN only moments earlier when Kirk had been sitting in his cabin, a drink in his hand, declaring with utter confidence and certainty to Dr. McCoy that he was going to join Spock in the conference room and together they were going to figure out a way out of this mess.

And what a mess it was. Garrovick dead, weapons systems out, helpless in orbit above Cragon V, with Weyland prepared to do who-knew-what. And worst of all, Sulu, Scotty, and Chekov were missing in action.

Kirk leaned against the railing of the turbolift, letting some of the self-doubt that he frequently felt wash over him.

The first rule they teach in command school—when you make a decision, stick to it. Even if it turns out to be the wrong one, see it through. Everyone makes wrong decisions. There's no such thing as a perfect commander. That's accepted. But a commander who reverses decisions, or displays doubt for the crew to witness—that was not accepted. That was intolerable.

So the crew never saw Kirk's indecision or regrets.

Instead they saw the calm, confident commander, and they drew their strength and assurance from him. And it was left to Kirk to reflect on his own decisions in private. The final, unchangeable decisions that he made, that sometimes cost him lives . . . and crewmen. Crewmen like Garrovick, Scotty, Chekov . . . Sulu . . .

"Captain, they're firing on us!" Sulu called out, tightening his grip on the helm.

Moments before, Kirk and the landing party had beamed up to the *Enterprise* and been met by a med team in the transporter room. McCoy had been first to meet them, of course, and he repressed his shock upon seeing the limp form of Garrovick that Kirk was carrying in his arms. He didn't ask details, didn't ask what had happened. He even refrained from uttering an oath or cursing the individuals responsible for this. Instead he immediately called for an antigrav stretcher to be brought forward, and without a word Kirk lay Garrovick down on the gurney. His voice a hoarse whisper, Kirk had said, "Do what you can for him, Bones."

Even as Kirk spoke, McCoy was already running his diagnostic instruments over Garrovick in preparation to rush him to sickbay. But his readings told him that no rush would be necessary, and the look in McCoy's eyes told Kirk the same thing.

"He tried to save a boy," whispered Kirk.

"Where's the boy?" McCoy asked.

"There wasna enough left of the lad to bring back up," Scotty had said softly.

"Who did this?" McCoy said, looking at the landing party.

For answer, Kirk had crossed quickly to the comm panel and hit it. "Kirk to bridge."

"Spock here," came the brisk reply. "Captain, your

return is none too soon. A Klingon ship has decloaked and is bearing," the most minute of pauses, "611 mark five."

"He wants to finish this," snapped Kirk. "That's what he'll get then. Shields up."

"Already up, sir. Phasers fully charged."

"If they're decloaked, they're about to fire. Evasive maneuvers. I'm on my way."

They were there in record time. Kirk heard the sounds of Klingon disruptor fire thudding against the *Enterprise* shields. Next to him in the turbolift he saw Sulu's fingers twitch slightly, as if imagining that he was returning fire. Chekov's face was set, and Scotty's was equally expressionless. Normally Scotty would be down in the engineering section, but it was clear from his face that he was intending to man the engineering station on the bridge. Obviously this was one encounter he wanted to bear witness to firsthand.

The four men virtually exploded out onto the bridge, lower ranking officers immediately vacating the stations to let the senior officers take charge. Spock smoothly removed himself from the command chair as Kirk slid in. Sulu and Chekov barely had time to seat themselves when Sulu called out the warning that the Klingon ship was firing once more.

The ship shuddered, and just as the word "Fire!" emerged from Kirk's lips, the Klingon battle cruiser vanished from the screen. Sulu sent out a torpedo spread in the area where the Klingons had been moments before, but his instruments told him that it was a clean miss.

"He took pot shots at us and then timed his vanishing act perfectly," muttered Kirk.

"He's good, Captain," Sulu said, his voice steady. Still, despite his calm, there was nothing in his attitude to indicate that battle was a casual experience.

"Helm, thirty degrees starboard," the captain ordered.

Sulu brought the ship around, and suddenly the engineering sections and underside of the engine nacelles were battered by phaser fire. The Klingon ship had rematerialized . . . directly under the starship. Then it vanished again. Hit and run.

Kirk was starting to get annoyed.

"Come about. Shields, status?"

"Shields forty-two percent and dropping, sir," Chekov said crisply.

And now Sulu spoke up. "Helm is sluggish to respond, Captain."

Scotty visibly winced at that, in anticipation of his captain's next question. "Scotty, why aren't we moving?"

"Sir, the right engine pod is down to fifteen percent, and the other is overheating. I canna give you maneuverability. I'm not sure I can give you warp."

"Captain," said Sulu crisply, "it's only approximate, but I believe I've got them nailed on the motion detector."

"Then hammer them, Mr. Sulu. Fire phasers."

And that was the moment when the mission, which had seemed incapable of getting any worse, got worse.

Sulu let out a cry, drawing his hands back. His skin was blistering and puckering on his palms. He gasped in amazement, and Chekov, thinking that somehow Sulu's board had overheated, tried to reroute phaser locking controls into his own console. A worthwhile but futile effort, for suddenly Chekov likewise found his controls unmanageable. The temperature had gone from normal to scalding within a nanosecond.

To Chekov and Kirk, it was momentarily confusing. To Sulu, it was a sensation that immediately brought back unpleasant memories.

"Sulu, what the devil's wrong?" demanded Kirk.

"Surface temperature of the weapons instruments has just gone nova, Captain," said Sulu. "Just like the time on Organia!"

"Forward drive is out, Captain," Scott told him. "We're not moving."

"The Organians?" said Kirk. "That's just . . . marvelous."

Uhura looked up. She was somewhat surprised that her comm board was still working, for when they had gone through this before, her station had become as overheated as anyone else's. "Captain," she said, "I'm getting a hailing frequency from the Klingon ship."

Kirk looked up at the viewscreen. Lo and behold, the Klingon ship had come floating into view, visible and helpless. Except for all that the *Enterprise* could do right now, they might as well still be cloaked and maneuverable.

Controls too hot to handle? Kirk was tempted to try and operate them using environmental gloves, but he had a feeling that wouldn't accomplish anything. Whoever was doing this—the Organians, apparently —might not take kindly to that, and cause the phaser banks to self-destruct, taking the *Enterprise* with them.

"On screen, Uhura," said Kirk.

The snarling and furious face of the Klingon commander—what was his name . . . Kral, was it?— appeared on the screen.

"All right, Federation bastards, you have us!" he snapped. "You've rendered us helpless! Destroy us and be done with it!"

Kirk's eyes widened momentarily and he glanced at Spock. The answer was clear—they thought the *Enterprise* had employed some sort of weapon against them and had incapacitated them. They didn't realize —at least not yet—that the starship was in the same fix.

"No," said Kirk sharply, barely containing his fury. "We'll kill you when we're damned good and ready."

"Rot in Dargoth's hell, Kirk," snarled the Klingon, and the transmission was cut off.

Kirk looked at his bridge crew. "All right. Now we wait for the other shoe to drop."

At that moment something began to shimmer into life directly in front of them on the viewscreen. Space seemed to cloud over and the cloud started to assume a shape.

"I believe, Captain," said Spock calmly, "that the remaining footwear you had mentioned is about to plummet."

Kirk wasn't sure what he expected. Ayelbourne, perhaps. Or one of the other members of the Organian council. Or maybe someone new. What he did not expect, however, was what he saw, and in retrospect he would wonder how he could not have seen it coming.

The screen dimmed, blocking most of the most painful glare. A man, ancient but still strong, full-bearded, with piercing eyes, stared out at them.

"Weyland!" Kirk muttered.

Spock raised an eyebrow. "The same Weyland, I assume, as the so-called god of the people of Cragon."

"A step above 'so-called,' I'd say," Kirk commented.

Weyland's massive face filled the screen.

"What . . . are you?" asked Kirk.

With a sepulchral voice, Weyland replied, "In charge."

"Vague but accurate," Spock observed.

Kirk did not have the time or enthusiasm to take pleasure in Weyland's brevity.

"You committed a crime against my people," Weyland said. "A child has died."

"Yes," said Kirk softly. "We know. We saw it. And we regret what happened."

"What happened was a direct result of your savagery," said Weyland, his fury clearly growing. "You doubtlessly think of my people as primitive—but the actions of the Klingons in their 'training' has destroyed my people's beauty of spirit."

"And where were you!" said Kirk sharply. "You claim to protect and love these people, yet you abandoned them for months, allowing the Klingons to do as they wished."

Weyland frowned, and then he said, "If it will make you understand what is about to happen to you more, then I will tell you . . ."

"What do you mean, about to happen to us?" said Kirk.

Weyland ignored him. "I was a part of a continuum of beings," he said. "Beings so evolved, so powerful, that they have taken to merely observing life in various universes, instead of using their abilities for helping lesser beings. I sojourned for a time in this universe, and found, purely at random, the good, simple people of Cragon. They touched something within me, and I knew that I would never be able to continue being a part of an entity that exists to ignore existence. I returned to them to tell them of my resignation from their alliance. But time is a subjective matter, far more so than I thought. I perceived myself as gone to my fellows for mere moments, but on Cragon months passed. Months that the Klingons put to use, and that you Federation men exacerbated. And your hostilities, Captain Kirk, resulted in the death of a child."

"It was a Klingon grenade that did it!" said Kirk. "I lost a man as well!"

"It was you who gave your word of honor to make sure no harm came to my people."

"You're the one who said you didn't need our help!" Kirk reminded him.

"That is irrelevant," Weyland said archly, and it was at that point that Kirk became convinced they were not dealing with a being who had any sort of solid grip on reality. "One of my people is dead as a result of an altercation between the Klingons and the Federation. The Federation is by far the worse aggressor, because of your moral posturing and high-minded ideals . . . when, actually, you are no better than the Klingons."

"That's not true," Kirk protested, beginning to feel like a broken record.

"Deny the truth of this, then—a child is dead because of the inability of the Federation and the Klingons to cooperate and act in a manner that betokens honor for all. Do you agree?"

Kirk paused. The bottom line was, Weyland was right. A child had been caught in the crossfire. The Klingons had initiated, the Klingons had caused it, but the Starfleet officers had been the target. How many times were innocents caught in between in the past of human history, because two groups were too thick-skinned to work out their differences?

But these were Klingons, dammit . . .

And they were the Federation. They believed in liberty and self-determination and the right of the weak to be defended and protected . . .

All of which made no difference to the charred corpse on the planet below, or the parents who were doubtless in mourning at that moment.

"I don't deny that," Kirk said softly. "But—"

"Good," said Weyland. "Sentence is carried out. Now."

There were three sounds, all the same, all simultaneous. Kirk looked around in confusion, trying to locate the source.

Spock was on his feet, his eyebrows arched, which was the closest he ever came to expressing surprise. Uhura gasped in shock, and then Kirk realized.

Sulu was gone. And Chekov. And Scotty. Gone, as if they had never been there.

"What have you done!" shouted Kirk. "I don't understand! If you're upset with me, punish me! I'm the commander. It's my responsibility!"

"But I am punishing you," said Weyland calmly. "Your punishment . . . is not knowing what happened to the fellow members of your landing party. The most effective way to discipline a commander of men . . . is to discipline his men, and leave the commander helpless."

"Where are they!" shouted Kirk.

"They are lost in time out of mind," Weyland told him. "And you can sit and rot waiting for them to return. This audience is ended."

And Weyland vanished.

Chapter Eleven

Scotland, 1746

MONTGOMERY SCOTT SAT in his comfortable loft, eating
the food the boy had sneaked him, and reveled in his
newfound understanding of himself.

He was a Miracle Worker. He knew that. He had the
ability to do things . . . things that no one else could
do.

At first he wasn't sure what that was. He had clung
to the description as if to a life preserver, and then
facts had started to float into his head. Facts as if they
had been given him from another time, another land.

Facts about his situation.

They tumbled through his head, names setting his
recollection off. Fat Billy, the boy had said. Prince
Charles, the boy had said.

Fat Billy was William Cumberland.

Prince Charles—Bonny Prince Charlie, as he was
known *(was* known? What sort of thinking was that?)
—who was . . .

Was what?

Scotty pulled at his memory.

Defeated. Fat William to his enemies and Sweet
William—for whom the flower was named *(will be*

named?)—to his friends. Either way, William had defeated *(will defeat?)* Bonny Prince Charlie.

His concept of past and future rushing together, Scotty remembered forward and backward.

Prince Charlie had landed in a remote part of Scotland, hiding out for months, gathering a ragtag army from the independent-minded clans that divided the Scottish highlands into a patchwork of holdings which were half feudal fiefs and half barbarian tribal lands. Then he proceeded to declare himself the rightful King of England and Scotland and commenced his march south. Needless to say, London was not amused, but the English crown had never been amused by any of the troubles caused by its Celtic peoples, be they Scot, Irish, or Welsh. It had been warfare in the long months that followed.

The Great Rebellion, it was called . . .

"Will be called," he muttered.

"What are you talking about?"

He looked up and saw the teenage boy again, looking at him oddly. "I'm remembering things . . . that haven't happened yet."

The boy's mouth dropped open. "Are you saying you have 'The Sight'?"

Bemusedly, Scotty rubbed his eyes. "If I do, my sighted eyes are fair tired about now. Still . . . I canna stay up in this loft forever." He looked at the boy with curiosity. "Tell me, lad—what's your name?"

"Seamus MacIntyre it is, but when I hired on here I told them to call me James. Lowlanders they are. *No* better than Englishmen. Damn Sassenachs," he spat, using the Gallic word for the English that was more a curse than a translation.

Inwardly, Scotty grimaced. Lowlanders. Highlanders. Clans upon clans that would cause the vision of a united Scotland, under the command of Bonny Prince Charlie, to split apart.

Interestingly, he realized that his own name, Scott, was considered a lowland name. Since this Seamus obviously had no love for lowlanders, it was curious that he hadn't remarked on it. Mentally he shrugged it off.

"Well, Mr. MacIntyre, what do you propose now?"

"Well, Mr. Scott, I think it would be best if you came in by the front door, and perhaps applied for day work. You were the one who got the slops the other day, were you not? But I'll wager the mistress will not know you. She is short of sight. So if you come as a man who needs work, what with the Duke coming, I'll wager you'll be welcomed, and make a penny on it."

"Aye, and perhaps hear a thing or two? That is a sharp plan, boy. After that?"

"After that I'm running off to fight with the prince. And you?"

"I think that might not be a bad plan, either," Scott said, offering his hand. The boy hesitated a moment before he reached out to shake hands, bowing slightly with gentlemanly courtesy.

"The prince could use someone with The Sight. Tell me, Miracle Worker . . ." And his voice was eager. "When will the prince win?"

Not if. When. The boy's confidence was boundless.

Who was he to tell the boy otherwise at this early date? Facts and dates still whirled in his head. He had suspicions, beliefs, but of nothing was he absolutely sure.

Scotty put a hand on the boy's shoulder. "When the time is right," he said. "When the time is right."

Scott managed to get clear of the inn, with the boy acting as lookout, and cut his way around a field. When he was safely out of sight, he turned back and marched up to the front door. In his new dry clothes Scott didn't look half disreputable or feel half bad.

His second encounter with Mrs. Nesbit, which was

the coarse woman's name, was fractionally more amicable. She growled and threatened and warned, but she did hire him. Her husband had no idea that this man was the one with whom he had struggled a couple days earlier. Seamus's description had been nothing like this man before him. The bandage Scott wore about his head was not even questioned— nowadays, with all the fighting going on, it was a rare man who was not injured in some way or other. So Commander Montgomery Scott, late of Starfleet, began his career as an apprentice publican at The Hanged Woman.

Chapter Twelve

Stalingrad, 1942

"OH, MY GOD!" Chekov muttered in English, a chill running through him. "Kirk, you say?"

The man was silent.

"Lieutenant Kirk, please, are you all right?" Chekov asked desperately, feeling in the dark for the silent man.

"Yeah," the flyer said. "I told you, you won't get anything out of me."

This couldn't be. This was too insane. John C. Kirk. Maybe, Chekov told himself insanely, the C stood for "Captain." It wouldn't be much crazier than what was going through his mind.

Kirk wasn't a rare name. It couldn't be what he thought. Whatever had happened to him, whatever fate had dropped him in another time and place with no explanation, it couldn't be that cruel.

Could it?

Chekov thought of some of the beings he had encountered in his life—everyone from Apollo to V'ger. Could it be?

"What does the C stand for?" he asked neutrally.

"Claudius," the man answered. He sounded charmingly defensive about it. "My grandfather had a thing about Latin studies. It's sort of a family tradition. I don't suppose that's giving away anything. Can't see Uncle Adolf getting much mileage out of that."

"You don't have to be embarrassed about it," Chekov said.

"It's not embarrassment. Not anymore," he added reluctantly. "Sure, I admit it was a real burden in school. Always hid what it meant. God, it's good to talk to someone, anyone. Got to shut up," he went on, more to himself than Chekov. "Got to shut up before I can't stop talking," he said, and then lapsed into silence. Then he added softly, "If you're a spy the Nazis put in here, you'll probably die of boredom before you hear anything useful out of me."

Chekov suspected he was right. He suspected a lot of things, none of which he liked.

It was too much of a coincidence, that odd Roman middle name. Like James Tiberius Kirk. Chekov struggled to calm himself. Where did the Prime Directive fit into the scheme of things here? he wondered. His captain's great-great-times-how-many grandfather? Was it possible?

"Have you any brothers, or uncles?" Chekov asked after a while. "Or a son?" At first the man wouldn't answer.

"What business is it of yours?" he finally muttered.

"None. Just trying to pass the time," said Chekov with an indifferent shrug.

Nothing got people talking quite like acting as if you couldn't care less whether they talked.

"All right," said Kirk gamely. "More important info for Uncle Adolf. My father is dead, I have no brothers, and one sister who works in the U.S.O. and is engaged to some guy named Capelli. Okay? I'm not married, and frankly, in these circumstances, the pickings are pretty slim. Unless you're doing one hell of an impression and actually you're going to turn out to be Betty Grable here to boost my morale."

"Afraid not," said Chekov.

Inwardly, Chekov's mind was racing. *Oh, God! The captain* . . . If he were right, this man was his captain's ancestor.

It was the no-win scenario all over again. He was not supposed to interfere. Such was the Prime Directive. Except he had, automatically, rather than let the Russians be shot down like dogs. And that action had seemed to backfire horribly—except it led him to someone who desperately needed his help, because otherwise the future that Chekov knew might not exist. Except he wasn't supposed to help . . . except if he didn't . . .

Chekov moaned softly.

"What's your problem?" asked Kirk.

"Time," replied Chekov.

"Well, we've got nothing but that," said Kirk.

The door creaked open and a man in a tattered German uniform came stumbling in. Chekov tried to stand, but his legs were shaky, and then the door slammed before he could do anything.

Anything like what? Get shot?

"Friend of yours?" asked Kirk.

The American airman leaned forward, the faint light from the single overhead bulb highlighting him. Now there was no doubt. Despite the terrible swollen bruises that deformed the airman's face, a young Captain Kirk looked back at him.

The man in the German uniform fell to the floor, looked up groggily at Kirk, and then at Chekov. They recognized each other at the same time.

"Oh, God," moaned the soldier in Russian. "You're the one I shot."

Kirk looked up at Chekov and, in flawless Russian, said, "You're obviously a very popular guy."

"It's a knack," replied Chekov. He remained where he was, staring at the newcomer. "You have an odd way of expressing gratitude, comrade."

"I am so, so sorry, as I cannot begin to express," said the soldier, sitting up. From the look of him, he wasn't in much better shape than Kirk. "I'm Ivan. Ivan Romanoff. A sergeant," and he looked around ruefully, "for all the good it did me."

"Romanoff. Why did you shoot me?"

"I saw you coming at us. In the confusion, it was automatic. Even as I was squeezing the trigger, I realized that you were the one who had created the diversion. What in the name of sanity were you doing inside of a German camp?"

Chekov thought fast. "Trying my best to do what I can for my people."

"Nice reply," said Kirk. "Very smooth."

Chekov did not reply. He saw no reason to. "What were you doing here?"

Ivan pursed his lips for a moment, then shrugged. "Transport plane they have on premises. Looked nice. We thought it would make a nice trophy."

Kirk looked from one man to the other. "We're quite trusting, aren't we, Romanoff? We know each other from before, but how do you know he isn't a spy?"

Ivan shrugged. "I've developed a talent for telling friends from foes. For example, I can always spot the secret police. A sixth sense. It tells me that this man is okay."

"Secret police?" asked Chekov.

Ivan looked at him strangely, and Chekov immediately realized that his obvious confusion about the secret police was obviously something that would not be shared by a present-day Russian. Already he was dredging up memories of it from who-knew-where, and he said without pause, "You can actually tell who

72

is with the secret police? Hard to believe. And where do you two know each other from?"

Kirk and Ivan looked at each other. "One wild night in Moscow," Kirk recalled with a smile that definitely evoked memories of a man not yet born.

"Um-hm," said Chekov. "So tell me . . . why am I supposed to trust the two of you? How do I know the two of you aren't spies out to trick me?"

A full grin split Kirk's face. "He's paranoid," said Kirk.

"That proves he's Russian," said Ivan.

Chekov shook his head. "Paranoia . . . secret police . . . it's difficult to think of these as part of what it is to be Russian."

"Welcome to the twentieth century," said Ivan.

It was a welcome the man from centuries hence could have done without.

Chapter Thirteen

VLADRA OF THE SCIENCE DEPARTMENT on the *Ghargh* looked up in surprise as the door to her quarters slid open. She was even more surprised when Kbrex stepped in quickly, his gaze moving sharply over the room as if taking in every corner. As if looking for a trap.

"I do not recall inviting you here, Kbrex," she said with deliberate informality.

The Ghargh had been sitting over Cragon V, helplessly, for twelve hours now. Vladra and her team had been exploring every possible means of breaking free from its helpless situation. So far, their efforts had proved fruitless.

"I think you know why I am here," he said. The door hissed shut behind him.

"Certainly. You are here to berate me for taking the first few minutes' rest in hours. I am sorry for being so lazy." Every syllable was dripping with sarcasm.

He stepped forward and put his hands firmly on either shoulder of the aristocratic-looking Klingon woman. "I have had enough of this nonsense. I have spoken to you in oblique, nondefinite terms as to my plans. You have chosen to remain oblivious of my meaning, so I shall be plain. I find you attractive, woman. I also find the prospect of command even more attractive. I would like to have both, and I wish to know of your loyalties to our present commander."

She looked away, her arms folded. "My loyalties are my own. As with any Klingon." She turned and stared at him with an icy gaze. "You will just have to take your chances."

Kbrex stared at her for a long moment. Then he nodded briskly, turned and left.

She waited for a full minute after Kbrex had left, her mind racing. It had been his murmuring and hints that had prompted her to go to Kral in the first place. It was clear that Kbrex was planning to gain from the debacle that was Cragon V.

None of this—none of it—was Kral's fault, Vladra told herself. He had done everything that any reasonable commander could be expected to do. But none of that was going to matter. In the Klingon empire all that mattered was results. Results got you promotion, command, and respect. Lack of results got you dead.

That was exactly what Kral was going to be. Dead.

Her mind raced. Kbrex was aggressive, experienced. More experienced, in fact, than Kral. That certainly had to be sticking in his craw, and pushing him into making a move against Kral. Who knew how many of the crewmen were on Kbrex's side? Some were always looking for excuses, always eager to hang any failure on one individual Klingon. So that they could tell themselves that the failure was the weakness of one individual and not a reflection on the entire race.

She might be better served if she aligned herself with Kbrex. It was clear from his demeanor, from words both spoken and unspoken, that he regarded her as far more than a potential ally. He was aggressive and powerful—all the things attractive in a Klingon male.

Kbrex was going to be the way of the future, and yet she called to mind an image of Kral. Young, vital, muscular and alive . . . so alive . . .

And he would be dead.

But not if she could help it.

Her mind made up, she reflexively reached for a comm unit. But that was not wise, she realized. Any communications might be monitored. She left her cabin and went down the hallway, first at a brisk walk and then at a run. Something was sounding an alarm in her head, a warning that time had run out much faster than she had thought.

She rounded the corner and banged on the door of Kral's quarters. The door hissed open, activated from within.

"Commander, I can't wait anymore, I must warn you about Kbrex—"

She stopped dead.

Kbrex was seated in leisurely fashion within, his legs propped up on a table, his blaster in his lap. He was smiling broadly.

"How kind of you to alert our beloved commander," said Kbrex in purring bemusement. "Unfortunately for you, he has gone back up to the bridge."

He stood and walked slowly across the room to her. Vladra stared at him, her chin tilted upward, her eyes defiant.

"So you have chosen," he said, shaking his head. "That is a pity. Let me show you . . . what you have missed."

He grabbed her roughly and fiercely slammed his lips against hers. She struggled in his grasp, her hands trying to reach her dagger. Kbrex grabbed her hands by the wrists and shoved her back down on the bed, dropping his bulk atop her. Vladra cursed and spat at him, her back arching in fury, a guttural cry of pure venom ripping from her throat.

"I'll kill you!" she snarled.

"I think not," Kbrex informed her, and he chortled low and started to do things to her . . .

And then a rough hand closed on the back of his neck.

That was his only warning—that, and a roar of anger, and then he was lifted bodily off Vladra and hurled against a wall of the cabin. Trophies and mementos fell clattering to the floor, and Kbrex looked up to see a seething Kral standing five feet away.

"You're dead," breathed Kral.

Kbrex launched himself at him with amazing speed, and Kral met the charge. They hurtled backward, the door politely opening to allow them to tumble into the hallway.

They tumbled about on the floor for a moment, and then Kbrex was on top. He clamped his knees about Kral's throat and started to squeeze.

Klingons passing in the hallway stopped in their tracks. They knew what was happening and what was at stake. They made no move. It was not their place to interfere.

Vladra felt no such compunction, and she dashed into the hallway and tried to pull Kbrex off of Kral. "You bastard!" she screamed.

Maltz, the second officer, grabbed Vladra from behind and yanked her away. "Don't disgrace him!" he snarled, and she knew that he was right. If Kral lived because of her interference, it would be a life without honor. Dying was preferable.

It was not, however, on Kral's agenda. He managed to shift his weight just enough to send Kbrex tumbling off him. Kral scrambled to his feet and aimed a kick at

Kbrex's face. It connected, sending the older Klingon sprawling.

Kral charged him, still greedily sucking in air through his aching throat. Kbrex got to his feet and met the charge. The two Klingons shoved against each other, grunting and swearing, struggling for leverage.

Abruptly Kbrex stepped back, the move throwing Kral momentarily off balance. Kbrex used the opportunity to grab Kral by the back of his neck and the front of his armor, turning swiftly and sending Kral head first into a bulkhead. The crash was so loud and crunching that Vladra almost felt ill.

Kral sagged, turned and faced Kbrex, wavering from side to side. Kbrex delivered a brutal blow to Kral's head, and that was all for the Klingon commander. He fell to the floor, gasping, the world spinning around him.

He felt the barrel of a blaster against the back of his head and muttered a quick prayer to his god. He looked up and Vladra was looking back, biting her lip. There was such sadness in her eyes that Kral's greatest regret in his imminent death was not the fact of the death itself, but the fact that he had let Vladra down.

Kbrex looked from Vladra to Kral and back again. His finger tightened on the blaster . . .

. . . and then relaxed.

He stepped back and waved the blaster. "Get up," he said.

Kral wiped blood from his lip and slowly stood on wavering legs.

"You are my prisoner," said Kbrex. "You are arrested for incompetence and failure to complete a mission. You will be held for future disposal, as I see fit."

The other Klingons blinked in surprise but said nothing. Kral glared at him steadily. Kbrex slowly turned and regarded Vladra. "Are you his or mine, Vladra?" he said.

Vladra said nothing for a moment, and then without a word she went to Kral, who was leaning against a wall. She took his arm and supported him.

"Don't do this," he whispered.

"You are no longer my commander," she said with surprising mildness. "You cannot order me. I do as I choose . . . with whom I choose," and she fired a look at Kbrex.

Kbrex made no reply, but merely nodded. He turned to Second Officer Maltz, who was now going to be the first officer. "Put them in the brig," he said, and Maltz nodded once and took them away, blaster leveled on them.

"You let him live," said one of the crewmen who had witnessed the battle. It was not phrased as a question. It was never healthy to question a commander, particularly one who had just come into power and was doubtless feeling his oats.

"I would have the woman," replied Kbrex. "If I kill him now, she makes a martyr of him in her mind. By imprisoning them together, I give her the opportunity to watch him descend into the frustration of losing his command and the humiliation of being left alive. I want her to remember him not going out fighting, but rather spending his last hours in misery and embarrassment. That way she will willingly come to me."

"As you say," said the crewman, and then deferentially added, "Commander."

Kbrex most definitely liked the sound of that.

Chapter Fourteen

Japan, 1600

SULU LISTENED CAREFULLY to what Sadayo, the formidable samurai, was telling him as they crossed the great courtyard of the castle. Sadayo had sensed Sulu's disorientation and seemed to have decided to singlehandedly bring Sulu up to speed.

"This is Fushimi Castle. It was the last to be built by the regent Hideyoshi, the great Taiko," Sadayo said. "See, here is the main keep, but there are also five fortresses in the garrison. Our strength is eighteen hundred men. Our lord Torii was assigned this castle by his lord, Tokugawa Ieyasu. Our lord has had the honor of being Tokugawa Ieyasu's retainer since he was a child, as his father served the Tokugawa clan before him and his sons shall after him."

As they passed by the gates to the inner court where the lord's wife and family were quartered, Sulu heard the chatter of women's voices. He found himself straining to pick out the voice of Lady Oneko.

The guards were quartered in dormitories, and it was there that Sulu was taken next. Packed with men and sleeping mats by night, the room was hollow and lonely by day. Sulu was issued two kimonos, appropriate undergarments and a *kami-shimo,* the two-piece uniform that he would wear on duty when he wasn't in armor. It consisted of the ankle-length pleated trousers called a *hakama,* and a stiff-shouldered vest.

When he was dismissed, he headed for the bathhouse, mumbling the complex directions in his head lest he wander off someplace inappropriate. As he went, Sulu tried to draw in everything, a lifetime of knowledge which he would be expected to know, and somehow did, but somehow didn't.

His eye caught the eye of an old gardener, a man extraordinary only for his ordinariness . . . and an odd scar that ran down the left side of his face. It looked like it had been made with a sword, although it was years old. The old man politely looked away quickly, returning to his task of pruning away faded camellias.

The bathhouse was thankfully quiet. The water in the scrub bucket was shockingly cold. Gingerly settling into the hot soaking tub, he watched the steam rise in lazy spirals, as the knots in his shoulders eased. His armor had been whisked away for repair, and removal of the considerable number of blood stains.

Blood. Blood from a fight.

He remembered how, years ago, he had run from an image of a samurai. Now he had become that which had terrified him.

And he accepted it.

Something was wrong.

He sat and pondered. Whatever damage he might have already done to the future was done, and whatever damage he might continue to do . . . He shook his head as if he could shake out the confusion. There was little help for it but to continue to play along . . . or live along. If there was a way out, he couldn't see it.

In the half sleep induced by the heat and comfort of

the bath, he accepted that it was clearly not going to be possible to get back home by his own efforts. After all, he couldn't just wave his *katana*—which turned out to be a particularly fine signed blade—and cry "Open Sesame" or something like that, and reappear on the deck of the *Enterprise.* Although, he considered wryly, that might work as well as anything else.

His gut hurt, like little twisted knives. He was never going to get back . . . never, never. He breathed in deeply and forced back the panic. It wasn't such a bad place to be, he told himself, more in black humor than in earnest. It *was* what he had always wanted in his most romantic fantasies.

But . . . to never fly among the stars? To do without all the conveniences of life that he had become accustomed to . . . everything from instantaneous travel to a hot shower. Separated from everyone he knew. To be dead centuries before they would be born—before he would be born?

He let the hot water soak away the fear which again had knotted his gut, and let himself think about all that had happened. But he couldn't quite remember the last moments, or was it hours, on the *Enterprise.* Then he thought he could see Oneko's face like an angelic spirit swirling out of the steam, and he caught his breath at the memory of her pristine beauty.

He saw that lovely face later that day, while sitting guard for Mototada.

Sulu was stationed on the other side of a privacy screen, and had been grateful that the screen had been pulled open to capture the slight breeze, although it was little relief against the summer heat. But the disciplined calm silence of his guard duty turned to self-conscious staring when the woman and her attendants shuffled in, artfully gliding through the yards of dragging silk that puddled like colorful sea foam around their feet.

"Tono, lord," she said, dropping to her knees and bowing before Mototada, her tiny hands delicately touching the ground. Two guards accompanied the women, and they dropped to the ground, also, in the cross-legged posture of men, bowing with choreographic precision, as two women attendants gracefully folded to their knees and bowed with their mistress.

"Oneko, how are you?"

"Well, my lord," she said, putting her hands to her belly and smiling warmly, her eyes flitting from the ground to her lord's face. "Forgive me," she said bowing low, "for causing you trouble. I had no wish to worry you. It was selfish of me to request the trip to the temple."

"No, it was my fault for not sending more soldiers with you. The physician said you should go there to rest, and I only endangered you." He smiled at her. "At sixty-two I hardly expected another child, but I am pleased, Oneko."

"I pray for another son for you, my lord," she said sweetly.

He laughed. "I have sons enough for ten men. So long as the child is well, and you are, too."

But the warm reunion of the daimyo and his youngest concubine was cut short by the announcement of a party riding to the fortress.

A messenger was brought in by an attendant. The man was in armor, sweaty and breathless from a hard ride.

"Tokugawa Ieyasu approaches," he announced.

Sulu's eyes widened upon hearing this. Mototada's lord, Tokugawa Ieyasu! Coming here! It was as if Uhura had turned and informed Kirk that the formidable and legendary Admiral Nogura was going to be swinging by for a stop. Part of him was thrilled by the honor, and the rest of him was wondering what sort of boom was about to be lowered.

The next hour was an ordered pandemonium of efficient chaos, at the end of which the lord of the hold sat cross-legged in the vast receiving room, his chief councillors lining both sides of the room. Sulu was now posted behind the closed screen, but he could dimly see through the thin, backlit wall, and he could hear everything.

When Tokugawa entered, all pressed their backs forward toward the ground, their knuckles on the ground to their sides, bowing with the obeisance due the overlord of this hold. Tokugawa took a seat on the raised platform where Mototada normally held court.

Through the stony-faced impassiveness of a guard, Sulu's eyes were riveted on the shadowy form of the man who would unite Japan. The man who would, for better or worse, create a postfeudal society, a society of art and culture, and one which would retain the pristine integrity of Japan for half a millennium.

Cool, almost cold, Tokugawa Ieyasu sat, his voice with a kind of lilt that inspired truth, or at least honesty, from others—the kind of voice that allowed his friends to prove their worth, and his enemies to make mistakes. Anyone who took this man as a mild-mannered patron of the arts addicted only to the sport of hawking and admiring famous scenery, was too stupid to live, and often didn't.

"Mototada, my old friend, the time has come," rumbled Ieyasu. "It comes as no surprise to you, but Ishida Mitsunari has gathered a western army against us."

Sulu cast his mind back to the stories that he had heard, of the political climate of this time. There had been a tremendous power struggle between Tokugawa Ieyasu—incredibly, sitting a few feet away from him

—and another man, Ishida Mitsunari. The entire business had involved control over the infant son of the previous regent, and eventually—eventually, hell, now (he had to stop thinking about the past in the past tense)—Mitsunari had raised an army, marching from the west toward the old capital of Kyoto, and beyond to Edo, Tokugawa's new capital.

"Fushimi Castle lies on the road that leads to my capital of Edo," Tokugawa lectured. "Would I have invested anyone less able than you to hold Fushimi Castle?" He laughed, but his voice was somber and cold when he continued. "I choose to meet the enemy at Sekigahara, where the Nakasendo Road runs between the Ai River and the Makita River. But it will take me time to assemble my troops. Not all my retainers are as reliable as you, my old friend, and there will be some who drag their heels, waiting to guess the outcome of the battle before they commit to the winning side. You must hold Fushimi Castle, thus holding back Ishida Mitsunari, as long as possible. I will send you more troops . . ."

"No, my lord," Torii Mototada said, his voice hoarse with emotion. "You must not. I have what men I need for what I need to do. To send more would only weaken your main force. We will do what we must, for as long as we can, but I implore you, my lord, do not sacrifice more men to this action."

"So," Tokugawa Ieyasu said, nodding in agreement. "It is settled. Thank you," he said with the slightest nod, causing his subordinate to lean forward in abject supplication, the honor of being thanked and so acknowledged by his lord leaving Torii speechless. And in that moment lay the unspoken volumes that the lord knew his retainer's worth, and the retainer accepted his fate with dignity.

And that was when it clicked into place for Sulu. Fushimi Castle, the home of Torii Mototada, had been laid siege to in September of 1600. They had fought against the forces of an overwhelming army for ten days, in order to buy time for Tokugawa Ieyasu.

And that time had been bought with the life of every man in Fushimi Castle.

Sulu had pledged, on his honor, to be bodyguard to a dead man.

He wasn't a sixteenth-century samurai, for pity's sake. He was a Starfleet officer. He wasn't in some wonderful, daydream fantasy. He was committing suicide.

Devil take honor. He had to get the hell out of there.

Chapter Fifteen

GARROVICK'S BODY was lying cold in sickbay, and the bodies of Sulu, Chekov, and Scotty had vanished into thin air. It was time, Kirk decided, to do something about it.

He exited the turbolift and entered the conference room. Spock was already waiting for him, and McCoy joined them moments later.

McCoy was impressed by the fact that the morose, self-doubting Kirk he'd seen earlier had, apparently, been left behind in the captain's cabin. Here Kirk was all business, utterly confident that he would be presented with options and courses to pursue, and from that would draw a course of action. His eyes were narrowed, his fingertips gently tapping on the top of the conference-room table.

It was the sort of conference that, normally, Scotty, Sulu, and Chekov would be attending. Their absence only drew that much attention to the need for the conference.

"Analysis. Where are my officers?" Kirk said without preamble.

"Difficult to be precise, Captain. Evidence is slight."

"Slight?" Kirk felt as if he were grasping at straws. On the face of it, there didn't seem to be any evidence at all. He was virtually on a fishing expedition.

"I would say that the only suppositions we can make are on the basis of what Weyland himself said."

"Now *there's* a reliable source," said McCoy crossly. "What the devil is that Weyland character, anyway?"

"There is no reason to believe that he is anything other than what he claims," said Spock. "A being of immense power who acts out of a rather singular definition of honor and obligation."

"Obviously he doesn't feel any obligation to our men," observed McCoy.

"No reason he should," said Kirk. "His concern is the people of Cragon V. Still . . ." His fingers drummed a moment more. "Time out of mind."

"What?" said McCoy.

"That's what he said. He said that our men were trapped in time out of mind."

"That could have two meanings," said Spock. "There is the figurative definition of that statement. 'Time out of mind' is generally used as a description of an infinity of time. Time beyond the human capacity to comprehend."

"You mean they could just be plummeting forward, or backward, in time, out of control, forever?" said McCoy in horror.

Kirk, in spite of himself, shuddered at the image that conjured.

"That is possible," said Spock neutrally, as if it meant nothing to him. He could just as easily have been discussing star charts or gravity fluxes. Or at least if he was feeling anything, he was hiding it with his customary efficiency. "The second possibility is the literal one. That they are in some other time, drawn from the mind. Their minds."

Kirk nodded slowly, trying to make sense of that, and then his eyes widened. "Of course! When we were down on the planet, they were discussing various time periods from their respective backgrounds. If Weyland was somehow able to tap into their consciousness or subconscious, then perhaps he sent them back in time."

"A lot of ifs, and a lot of maybes," said McCoy. "How do we know he can do all that?"

"Thus far all we've done is underestimate him, and it's gotten us into nothing but trouble," replied Kirk. "It'd be better if we started giving him the benefit of the doubt. And if they've gone back in time, then we can get them back. I remember the time periods they were discussing. We have ways of going back in time."

"May I point out, Captain, that the engines are still not functioning, courtesy of the immortal Weyland," said Spock. "Furthermore, may I point out that when you and I returned to the past, to 1938 on Earth, it was only with luck that we were able to locate the doctor. And it was at the cost of a personal tragedy to yourself that current history was preserved. All lies in the balance, Captain, and we are unable to do anything to change that. That is unfortunate, but logical. Either the men made no significant changes in history, and they have long since lived out their lives in another time, or they will return to us in our future. We must wait."

"I cannot accept that. I will not." Kirk sighed deeply and dropped his head, closing his eyes as if to shut out the clear and irrefutable argument of Spock's analysis. He looked back up, fixing his eyes on Spock. "And there is nothing we can do?" he asked coldly.

"We can make a computer search for clues as to their actual presence in past history, but records in precomputer time are incomplete. As to what we could do to reverse their trip into time, I do not think there is anything we can do."

"Then I must try to contact Weyland, and convince him to reverse this terrible thing."

Chapter Sixteen

Scotland, 1746

IT WAS ACTUALLY half a day before the command staff of William Hanover, Duke of Cumberland, came riding in, accompanied by a number of young sports in expensive and well-tailored coats, and an even larger number of support personnel less regally appointed.

Scott stared, fascinated at the famous general. "Fat Billy" was an understatement. The man, fastidious in his remarkably clean uniform and lace-trimmed shirt, was huge both in stature and as a product of good living. His horse was as large as a racing stallion could get and still not qualify as a draft horse.

The Duke shouted encouraging epithets to the assembled soldiery, the cheapest form of largesse, and was rewarded with loud but unenthusiastic cheers and waving hats. When the Duke actually dismounted in the yard of The Hanged Woman, Mr. and Mrs. Nesbit were all but overcome with humble appreciation of the honor.

Despite his grandiose and foppish manners, Scott recognized in Duke William a razor-sharp mind and the carriage of a soldier who, despite his indulgences, had seen a lot of death and deprivation.

"I'm not paying you to gawk at the gentlemen," the proprietress bellowed, breaking the reverie of the assembled servants, and Scott put his back into unloading the wicker baskets of fine food and the chests of clean clothes the noble Duke and his entourage had brought for the night's stay.

The excitement of the exalted company was a blessing for Scotty, who was quickly lost in the shuffle. He soon found that his willingness to work and gentlemanly manners bought him a certain acceptance.

It certainly afforded him the opportunity of listening in on the conversation of the great; unlike Seamus, who was kept busy in the kitchen and out of the way of the gentlemen guests.

The company at table was certainly impressive. A fair bit of the Duke's senior staff, and other key persons from the various armies under his command, had been gathered here for some serious strategy. And although it was clear that the secret talks would take place in more private circumstances, there was enough table talk to make Scott almost tremble with the excitement of it.

The excitement Scott felt, however, quickly turned into carefully controlled, but nonetheless quite real, inward rage. The English officers, each competing to gain the favor and attention of Fat Billy, thought nothing of endeavoring to undercut each other's achievements while, at the same time, aggrandizing their own. William Hanover, for his part, seemed to gain a good deal of mental exercise playing one of them against the other, and watching in amusement as they had at each other.

And in each of their recountings and retellings, the withering and nasty descriptions they gave of the Scotsmen they were battling—"bastards," "damned barbarians," and the like—gave rise to a fury that Scotty could barely contain.

Finally, one of them—a Lord Bury—held up a hand to try and still the sniping. "Should we continue this bickering, we shall come to resemble the Celt himself, strutting and braying like so many jackasses," he said with a self-satisfied smile.

"And how their brutish tongue is as the braying of an ass," another young rake opined, snorting and hee-hawing to make his point. This was greeted with hoots and hilarity from his fellows.

"Best to let the Campbells loose, or other of the lowlander, to lead the highland Celt, as one leads the braying jackass with a carrot on a stick," said another. "Is there a 'mack' whatever worth his fodder who would not chase bare-legged and bare-assed across the heather for the nip at any Campbell? And what better food for the impetuous asses than a Scottish-held carrot?"

As furious as the words made Scotty, he knew the truth in them. The greatest enemy of the people of Scotland was the people of Scotland. The conflict of interest between the chiefs who adhered to the old clan ways and those who threw in their lot with their English masters had hit an all-time high in the rebellion of 1715, and the massacre at Glencoe. The bad blood between the Donalds and Campbells would endure a millennium, not just the thirty or so years that had just elapsed.

While the young dandies chortled over their puns and clever repartee, Scotty still felt the flush of humiliation. He found them patronizing and shallow. And he felt ashamed for the noble clans who were being treated with such a lack of honor.

The ranking officers retired to the privacy of the large upstairs room, while some of the younger dandies made themselves available to the country girls who had gathered to see and be seen, and also to earn a coin working in the kitchen for the day—or if luck would have it, working in the bedrooms at night. The men who had no interest in risking a case of pox for a night's diversion went off to their bivouac to gamble, a privilege that would have earned a common soldier a flogging but was considered a harmless pastime for a man to the manor born.

After supper Scott addressed himself to the chore of cleaning up the mess. He reflected that it gave new meaning to the traditional military use of the word.

"Mr. Scott, Mr. Scott." The boy's insistent voice took a moment to ooze through Scott's confused and dark private thoughts.

"Ah, yes, lad. And what did ye make of that?" he asked in a jovial but careful way.

The boy looked at him with a hostile curiosity. Scotty could almost hear the boy's thoughts, guessing about this stranger who had appeared wild-eyed and lost in a worn kilt, but who fit in so well with these gentlemen soldiers. If he had been seated at table with them, the boy's eyes begged, he would have gone unnoticed and unremarkable.

"Nothing, sir," Seamus answered quietly, and he slipped off about his chores.

Scott sighed. What could he say to the boy? Certainly he was grateful for the clothes and the help. Without them, by now he would be jailed or hanged as a traitor to king and country.

His thoughts wandered as he thought of what he knew.

Bonny Prince Charles would lose.

Or . . . might he lose?

Was there something that could be done? Was the sight that Scott saw absolute . . . or could it be changed by the actions of man? And . . . should he?

94

Did any man have the right to attempt to thwart destiny?

"Are you planning to wipe the pattern off the plate?" Mrs. Nesbit shouted at Scott, causing him to start so suddenly he nearly dropped the precious piece of real china.

"Ach, no, indeed, madam. I was only thinking of this evening and all the famous men I have seen," he said, attempting to sound as much the country bumpkin as he could.

"Well see to it that you do your dreaming in your bed, man. Candles cost good money, and that dish is now quite dry." She fussed about the kitchen, setting things in order with the peculiar fashion which was her own, as is the kitchen of every housewife, and snapping little curses whenever she found an item relocated.

"May I be off to bed then, ma'am?" Scott gallantly asked.

She shot him a disapproving look which was her all-purpose ploy to keep from agreeing to anything, but she nodded him away, the wrinkles around her eyes softening a bit, moved by his sweet manners.

In his bed, the questions returned and whirled in his head. But whether by plan or despair, the best he could come up with was wait and see what else happened. More data, Scott, he told himself. You need more data. Then he wondered why such an odd word as "data" came to his mind.

As he dropped off into a fitful sleep, he prayed, "Please Lord, make this go away. Let me go home."

And he was awakened by the shouting, and a shot being fired.

And then everything fell apart.

Chapter Seventeen

Stalingrad, 1942

CHEKOV BLINKED into the light that was shining into his face. Standing just beyond the rim of the light was a man in a uniform Chekov recognized as belonging to the SS. He stood over Chekov with the sort of calm, confident expression that indicated he knew that Chekov would tell him what he wanted to know, sooner or later.

There were other Nazi soldiers in the room. They were secondary to the main problem of the SS man.

"Who are you?" said the Nazi.

"Chekov."

"Really. Gentlemen, we have a playwright with us."

Chekov sighed. That joke was wearing thin with him very quickly.

"How did you get here?" said the Nazi. "How did you get a German uniform?"

"I don't know," said Chekov.

"You don't know?"

"I don't know."

"Tell us your troop strength."

"I don't know."

"Tell us how many rifles you have."

"I don't know."

The Nazi's eyes narrowed. "Do you know what will happen if you refuse to cooperate?"

Chekov thought about the men back in the cell, covered with bruises and cuts. "That I do know," he said softly.

"I will give you one chance to cooperate."

Chekov shrugged. "You would not believe me if I told you."

The Nazi smiled. "Try me."

Chekov tried.

He was right. They didn't.

When he was brought back to the cell, it was with a swollen lip and a cut over his eye. Those were just the visible injuries.

They hurled him into the middle of the cell, where he landed heavily, a gasp knocked out of him. The door slammed shut behind him, plunging him once again into the dimness of the cell.

This was insane. He had never had the opportunity —unlike other members of the crew—of being to the past. It had always sounded, from what he'd heard, like a grand adventure . . . although Captain Kirk never wanted to discuss his experience with the object called the Guardian of Forever.

This, though, was no grand adventure. Since the moment he'd gotten there, Chekov had felt dirty, harassed, or just plain scared. This was no grand adventure. This was something he'd just as soon get out of, except he didn't have the faintest idea how to go about it.

Cells, interrogation, secret police. The clean, pure world of the *Enterprise* seemed far away. He was beginning to understand why people of this time considered space travel and creatures from another world to be patently absurd. To him it was his reality, and it already seemed unreal.

He heard the voice of John Kirk say, "Well, if your

being here is a Nazi trick, you've certainly thrown yourself into it."

Chekov looked around. "Where's Ivan?"

Kirk shrugged. "Don't know," he said with careful control that was clearly covering his concern. "They came for him right after they took you. I imagine they wanted to ask him some of the questions they asked you." Then he paused and, with some of his real emotion showing through, added, "He was in pretty bad shape when they took him. I don't know how much more he can take."

"How much can any of us take?" said Chekov.

Again Kirk shrugged. There was no answer, and Chekov hoped he wouldn't have to find out.

Ivan did not come back.

The next day the Soviet shelling kept the Germans busy enough that Chekov and John Kirk were spared further interrogation. The throbbing pain was terrible, but the thirst was worse. They didn't talk—it hurt too much. But in the dull light the two men became friends in little ways: a smile of hope, aid in moving a broken body to a more comfortable place on the filthy floor. Things that mattered.

Chekov awoke from a troubled sleep by the door being burst in. He looked up, as did Kirk. The SS man was in the doorway with several soldiers standing behind him, looking as if they meant business.

Without a word the soldiers stepped in and grabbed both Chekov and Kirk by the arms. They were dragged out and into the main courtyard. The sky was as slate-gray as it had been when Chekov had first looked up at it.

"You think they're letting us go?" said Chekov, in a tone that indicated that he, for one, certainly doubted it.

"Oh, they've just come to realize that they'll never

win, and they've decided to be nice to us," said Kirk. "They figure that it'll do them good later."

Then Chekov and Kirk saw where they were being directed. It was a free-standing brick wall, with enough pockmarks in it to show that it had been hit with lots of bullets. Chekov suspected, correctly, that it hadn't been simply used for target practice.

There was blood on the dirt in front of the wall— blood directly at the feet of where Chekov and Kirk were made to stand.

The Nazi SS man smiled into Chekov's face, his jaw jutting outward in a cocky grin. "Do you have any final things to tell us?" said the SS man.

Chekov smiled, inwardly pleased at his total cool in what were undoubtedly his last moments on earth. "Your Führer is going to kill himself, and your precious Reich is going to stand as a symbol of all that's vile," he said in Russian.

The SS man shoved them against the wall and stepped away. Chekov stood next to Kirk, and the American muttered, also in Russian, "Don't worry."

"No?"

"No. I'm working on a plan."

Chekov looked at the firing squad before them, raising their rifles and taking dead aim.

"I can't wait to hear it," he said.

Chapter Eighteen

KRAL SAT across the tight, unpleasant room from Vladra. She was not looking at him, but staring straight ahead. He, however, was looking at her and shaking his head. His lower lip was swollen, and dried blood caked his beard.

"Why?" he asked at length.

She turned to look at him. "You have to ask?" she said softly.

"Yes. I do."

"Because I love you."

His eyes widened and his voice shook with fury. "You tried to dishonor me because you love me?"

"Dishonor you?" She shook her head. "I don't underst—"

"Coming to my aid! Acting as if I could not take care of myself."

Now Vladra was incensed, and she stood and waved her arms. "Well, now I wonder, *Commander,* why anyone would ever think such a thing? After all, you've only been beaten, bloodied and bruised, stripped of command and defeated in combat. Who in the galaxy could possibly think that the great Commander Kral could not take care of himself!"

He sat with his arms folded, smoldering. Vladra threw herself back down on a seat, and then she said slowly, "Why did you come down at that particular moment?"

"What are you talking about?"

"When I went to your cabin to warn you . . . and you showed up, just in time . . ."

He shrugged. "I am not sure. I was on the bridge, and Kbrex was not there, and suddenly I simply got this . . . feeling. I cannot explain. I only knew that I should get back down to my quarters. That something was definitely wrong."

"Oh," she said.

Kral leaned back, his head against the stark wall. He closed his eyes and sighed softly.

"Love," he said. "What a truly alien concept."

"I'm sorry that you think so," she said sharply.

He spoke as if he hadn't even heard her. "I have never been in love," he said, "or had a woman say she loved me. I have spent my life in my constant endeavors to conquer, to rise in the ranks and conquer others. Such softer emotions seemed a waste of time and useless. And yet perhaps," and he turned and looked at her, "perhaps those emotions that I've considered to be too soft are, in fact, the only ones that really matter."

She stared at him. "Such things you're saying . . ."

"It is amazing what one thinks of when death beckons. Once you've made your peace with death, then thinking about love can hardly be too frightening a prospect."

On the bridge, Kbrex sat in the command chair and stared in frustration at the peacefully orbiting globe below.

"Sir," came the quiet report from the engineer, "our orbit is starting to decay."

Slowly Kbrex turned and eyed him. "What?"

"With our engines inoperative, we are unable to adjust our orbit. Our orbit is decaying. It's not immediate, but within twenty-four hours we will begin our descent into the planet's atmosphere."

Kbrex felt all eyes on him, and he felt a slow, bubbling fury. "Summon Weyland on the communications grid."

"I had been trying to, sir, for some hours. Those were Commander Kr—ex-Commander Kral's orders, and I assumed you wanted me to continue."

"That was a dangerous assumption," said Kbrex warningly. "I will excuse it, however. Any word?"

"None, sir."

His fury mounted. He had staged a coup, unseated the young upstart Klingon, and taken over command . . . of a powerless hulk that would be a fireball before too long.

It was all Kral's fault. The fool had left him with an impossible situation, and Kbrex could tell from the way that eyes were on him, that they were already blaming him for a situation that he had inherited.

It was time to refocus blame where it belonged.

"Damn Kral for getting us into this. Honor guard, attend for an execution," and he walked briskly for the turbolift, four Klingons following him.

As they headed for the brig, Kbrex was running through his mind all the things that he would say to Vladra to convince her of the folly of her preferences. He would be alternatively calm, reasoning, and firm. He imagined lines of dialogue, and polished his intended speech to a gleaming shine.

When they arrived at the brig, Vladra and Kral were locked in a passionate embrace. Upon seeing it, all of Kbrex's high-born plans went out the torpedo chute.

Klingon ships were built with airlocks. They were emergency portals only, to be used in the unlikely—

but not impossible—event that some sort of exterior work had to be done on a ship and the transporters were out of commission. After a major battle, for example.

Seeing them entangled in each other immediately gave Kbrex another use for an airlock.

Suddenly aware that they had an audience, Kral and Vladra broke their clinch and looked at Kbrex and his followers. Kbrex told himself that, at this moment, the decision was still Vladra's. She held her own life in her hands.

She spit at him.

It arced through the air and sizzled into nonexistence, several inches short of Kbrex's face, thanks to the brig force shield. But the gesture was more than enough to decide matters for him.

"Careful now," he ordered the half dozen guards who held the commander aloft by his twisting, kicking limbs. "We don't want the damned superbeing alerted." Kral screamed and thrashed like a spit lizard. They threw him in, punching Vladra out of the way as she charged with crazed fury to Kral's aid.

"Kral," she screamed with despair as the heavy door of the airlock slammed on them.

A brusque, recorded Klingon male voice said curtly, "Thirty seconds to vacuum. Thirty seconds to vacuum."

Kral sat stunned for a moment. Vladra knelt by his side, burying her head into his shoulder.

"Twenty seconds to vacuum. Twenty seconds to vacuum."

The growling male voice of the computer galvanized Kral into action. He scrambled to his feet, pushing Vladra away, and lurching toward a storage cabinet marked "Environmental Units." He fumbled with the door.

"Damn it to Cymele's Hell," he screamed as he tugged at the door. It sprung open. It contained environmental suits, all right; the damaged ones destined for salvage.

"Fifteen seconds to vacuum. Fifteen seconds to vacuum."

"Shut up!" he bellowed at the wall speaker. He looked around wildly. There were two more storage cabinets, but no time to try them.

"Here, get in this," he shouted at Vladra, thrusting a mostly intact environmental suit at her. As she slithered into hers, he struggled into his, a heavier model designed for extensive use and even, in an emergency, for an escape pod.

"Ten, nine, eight . . ."

Before he slammed down the mittenlike paws of the suit, he fished around for a roll of silver repair tape. "Damn it," he screamed, as the hiss of the escaping air grew more insistent. "There," he shouted, and he drew a great strip of the stuff and grabbed her up, strapping her to himself. He was about to fling the tape aside when he saw a dangling flap of torn silver fabric in her suit.

"Seven, six, five . . ."

"Bunch it up. There's a tear in the arm of your suit. Squeeze your arm down. There," he said, making a futile attempt at a patch with a final strip of the tape.

"Four, three, two, one . . ."

As he reached around her to turn on her air, the great airlock doors whisked open and they were sucked out in a whirlwind of debris and what little air remained.

Chapter Nineteen

Japan, 1600

"COME ON, Great One Cut." The shrill voice had feet, and Sulu felt himself booted out of his blankets by one of them.

He recognized the voice immediately. It was Motonaga, the youngest son of one of Mototada's retainers. The last person Sulu needed to see after a sleepless night of wishing that his comfortable bed on the *Enterprise* were beneath him.

Sulu groaned, opening one eye to Motonaga's nasty grin. The sun wasn't up yet, although the sky was already a warm slate-pink.

"Shut up," one of the pile of sleeping men grunted.

"Come on, demon slayer," the boy taunted.

"Come on, Motonaga, give it a rest," Sulu mumbled in colloquial Japanese. Motonaga was only sixteen years old, but being the son of Naito Ienaga, a garrison commander and one of Torii Mototada's generals and trusted retainers, gave him much license. He was hell-bent to prove himself a samurai worthy of his father, his older brothers, and his lord. As a result, he was something of a pain in the neck to the samurai of more years but less rank.

"That's what I like about you, Heihachiro," the boy

105

said, grinning and dragging Sulu up. "You have no manners, and that makes me look good."

Sulu made a quick lurch at the boy, grabbing a handful of kimono as Motonaga darted back.

"You'll have to get your satisfaction later. The lord wants you."

"Why didn't you say so?" Sulu burst out, scrambling to pull out his clothes from the chest against the wall, wading over the snoring men.

"Well, I'm saying so now," the boy taunted, striding out with such an exaggerated gait that he almost looked like a caricature of a samurai.

Sulu dressed quickly, slicking back his hair. He stuck his small sword in his belt, took his *katana* in his hand, and with a last minute tug on the front of his kimono and uniform, strode to the master's quarters.

All the way there his mind was racing. He was too visible and, for that matter, the land was too wild, to just go sneaking out. He was going to have to figure out some graceful way of getting out of this. At least, he knew, he had a little time.

And, although he hated to admit it, the concept of running out on his "lord and master" was rubbing him the wrong way. He reminded himself that he was a Starfleet officer, and tried to remain detached.

But it was not easy. To read history books, when people are reduced to glowing letters of text, or to hear stories from one's mother—that was one thing. This, though—walking with people of flesh and blood, who look at you and smile and nod their head—that precious detachment was no longer easy. The question became—was it even possible?

He knelt outside the screen and called out, "Okiri Heihachiro here," politely announcing himself before he opened the screen and entered. He bowed low, and dropped cross-legged to the ground, bowing again. He quickly assessed the men assembled and scooted on the ground to take the place to which he was entitled. It looked as though none of them had gotten any sleep that night.

"Heihachiro-domo," the lord called out, using the honorific which reinforced Sulu's status as a retainer.

"Hai, tono." Sulu scooted forward again, bowing low. Mototada waved his hand toward the ground, motioning Heihachiro to a place closer to his presence. Again Sulu scooted forward, the kind of dignified crabwalk which was the customary method of locomotion in formal situations. He sat cross-legged and waited.

"Lord," he snapped efficiently.

"I want you to lead a guard and accompany my concubine, Oneko, to her uncle's house in Edo."

He couldn't believe it. The problem was solved. He was being given a free pass out of there—at the request of Mototada!

"Hai," Sulu snapped, the word yes coming out like a blast of air. "I am honored by such a responsible duty," Sulu added, again pressing his back forward, his fists on the ground to his sides.

"Tono! Lord!" The emotional cry came from the open doorway. It was young Motonaga again, this time his slender form and angular face almost quivering with restrained anger. "Why is this upstart, this unknown, allowed the honor? When will I be able to prove my worth as a samurai to my lord? Do we even know we can trust this one?" he screamed, pointing his finger accusingly at Sulu.

Naito Ienaga, the boy's father, bellowed back, "Such insolence," and turning to the daimyo, whose frown seemed to harbor some amusement, "Forgive my son, lord. He is impetuous."

"Motonaga," the master said sternly, "you must learn when to attack and when to wait, if you would be a great war leader. Your turn will come, soon enough.

It is important that no one know who she is. You are known, but our new retainer is not, and so he shall accompany her. If Tokugawa does not win the battle to come, then my surviving kin may not be safe, and if she carries a son, it will be her duty to hide my remaining heir and rebuild the Torii clan."

He turned again to Sulu. "There is something about you, something not of this land. Perhaps the gods of my family have sent you for luck. But no matter. Do you understand that this task is very important?"

"Hai, tono." The irony was staggering. Oneko, the woman he'd saved—and endlessly second-guessed himself over—was being entrusted to him once more. It was a bizarre situation. If they were attacked en route, he could then stand aside and let her die and rectify the original error . . . except, what if it wasn't an error? What if he was supposed to be her savior? What if letting her die was wrong?

Once again he told himself that he should trust his instincts. And his instincts were telling him that drawing this assignment—and having the opportunity to spend time with the fascinating Oneko—was luck of the highest order.

"When she is safe," said Mototada, "you will return with what new intelligence our allies have been able to gather. I only pray to the gods and the buddha we will not be engaged by our enemy until we have that information," he added, the fire of an old campaigner in his voice. "Do you understand?"

"Yes, lord," Sulu snapped.

"Good. My administrator shall give you funds and tell what arrangements have been made for the trip."

With that Sulu was dismissed.

At breakfast he toyed with his rice, still in a daze as he reviewed every word of the interview with Mototada.

He was expected to return. Well . . . he just

wouldn't. As difficult as it was to simply abandon Mototada, there was no point in just giving up his life for no reason.

Was there?

For the first time he started to toy with the idea that he should return. That he owed an obligation to . . . to whom?

To Mototada? His lord? Nonsense. He owed his allegiance to James T. Kirk. No one else.

Besides, what did he know about this world? It was all so new, so fragile. And what did the world know of him? Could he change something important, something sacred to the history of his people?

Midmorning found him on an errand in the inner court.

"Wait. Young man. Come here." The sweet singing voice of the woman rang out to him like a bell in the breeze.

His heart almost stopped. Oneko! "My lady," he said, turning and bowing.

"I hear that you are to be my escort to Edo," she said gently.

"Yes, my lady," he said, suddenly remembering that Edo was the old name for Tokyo. Sometimes it was too confusing to think about.

"They say you fight like a mountain demon. Tell me, are you a god? Or a ghost?"

"No, my lady," he said.

"And yet, they say you are strange, different. Perhaps I will uncover your secret on the road." With that she swept off in a gliding shuffle of little steps, followed by her attendants.

"Pretty, isn't she?" The voice was behind him. Sulu spun around.

"Oh, it's you, Watanenabe Sadayo-domo," he stammered, still red-faced.

"Some warrior! The god Hachiman would never let himself be snuck up on while he was gawking at a lady."

"Er, I, er, that is . . ." Sulu stammered.

"Don't worry," the man said, clapping him on the shoulder, laughing. "She does that to all of us. Come along to the sword dojo. I've been watching you practice the past few days. You are one of those fellows who is inspired in battle, but not so in practice. I think I have a few tricks to teach you. I am the lord's sword master, in case you didn't know."

"No, I didn't," Sulu said, bowing politely. "I would be pleased to learn from you."

"Besides, working up a good sweat is the best way to forget women," Sadayo added, grinning as they marched along the paths and verandas of the great estate to the practice hall.

Already they could hear the echoing shouts, the dull thud of bare feet on the wooden floor, and sharp snapping clacks of wooden swords on wooden swords, as the young samurai practiced *katas,* the formal exercise sets, and tried out their cuts in free-style duels with wooden practice weapons.

Sulu had already worked up a sweat, and had almost forgotten about Oneko, when the young hothead, Motonaga, swaggered in.

"Well, let's see how good you are," he challenged Sulu.

Sulu shrugged. He didn't want to make an enemy of this boy, but on the other hand, if he didn't hold his own with a sword, he would never get the kid's attention long enough to explain that. Motonaga was galloping across the floor before Sulu was even in position. He sidestepped the charge but was unable to bring down his own cut before the boy was out of range and had turned again to face him.

Motonaga struck downward with a strong cut to the

head. Sulu blocked, the shock burning through his tired arms. He disengaged his sword, using the boy's own strength against him as Motonaga's sword swept uselessly down, unable to stop Sulu's cut to the boy's head. Sulu stopped it short of contact. It was, after all, practice, not war. The boy bowed stiffly, turned and left.

"There! That's better. More like battle fighting," the sword master said, coming up to Sulu, reaching out to correct his grip on the wooden weapon. "Practice that cut," he ordered.

And then his voice went low and he said, "Are you familiar with the story of the samurai who was sent by his lord to deliver a treaty, but an enemy changed letters and the man carried his own death warrant?"

Sulu stared at him, uncomprehending.

"On the road," continued the gray-haired samurai, "he meets a samurai in a lion-face helmet and fights him, only to find it is his own brother, who in dying confesses that he was the treacherous enemy, and bids him destroy the letter. Now . . . to whom do your sympathies go?"

Sulu frowned, still not getting what he was driving at. "The dead brother, I suppose. He tried to make up for a misdeed and wound up dead."

"He was a traitor," said Sadayo through thinned lips. "Remember that, when you are on the road with the lady."

And he walked away from Sulu like a ghost on glass.

Chapter Twenty

"UHURA, KEEP TRYING to raise Weyland."

Uhura sat at her station and shook her head slowly. "You realize, Captain, that I'm broadcasting blindly here. The tech readings on Cragon V say that they don't have the facilities for receiving starship communications. Or any communications, for that matter."

Kirk sat in his command chair and nodded, staring at the image of Cragon on the screen. He was stroking his chin thoughtfully as he said, "Yes, Uhura, I'm quite aware of that. But if the immortal Weyland is as powerful as he seems to be, then I'm sure he can read our signal if he chooses. Keep trying. Likewise, keep trying to raise Starfleet."

"Negative response, Captain. Would you like me to try and raise the Klingon ship?"

Kirk thought about the Klingon grenade detonating, blowing up a good young officer and a boy who hadn't even had the opportunity to live yet.

"I have nothing to say to them," said Kirk tightly.

At the helm, Lieutenant Ryan was filling in for Sulu, and she turned in her seat and said softly, "Captain. I hate to bring this up . . ."

Ryan was new, and cautious. Kirk could understand—no one wanted to be the bearer of bad tidings, least of all someone who had just arrived on board. Nevertheless, Kirk was not in the mood for prevarication. "Go ahead, Lieutenant."

"Instruments indicate that our orbit is beginning to decay. In approximately," she glanced at her controls, "25.3 hours, we're going to descend into the planet's atmosphere and . . ."

She didn't have to complete the prediction. Everyone on the bridge knew what it was.

"Thank you, Lieutenant," was all Kirk said. What he thought in addition was, *My day is complete.*

"Bad news?"

The question came so abruptly, and from such an unexpected spot, that everyone on the bridge jumped involuntarily. There on the screen, replacing the image of the planet, was Weyland's face, much as it had been the last time they saw it.

Kirk's mouth moved a moment, and then he found words. "We wish to speak with you."

"Speak," said Weyland noncommittally.

"I wish to know how long you intend to keep us here."

"I have already told you that," said Weyland.

"Telling us we will stay here until we rot is not what I would call a useful answer."

"If that is what you heard, then that is your answer."

Kirk shook his head. "I don't understand."

"Then that, too, is your answer."

"I'm getting tired of your riddles," said Kirk, trying to keep a rein on his anger and only partly succeeding. "You can't simply keep us trapped here indefinitely. Sooner or later the Federation, and the Klingon empire, will send ships to investigate our absence."

"That would be most unfortunate for them," Weyland said mildly.

"Are you saying you're powerful enough to stand up against the might of the Federation and the Klingons?" demanded Kirk. "Because that's exactly what you're going to have to do."

Weyland actually seemed to consider that a moment. "What would you suggest?"

"Return my men to me and restore our power. We will leave you as we found you."

"Why should I believe that?" demanded Weyland. "You've not been trustworthy thus far. Why should I believe you to be beings of honor?"

"I'm trying to convince you, dammit. Restore our transporter, and let me come down there and speak to you directly."

Again Weyland gave it some thought. "Very well," he said. "The time is right. I shall give you the opportunity to use your transporter one time . . . one time only. Do as you see fit."

He vanished from the screen.

Kirk blinked in surprise. "I didn't think he'd agree to it."

"Nor I."

"Perhaps he hasn't. Kirk to engineering."

"Engineering," came the brisk reply.

"Mr. Sco—" He corrected himself immediately. "Mr. Two Feathers, kindly run a check on transporter circuits."

There was a brief pause, and then the surprised response came back. "Sir, transporter circuits are clear for Transporter Room A."

"No glitches or energy disruptions." Kirk was wary of a trap, although he wasn't sure why. A being like Weyland didn't need to resort to trickery if he decided to dispatch someone. That much had been proven.

"None, sir. It's clear."

"Thank you, Mr. Two Feathers. Kirk to transporter room. Two to beam down. Come along, Mr. Spock. Perhaps the logical approach will work."

"It frequently does," Spock told him serenely.

Moments later they were in the transporter room, Kirk issuing last minute instructions to transporter chief Kyle. Spock was already on the transporter pad. And that was when the alert came down from the bridge.

Kirk immediately tapped the comm panel. "Kirk here."

"Captain, this is Ryan. Sensors have detected two figures outside of the Klingon ship."

"Outside?" Kirk couldn't believe it. "Are they performing some sort of repair work?"

"Negative, Captain. We have them on screen. They appear to simply be flailing around. Whatever they're doing out there, I don't think they are there voluntarily, sir."

"Ryan—" and then he stopped.

One shot with the transporter. That was what Weyland had said. And Kirk had promised to come down. Weyland had been contending that they couldn't be trusted, then he gives them a chance to show they can, and Kirk doesn't even show up? Uses the transporter for something else . . . perhaps even a move that could be perceived as an attempt to take a prisoner or two. After all, the Klingons might still be performing some sort of necessary maintenance.

Even if they were in trouble, so what? They were just two Klingons, after all. Two murderers. Just two lives . . . and even if they were in space involuntarily, so what? Who would care if they were dead? Just two lives . . .

"Damn," muttered Kirk, after a hesitation that had

actually been less than a second. "Ryan, feed the coordinates to the transporter room. Kyle, lock on and beam them here immediately."

"Captain," Spock said, stepping down off the transporter.

Kirk looked at his first officer and said, "What else can I do? Are there any logical alternatives?"

Spock nodded. "Yes. But only one correct alternative."

"That's good to hear." He hit the comm panel once more. "Transporter room to sickbay. Bones, get up here. We're about to have company."

The transporter beams hummed, their familiar lights cascading across the pads. Kirk and Spock waited, and moments later two silver-clad forms appeared. Their hands were outstretched toward each other, as if they had been trying to reach out to one another in one last, desperate act. The moment their molecules were fully integrated, the two of them collapsed to the floor of the transporter. Kirk noted incredulously that there seemed to be some sort of patching here and there to hold the suits together.

"Sir," said Kyle in confusion, "the transporter circuits just went dead again."

Kirk nodded. He'd expected that. Weyland was a man of his word, if nothing else.

McCoy entered quickly with his medical gear, and his eyes widened. "Where the devil did they come from?"

"From the Klingon ship, apparently. So adjust medications appropriately."

"I'm not sure what's appropriate for a Klingon," said McCoy, approaching the individuals on the platform cautiously. One always had to be careful when dealing with Klingons, but these two hardly seemed to be in shape to give McCoy any grief.

The larger of the two figures removed his head

covering. Kirk's eyes went wide with surprise, and then he shook his head. The Klingon rites of succession in action once again. All things considered, it was amazing the individual was alive.

He looked up at Kirk with amazement. "Gods. I'm dead."

"No," said Kirk. "You're on the *Enterprise.*"

"I assumed I was dead, since my personal picture of hell is being trapped forever with you."

"Good to see you too, Commander Kral."

Chapter Twenty-one

Scotland, 1746

MONTGOMERY SCOTT ROLLED OFF his straw pallet, ignoring the protesting creak of his back. What had just happened? There had been a shot, and some shouting, and now the sound of running feet and the sound of angry voices raised. He thought he heard the Nesbits, begging and pleading about something. The inn was ablaze with light, and Scotty burst out, almost tumbling down the stairs to the main room.

There was William Hanover, Duke of Cumberland, in his night clothes. He was holding, by the scruff of his neck, a furious and kicking Seamus.

"What the blazes . . . ?!" Scotty gasped.

Hanover was paying no attention to Scotty. Instead he was addressing the Nesbits, shaking Seamus for emphasis. "So are you claiming that you were unaware that this little rebel was under your own roof?"

"I am no rebel," shouted Seamus, red-faced, "but a patriot, who will gladly die for the prince who, by God, is your king!"

"Oh, shut up," said Hanover in annoyance. "And next time you attempt to shoot someone in their sleep, be certain that your hand is not shaking with fear."

"If my hand was shaking," snapped Seamus, "it was

with excitement at having the chance to rid the world of you! And strike a blow for the prince!"

"You had your opportunity," said Hanover, "and you missed it."

Seamus kicked him in the shin.

William Hanover, the Duke of Cumberland, let out a yelp and lost his grip on the boy. Seamus made a break for it, leaping toward a window. He almost made it, but one of the soldiers lunged forward and snagged him by the ankles. Seamus went down with a crash, amidst a tumble of chairs. It took three soldiers to haul the struggling teenager to his feet, and Seamus promptly sank his teeth into the forearm of the nearest one. The soldier yelled and, drawing back his hand, cuffed Seamus once hard across the face. The boy moaned and sagged in the grip of the other men.

"What shall we do with him, sir?" said the officer who was holding Seamus from behind.

"Shoot him," said Hanover, sitting and nursing his throbbing shin.

"In here, sir?"

Hanover stared at him in disbelief. "Of course not in here! Do you think we're as barbaric as the enemy? Sink me, man! If you shot him in here, you'd get blood all over the floor."

"Sorry, sir," said the officer, properly chastened.

"Decorum at all times," said Hanover. "We are English, you know. We stand for something. Take him outside and shoot him."

"Right away, sir."

Seamus was dragged out into the street. It was dark, the small amount of light being provided by torches held by some of the soldiers.

No fancy firing squad here. Seamus was simply hurled into the middle of the dirt road like so much baggage. He tumbled and fell onto his back.

He started to scramble to his feet, and one of the

officers, swinging up his musket, called out, "I wouldn't try to run, boy. If you do, then you'll be wounded and we'll have to finish you slowly. If you stand still, then we can make it quick. You won't feel anything."

"I already feel revulsion! Whenever I look at you!" said Seamus defiantly. He stood, arms drawn back, facing them. "Go ahead! I'm not afraid!"

"You've got spunk, lad. Too bad you're on the wrong side," said the soldier. The others brought up their muskets as well.

And then there was a pounding of hooves and the loud whinny of a horse.

The soldiers spun around, unable to make out who was galloping down on them in the dark. Suddenly a horse burst into the circle of light, plowing right through the soldiers before they could do anything other than scatter to get out of the way.

The boy's eyes widened in amazement. "Mr. Scott!" he cried out.

Scotty bore down toward the boy and extended an arm. "Hurry! Now!"

Seamus leaped upward and Scotty hauled him onto the back of the horse as if he were completely weightless. He snapped the reins and the horse charged forward. There was the crack of musket shot just past his head, but Scotty wasn't concerned. Even under the best of circumstances, muskets weren't *(Aren't! Aren't!)* very accurate.

And within moments Seamus and Scotty had pounded off into the darkness.

Hanover looked up as his men, looking somewhat shocked, slowly reentered the inn.

"Is he dead?" asked Hanover.

"Uhm . . . no, sir," said an officer. "He, uhm . . . he got away, sir."

Hanover's stare was acid.

"Got . . . away?"

"He had help, sir."

"Really?" He regarded them carefully. "Not a mark on you. You must have put up a fearsome fight."

"He surprised us, sir. A man on horseback—"

Hanover slammed a fist down on the table, causing dishes to rattle. "I don't care if a hoard of rampaging Huns helped him! Get him back here!"

"Yes sir!" said the officers, and hurriedly they ran out to mount a pursuit.

Hanover shook his head. "Damned disappointing performance, I must say. Impossible to find good officers nowadays."

Chapter Twenty-two

KBREX BELLOWED in utter fury, "They were *what?*"

"Transported away," said Kevlar at the sensor station. "They were on our screen and then they vanished."

"Raise the *Enterprise*," snarled Kbrex. "Raise those bastards immediately. *Enterprise!* Answer us, damn you!"

"*Enterprise* here," came the unflappable voice of a human female.

"I want to speak to your slime bastard of a dung-brained commander, now!"

There was a pause. Then, when the woman came back on, she sounded amused. "I'm sorry, but there's no one here by that name."

Dead silence.

"They've cut off, sir."

"Get them back!"

Moments later . . .

"*Enterprise* here."

"You stupid targ!" bellowed Kbrex, waiting for her to sound intimidated, as he added, "Do you know who you're dealing with?"

"You called earlier, didn't you?" said the woman calmly.

"Put your brainless captain on immediately, or so help me Kahless, I will rip out your living heart and strangle you with your own entrails!"

There was a pause.

"Who did you want to speak to again?"

His face was turning purple. "Your flea-bitten, cowardly, son-of-a-whore captain!"

"He's out walking the dog," the woman informed him. "But I'm sure he'll be back when you're ready to be polite."

Dead silence.

"They disconnected again."

"Get them back!!"

"Enterprise here," came that same maddening voice.

"You weak vomitus—" began Kbrex.

But he was cut off as the voice continued smoothly, "We're not home right now, but please leave a message and we'll return your communication as soon as possible."

Kbrex sputtered for a moment, and then the communications officer, fearing for his life, informed Kbrex that the *Enterprise* had severed communications once more.

On the bridge of the *Enterprise* the crew was as close to full-fledged hysterics as Kirk had ever seen them.

After hours of sitting helpless, in the hands of some superbeing with his own motives and unknowable thought process, having the opportunity to let off some steam was proving a blessing for the crew.

"We're being hailed again, Captain," said Uhura. As opposed to the barely controlled giggling from the rest of the bridge crew, Uhura maintained the absolute deadpan that she used with the Klingon. "How long shall I keep this going?"

"Until he's ready to behave in a respectful fashion," said Kirk, casually studying his fingernails. "In my younger days I might have taken his abuse. But I'm getting too old to put up with this sort of treatment."

"Yes sir," she said, ready for another round. Adding a honey-dripped drawl to her voice, Uhura picked up the communications band and said, *"Enterprise here."* As before, she immediately had it on audio for the crew to hear.

There was silence for a moment, and then a gruff Klingon voice, sounding as if he were strangling on every syllable, said, "Is . . . Captain . . . Kirk . . . there . . . *please?"*

Kirk and Uhura looked at each other, and Kirk smiled, inclining his head slightly. "On the screen, Uhura."

The infuriated face of the Klingon appeared, and he snapped, "Have I provided you with sufficient amusement?"

"Is there some way I can help you?" asked Kirk.

"You know damned well what you can do," he snapped. "I am Commander Kbrex, and you have our former commander and his companion over there."

"You seemed to be finished with them," said Kirk neutrally.

"They have been sentenced to die," came the angry reply.

"Well, then you will doubtlessly get your wish. I can assure you that they will die."

Kbrex actually seemed surprised at that. "You mean you will interrogate them and then kill them yourselves?"

"No. I'm just assuring you that they will die. Sooner or later. We all will."

Kbrex's face darkened. "And some of us, Captain Kirk, sooner than others." The image blinked out.

"I don't think he likes us," observed Kirk.

Spock stepped to the side of Kirk's command chair, staring straight forward as he said, "The question remains as to your intentions toward our guests."

"I have no intentions toward them," said Kirk tightly, the faint amusement he'd derived from Kbrex's discomfiture quickly fading. "I have nothing to say to them."

"You are irritated over the recent events on Cragon."

Kirk looked up at him sharply. "They were responsible for the death of one of my men."

Spock inclined his head slightly in deference to the captain's statement, but with Spock what was unsaid was frequently as important as what was spoken.

Kirk thought for a moment, and then stood. "You have the conn," he said.

It was fairly clear where the commander was quartered. It was the only cabin with a pair of heavily armed security guards posted at the door.

The captain knocked, and waited for a moment before he let himself in. The two Klingons rose when he entered.

There was dead silence as the two men sized each other up. The captain studied the steady poker face of the young Klingon commander. If he could read those inscrutable Klingon features, there was something beyond the usual warrior stiff-necked snarl. Kirk's eyes flicked to the woman, just barely. That could be a sore point with a Klingon male. But even in his brief scan of her face, he saw not only her noble beauty, which was breathtaking to any humanoid, and a haughty braveness, but a hint of fear. And fear in a noble Klingon wasn't a casual thing.

"I want to know the status of your ship, Commander," said Kirk briskly.

"Rot in hell," said the male. There was a sharp intake of breath from the female, but otherwise she said nothing.

"That is not the best attitude to have with your savior," Kirk said.

"A savior? That would imply that you had some sort of altruistic motives behind your action," replied Kral. "Your reason for rescuing us is governed entirely by your desire to torture us to derive information."

Kirk shook his head. "They certainly have you brainwashed about us, don't they?"

"We know the goals of the Federation," said Kral.

"We've never made a secret of our goals," Kirk told him, getting angrier by the moment. There was something about the arrogant and defiant stance of the Klingons that was absolutely infuriating. "To promote well-being and understanding throughout the galaxy. Just as the Klingons have made no secret of theirs: conquest and obliteration of all races but theirs."

"We are the stronger!" declared Kral.

"I've heard those claims before, Kral. Years ago, spouted by Klingons who looked different from you but had the same obnoxious and arrogant attitudes."

Kral turned his back on Kirk. "I see no point in continuing this discussion. Bring us to the nearest starbase, where we will assume our status as prisoners of war."

"There is no war!" said Kirk in exasperation. "As for the nearest starbase, what do you suggest we do? Get out and push? We have no power!"

Vladra seemed surprised by this. "You don't, either?"

Kral turned and made a sharp hissing sound, indicating that she should keep quiet. But defiantly,

Vladra said, "Commander, what does it matter anymore? We're not welcome aboard the *Ghargh*—"

"Be silent!" he snarled, his fists clenched.

"Do you think I'm stupid, Commander?" demanded Kirk, trying to distract the Klingon's growing fury away from the woman. "Dropping a commander into space isn't exactly a sign of respect. Obviously your crew has decided they have no further use for you. And frankly, if you were as cooperative with them as you are with us—"

Kral launched himself at Kirk.

Vladra cried out a warning, but it was, of course, a bit late. Kirk sidestepped quickly and Kral slammed into the wall. Kirk backpedaled as Kral spun and faced him, fists clenched and teeth gritted.

The doors to the quarters hissed open and the two security guards entered. They interposed themselves between the Klingon and the captain; each of them trained a phaser on one of the Klingons.

Kral, blinded by fury, charged at the security guards. The closest of the guards immediately took aim and, just at the moment Kirk shouted "No!" the phaser whined. Kral went down, enveloped in a burst of stun energy. He hit the ground, cracking his head against the edge of the bed.

"Sorry, Captain," said the guard apologetically.

"It's all right," said Kirk reluctantly, going straight to the comm panel and, once again, summoning McCoy from the sickbay. Vladra was rolling the unconscious Klingon commander onto his back. It was a nasty gash, but nothing McCoy couldn't deal with.

"He's upset," Vladra said, sounding almost apologetic.

"It's a common mental state among Klingons," said Kirk as he turned to leave. He saw little point to remaining.

"He appeared," Vladra said abruptly.

Kirk turned. "He?"

"The thing called Weyland," she said, repressing a shudder. "He made our weapons useless. We're trapped there. That's why Kral was thrown out of command. The crew wanted someone to blame our situation on."

"Any men?" demanded Kirk. "Did he take any of your men away?"

She frowned. "No. Why? Did he take some of yours?"

For a moment Kirk didn't want to reply. But then, he reasoned, that was the same sort of paranoia that motivated the Klingons. The last thing he wanted to do was emulate Klingons. "Yes," he said tightly. "Three of my men vanished."

"I can understand your anguish," she said softly. Then she glanced at Kral. "Perhaps you can understand his."

Kirk looked at the unconscious Kral, the Klingon's chest rising and lowering irregularly.

He thought about Garrovick dying at the hands of Klingon weaponry.

"I wish I cared," said Kirk, and he turned and left the room as McCoy stepped past.

He looked neither left nor right as he strode down the hallway, fists clenched. Replaying in his mind was scene upon scene of a history of Klingon violence and maliciousness, up to the most recent—Garrovick's death.

"We can all rot together," said Kirk.

Chapter Twenty-three

Stalingrad, 1942

THE SS OFFICER stood to the side and called briskly, "Ready! Aim!"

Chekov muttered to John Kirk, "This had better be a damned good plan you're working on."

"You'll love it," said Kirk.

"Fire!" shouted the SS man.

Chekov braced himself, his eyes closed, and the guns went off.

He waited for pain, for excruciating agony, for his blood to gush from perforations and his legs to collapse under him. For something!

Nothing.

Almost afraid to believe it, he opened one eye and then the other. Kirk was next to him, and they were looking at each other with equal befuddlement.

They turned then, upon hearing the raucous laughter of the German soldiers.

"Blanks," muttered Kirk. "They used blanks. The idea is to bring us out here and convince us we're going to die. They can do this any number of times, trying to soften us up."

"Effective," said Chekov, trying to stop his voice from quavering.

"Now," said the SS officer, approaching them briskly, "we'll bring you back to your cell. And then we'll talk. And tomorrow, well . . . one never knows when the real bullet will be lodged in one's chest, does one?"

Then there was a rifle crack, and the SS officer pitched forward with a bullet lodged in his chest.

Chekov and Kirk looked around in confusion as, all of a sudden, there was pandemonium throughout the camp.

The firing squad swung their rifles around and automatically started firing about them, forgetting that they only had blanks in their rifles. They toppled back, twisting and writhing, crying out and shouting profanities.

Chekov suddenly felt hands at his back, undoing the bonds. To his left he saw that Kirk was likewise being freed, and Chekov's eyes went wide when he saw who was responsible.

"Ivan!" he said joyously.

Ivan said briskly, as he finished undoing Chekov's bonds, "They thought I was dead, after my most recent questioning session. They dragged me out and dropped my body with a pile of unburied corpses. Then the shelling started. I came to and crawled to a farmhouse and told the farmers what happened. We ran out and pleaded with a group of Russian laborers. A few, mostly the anti-Soviet Mongols, refused to help, but the others were patriotic. Some were even partisans spying on the Germans."

Farmers, thought Chekov. He owed his life to determined farmers, sniping from nearby. "And the Russian army?" he gasped.

"Responsible for mortars and sharpshooting."

And suddenly they looked up as they heard an incoming whistle.

Ivan's eyes widened. *"Scatter!"* he shouted. The

mortar did not know, apparently, who was friend and who was foe.

Chekov dashed madly, and seconds later was hurled forward by an explosion from behind him. He glanced back, but the rising smoke didn't permit him to see anything, and he didn't have the time to go back and check things further.

He was barreling forward when a German soldier blocked his way. Chekov drove forward, smashing his shoulder into the soldier's stomach. The soldier went down, gasping, and Chekov slammed a knee on the man's chest, fist drawn back to knock him out.

The skinny, acne-scarred kid stared up at Chekov, terror in his eyes. Fringes of red hair were visible from under his helmet. Was this the Nazi threat, the fanatical product of the Hitler Youth? Or a scared kid who would rather be worrying about his school exams or his future with the girl down the block than fighting in an ideological war about which he neither understood nor cared?

"Get out of here," Chekov yelled at him in Russian, but his meaning was clear. The kid stumbled to his feet and ran.

Chekov ran into the darkness, the sounds of gunfire and screams and death all around him.

He heard his name shouted and turned in time to see Kirk, twenty yards to his left. Kirk was gesturing to him, and Chekov dashed in his direction.

He was supposed to be saving Captain Kirk's ancestor? Somehow it seemed that John Kirk had matters firmly in hand.

Chekov stumbled over a still warm body of a dead German soldier. The back of the helmet was cracked open, and he saw red hair, now soaked in redder blood. He didn't turn over the body to look at the face.

Kirk led Chekov with single-minded purpose, muttering, "It's over in this direction. I know it. I—There!" And he pointed.

There was a runaway, and on it stood a Ju-52 transport plane.

"It's what Ivan said he was after," said Kirk, grinning. "Let's give him an early birthday present."

"Can you fly one of these things?" said Chekov.

"We'll find out," the American said.

Now that, thought Chekov, *definitely sounds suspiciously like James T. Kirk.*

Chapter Twenty-four

WHEN KRAL OPENED HIS EYES, he saw that same medical officer, in the loose blue tunic, waving some damned Federation device over his head. With a low snarl he brushed the hand away and started to sit up with a curse.

To his amazement the apparently soft and lily-livered medical officer shoved him back down onto the bed. The Klingon looked up at him, shocked.

"How . . . how dare you?" said Kral, but he was surprised at how shaky his voice sounded.

"You injured one of your frontal vertebrae," said the doctor briskly. "I've patched up the abrasions, but you're still going to be dizzy for at least an hour."

"I should have known," muttered Kral. "No weak, thin-blooded Federation man would be able to handle me in such an ignominious fashion if I weren't injured."

The doctor harrumphed loudly. "You may consider us a bunch of soft-skinned cowards, but I'll have you know that my bloodlines are as good as yours. And my great-granddaddy, ten times removed, was as tough a general as ever sat a horse. And furthermore he, unlike yourself, was able to listen to reason. Which puts him a damned sight ahead of the more 'advanced' Klingons."

Kral's eyes narrowed. Nearby sat Vladra, her hands interlaced and on her lap. "If you were on my ship, you would be disciplined for that."

"Really." The doctor raised an eyebrow. "My understanding is that you were found doing the backstroke in a vacuum. So what was it you said that prompted that treatment, eh?"

Kral said nothing.

"No answer. I wasn't expecting any." The doctor stood and addressed Vladra. "Tell your commander that he'll be fine in an hour or so. And tell him that, if it's of any consolation, he's as boneheaded as my commander."

Kral half turned, and ignored the brief dizziness that provoked. "How dare you compare me to your weak captain!"

"Well, this is my ship, so I get to dare a lot," said the doctor tartly. "You have your opinions about Captain Kirk. He has his opinions about you. And while the both of you are making noises at each other, we're stuck up here and might be here forever."

"If we're that lucky," said Vladra.

McCoy glanced at her. "What are you talking about?"

Vladra opened her mouth, then closed it again.

To McCoy's surprise—and to some degree, Vladra's—Kral said, "If your ship is being affected the same as ours, then the orbit is decaying. We have less than twenty-four hours to rectify that situation."

"And how would you suggest we do that?" asked McCoy.

Kral's head sagged back on the pillow. "I haven't the faintest idea."

Chapter Twenty-five

Scotland, 1764

"MR. SCOTT, you saved me," Seamus screamed jubilantly, his voice coming in jerky spurts as the wind was knocked out of him by every pounding of the animal's hooves. By now the chaos had given way to pursuit.

"You ride like a lord," the boy said.

"I did'na know I had the skill, myself, but having the hounds of hell on your heels is a good incentive. Which way, boy?"

"At the crossroad, left. There is heather and hills beyond, all the way to the highlands, sir, all the way. They'll not follow us there."

Well and good, Scott thought, but he would need to put a few more miles between him and the pursuers before he would breathe safely.

As the wild ride sped on, the boy muttered a prayer whose origins were as rooted in pagan antiquity as in Christian doctrine.

> "Briget and Bran, protect us,
> Wild Queen Meave, protect us,
> Mary, Virgin Mild, protect us,
> Michael, protect us,

And Brian, steed of Michael,
Put fire to this stallion's hooves,
Oh, Christ, and all the saints,
Protect us."

The guttural rhythm of the magical poem, which the boy repeated over and over again, matched the rhythm of the horse as it galloped down the road turning north to the highlands almost by its own will.

"By God, we've lost them," Scott pronounced with relief, daring a quick glance back. He reined in the frothing animal. "Lad, lad are ye well?"

"I'd be more well if I'd done what I'd set out to do. A world rid of that fat oaf—"

"You wouldn't have succeeded. Hanover—"

Seamus looked up at him. "What? Hanover what?"

"Hanover . . . was too much a veteran to have been caught like that."

"No." Seamus's eyes narrowed. "That's not what you were going to say. You know something. Something in The Sight . . ."

Scotty sighed, and then said softly, "Lad . . . perhaps ye should reconsider joining the prince."

"What're ye saying? That Hanover is destined to defeat him? That the prince canna win? Is that what your sight tells you?"

Scotty made a rude noise. "My sight. My sight can't even see where I've been. Yet somehow I know, lad . . . yes. The prince canna win. There are greater forces than your trembling aim in your first murder attempt working against ye. You have the weight of history on your shoulders. History that has yet to happen."

Seamus's face was set. "If it hasn't happened, then I can make it happen the way I want."

"I wouldn't have it any other way, lad," Scotty said.

The boy dismounted and walked around, shaking out his legs. Scotty stayed atop the horse and looked at him with open curiosity.

"So you are a spy, then?" he said to the lad, shaking his head in disbelief.

"Aye, sir," Seamus said, shivering. "I was a ship-wright's apprentice in Skye. But the call came, and I was sent to the lowlands to spy. I was the king's own drummer boy for a year, and I've the scars on my back to prove it. Then I deserted, following the army, taking work as I could. I sent reports to General Murray, of Prince Charles's army, by pigeon."

They rode and walked for a time. The lemon-yellow sunlight, which had cast lovely lavender shadows on the rolling gray land, dotted with mounds of snow, was all too soon overshadowed by rolling clouds more gray than even this vast and lonely land.

"It's warming up a bit," Scott said, sniffing the air.

"That means more snow, Mr. Scott," Seamus said with certainty.

True to his prediction, the big wet snowflakes began to drop gently, plopping themselves on the two men, only to melt at the first touch. But soon the snowflakes were small and hard and stuck tight to the men as they rode slowly into the wind toward safety.

"Hungry?" the lad shouted to Scott through the windblown snow. They were riding double, huddling close for warmth.

"Aye, Seamus, I am that."

"I spy a cottage ahead. See, the smoke there?" Scott kicked the horse to a trot.

"Hello," Scott shouted, dismounting and banging on the door. "Open up for two freezing travelers, will ye?"

There was no answer. Scott thumped the door again, hoping to rouse the householder from his slumber. In response to Scotty's insistent banging, the door creaked open, but there was no one in evidence inside. The two men cautiously stepped over the threshold. Still they saw no one, although the evidence of recent habitation was clear. There was a pitiful peat fire in the hearth, sending up more smoke than heat, and a near empty pot of thin porridge hanging over it. There were also several long, thin pieces of wood in the corner that had been part of a load used in constructing a simple lean-to that Scott noticed out back. Even though it was left over, it still remained, for poor people wasted nothing.

"Damn it all, Seamus," Scott said, ready to turn and leave, "I cannot take the last food from this poor soul, wherever they have got to. Come, let's go."

"Mr. Scott, I beg of you. We cannot take a night out on the heath. I tell you, man, we'll find our death out there tonight. I say we stay the night and take what we need."

"Do as you will, lad. I'll stay indoors, but I will not eat of this poor man's food."

Seamus grumbled, eyeing the unappetizing gruel as if it were a savory stew, but he contented himself to drink some water from a pitcher and settle down to sleep by the hearth, after stabling the horse in the crude lean-to out back.

Scotty sat down on the packed dirt floor, leaning against the stonework of the hearth. He would try to stay awake, at least until the boy had caught some sleep. Someone had to keep watch for the return of the homeowner.

A rustling sound caught his attention. He strained to listen. He was ready to dismiss it as mice nested in the meager stores which were stacked in a shadowy corner, but it was too . . . well, too purposeful, too large. Then he noticed that one particular lump among the stores moved.

Stealthily he got up. Seamus awoke again, but Scott hushed his question with a warning gesture, first placing his finger to his lips, then pointing to the corner. Seamus nodded and rolled quietly to his knees, pretending to snore even as he moved silently to his feet. Scott circled to flank the hidden person, and then at his signal the two men swooped down, pinning the squealing prisoner.

"Don't move or I'll be forced to kill you," Seamus said grandly. He pulled aside the sacks and clothes that hid the person.

"Do what you will with me," the prisoner shouted defiantly.

"A lassie!" Seamus choked, his face now only inches from her. One of his hands was clutching something rather soft. He turned beet-red, let go and leapt up. "Oh, I'm so sorry!" he stammered.

Scotty also released her, and gallantly offered her a hand up. But she lay huddled, her eyes wide and frightened, her face smudged and her long dark hair wild and matted. Scott left his hand out reassuringly for a long time before she shyly reached for it and allowed herself to be lifted up. She was scrawny with starvation, but for it all, she was still a handsome lass, perhaps no older than Seamus. Yet she had the old eyes of someone who had been very badly hurt.

"Forgive us if we frightened you," Scott said with stiff formality. He wasn't sure what to say to her. After all, he had trespassed on her home, and terrified her to boot. "We only came in because of the snow. Please, don't cry," he begged. But she was shaking and sobbing uncontrollably.

"What are you going to do to me?" she wailed.

"Nothing. Please. We'll leave, won't we, Seamus?" Scott said sincerely.

"Please. Please," Seamus begged, totally unnerved by her tears. "We are being pursued by the English, and we are only trying to reach the prince in Inverness. They say the clans are gathering there. Please. Don't cry!" Seamus moved as if to catch her up in his arms to comfort her, but the shyness of any lad, coupled with the emotion of the moment, made him stop in his tracks, his mouth gaping and his hand hanging uselessly by his side.

"There, there, lassie," Scott said, coming to the rescue and reaching out to her. He enfolded her in his arms and held her as she sobbed out the terrible story.

"My father and brother are both dead by hanging. Fat Billy's men came through here. They . . ." She looked down, the pain in her face beyond endurance. "They did unspeakable things to me, and left me for dead. But the men, they hung them for being Scots. For naught else."

Scott held her for a long time, until she finally pulled away, mopping at her face with her apron. Scott looked down at the poorly repaired rips in her shift and petticoats, but quickly looked away, ashamed of the brutality she had been forced to endure.

"Come, please share my food," she offered, still shaking, but making a brave attempt to be the good housewife. She got bowls, Seamus scurrying to her side to help her set them out. The gruel was as tasteless as it looked, but in the cold cottage filled with sorrow, it was a feast of love and comfort, the two men offering their best cheer for what little it was worth to the girl.

After dinner the girl, whose name was Megan, rummaged through the baskets that held her worldly goods. She pulled out two large woolen kilts, hand woven by herself, no doubt, and presented them to Scott and Seamus.

"Here, take these, and burn those Sassenach rags," she said, with a cold rage. "And there is more," she continued. She dropped to her knees, scrabbling at the dirt floor. Scotty was the first to see what she was doing, and he took down the iron pot hook to use as a tool in the excavation.

Before long Scott and Seamus had uncovered an old box covered with the dust of a generation of men and the cobwebs of dozens of generations of spiders. Scott hauled it up, squinting and coughing as he brushed off the top.

Megan caressed the lid, then got to work prying it open. Inside the chest, reverently wrapped in an ancient plaid and tied with sturdy twine, were two fine *Claidheamh beag,* the basket-hilted broadsword of the highlands.

"These were my father's and his brother's. They were hidden after the rebellion in 'fifteen. I would to God that they had not been under the ground, for if they had been in my father and brother's hands, they might not be now under the ground. Take them," she said passionately, forcing them on the two men. "Take them and fight for the clans in my family's stead."

"I'll not dishonor his blade. I'll fight the enemy with heart and soul and flesh, before Mary and all the saints I will," Seamus swore.

Scott looked at the girl. "I'll fight as I have to," he said. "But I'm not a young firebrand like Seamus here. I must admit to you, lass—I hope I don't have to raise my arm in combat any too soon."

And from outside came the shout of a voice with a clipped, annoyed British accent.

"Come out here! We know you're in there! You left a trail a blind man could follow. Come out here and, instead of savages, die like the men you would pretend to be!"

Chapter Twenty-six

Stalingrad, 1942

"I'LL FLY LEFT SEAT if you want," Chekov said, offering to pilot the craft and dredging up a term he remembered from historical novels about the ancient war. John Kirk turned to look at him with a raised eyebrow and a smile.

"Should have known you were a fly boy. Too crazy to be anything else. Let's go. I'll fly left. You copilot. Where are we flying?" he asked as they scrambled onto the flight deck. Russian soldiers were already there. Ivan hadn't been kidding when he said they wanted to get the transport. It had been made one of their priorities, obviously. The ground crew was doing its best to prepare for takeoff, as the partisans who chose to leave piled on board. The rest ran off to provide ground cover from any German forces, although the most serious danger was from friendly fire.

"Over the Volga, east of Stalingrad. There's an airstrip," said Kirk. "Trust me on that. I was ferrying lend-lease P-39s when I was shot down, so I know what I'm talking about. We can fly visual. I'll point it out. You gonna make it, Chekov?"

"Easily," replied Chekov. Yet for all his apparent cockiness, Chekov was in a cold sweat at the prospect of copiloting the strange aircraft and of risking not only his life, but that of the young Kirk, over the war zone.

"You'd also better get on the radio and start talking in Russian. I don't think that your people are going to take kindly to this thing in their airspace. Flaps," he snapped, beginning a very quick checklist.

"Flaps," Chekov echoed.

Soon the ground crew was aboard, the propellers an invisible blur. The great plane started to roll forward, and suddenly Chekov heard from the back, "Look!"

There was a furious burst of arguing from the rear. Kirk said briskly to Chekov, "Settle them down. I'm not going to need distractions." Chekov immediately unbelted and dashed to the back, where men were grouped around the rear hatch. It was hanging half open.

"Close the hatch!" Chekov ordered. "Are you crazy?"

But one of the ground crew was pointing and saying, "Look! Look!"

Chekov leaned out and his eyes widened.

Ivan was madly running down the runway after them, his arms pumping, his mouth open and gasping.

"Kirk!" shouted Chekov, finding it odd to be barking orders to someone with that name. "Slow down! Ivan's out there!"

"If I slow down I might not make speed to clear the end of the runway," shouted back Kirk, but nevertheless he slowed down just a bit.

Ivan was running like mad, and Chekov hung out of the hatch, extending his arm as far as he could. Ivan's legs were churning, his arms pumping. In his eyes, Chekov could see desperation.

"Hurry!" shouted Chekov. "Hurry!"

Suddenly Chekov heard machine-gun fire. Swinging in hard from the left came a jeep with a mounted machine gun. The bullets chewed up the runway behind Ivan, nipping at his heels.

It was all the additional spur Ivan needed, and with an extra burst of speed, the Russian hurtled forward and leaped, desperately, almost with an air of resignation.

Chekov's hand snared Ivan's wrist. "I've got him!" shouted Chekov. "I've—"

The machine gun spat out death, and Chekov felt, in a rather distant way, some sort of pain. He saw Ivan's eyes widen in despair.

He sensed, rather than saw, warmth on his right arm, and he refused to acknowledge it. Additional hands were grabbing him now, pulling him into the plane, and still he held onto Ivan's arm. His hand had closed around Ivan's wrist with a single-minded determination that would defy death itself.

He tumbled back into the plane and felt a heavy weight on himself. Then he realized that it was Ivan.

"Move!" shouted Chekov. "Move!"

The hatch was slammed shut, and Chekov staggered forward as he heard the roar of the engines increase.

Kirk glanced at him as he dropped into his seat, then did a double-take. "My God, you're hit!"

Chekov glanced at his right shoulder. There was a huge ugly red blotch on his shoulder, spreading rapidly.

"It's nothing," said Chekov briskly, ripping the sleeve off his left arm. "Do your job."

The plane picked up speed, the chattering of the machine gun fading as the plane left them behind. Then Chekov saw, even as he made a makeshift tourniquet, that they were coming up fast, too fast, on a grove of trees at the end of the runway.

"We going to make it?" he grunted, ignoring the dizziness.

"Oh, we'll make it," said Kirk. "Don't you worry about a thing."

He drew back on the stick, and the airplane started to rise into the air. Chekov gritted his teeth against the pain in his arm and the pounding in his head.

The plane rumbled, rising higher and higher, vibrating with urgency. The trees were coming up fast, too fast.

Chekov gripped the sides of his seat and risked a glance at Kirk. The American was grinning broadly and was whistling a tune of some kind . . .

"What is that song?"

"What, you've never heard 'Off We Go into the Wild Blue Yonder'?"

The plane leaped with an additional burst of energy, the landing gear just clipping the top of the trees.

John Kirk turned and looked at Chekov cheerfully. "So . . . how do you like my plan so far?"

Chekov made no reply, but instead put all his concentration into not passing out.

They climbed higher and higher. Chekov looked down at Stalingrad laid out below them, and felt more remote from it than ever before.

Then he heard Kirk give a low oath. "Vat?" said Chekov in English, not really in the mood for surprises.

"They clipped our fuel line," Kirk informed him. "We're losing fuel fast."

"Ve going to make it to the airport?"

"Either that or crash," Kirk told him. "Maybe both."

"Oh good," said Chekov. "For a moment I thought ve vere in trouble."

"Naaah," Kirk assured him, even as he watched the gauge drop precipitously. "You'd better get on the radio and start talking in Russian, or we will be in trouble."

Chekov reached for the microphone and pain stabbed through his right arm. He bit his lower lip to prevent himself from crying out, and then reached around and picked up the mike with his left arm. He risked a glance over at his tourniquet and saw that it didn't seem to be slowing the flow of blood very much.

"Wonder how much fuel we'll have left when we get to the strip?" Kirk mused.

Chekov was wondering the same thing about himself.

Chapter Twenty-seven

McCOY ENTERED Kirk's quarters to find his captain staring at the computer screen.

"It seems we have a deadline," said McCoy briskly.

"You're referring to the decaying orbit."

"I'm not referring to an overdue library book," he replied, surprised at Kirk's calm. "Dammit, Jim, you have to do something."

"I know," said Kirk slowly. "I know. And I know what. But that doesn't make it any easier."

"You know what to do?!" said McCoy with amazement. "Then why don't you do it? What are you supposed to do, anyway?"

"I've been reviewing the ship's automatic log of when the immortal Weyland took the wind from our sails." He turned the screen of the computer around to face McCoy. There was an image of the *Enterprise* bridge crew facing a screen on which the massive head of Weyland appeared. "The key to this is how he faced things. He said that we can stay here and rot. Not that we *will*. But that we can."

McCoy frowned. "You're saying that he suggested that it's up to us."

"That's right."

"Even though he's the one who disabled us and left us floating around like a prize turkey."

"To him," Kirk said slowly, "his reactions are being dictated by our own. He reacts to what we do. And there're things that we can do to make him react the way we want him to react. Every single thing he's said to us is in that same, cloaked manner. If we wish it. If we allow it. And I'm damned annoyed with myself that it took me this long to realize it."

"Why do you think that is?"

Kirk glanced at him. "Why do you think?"

"Garrovick?"

Kirk nodded. "There was something special about him, Bones. You said once he reminded me of myself. When he came aboard ship this time, I saw it more than ever. I saw myself." He paused and said softly, "I've told you about David."

McCoy was surprised. Kirk had mentioned David to him only once, and that was when they were deep in their cups. Come the dawn, there had been an unspoken agreement between them not to mention it again. But now Kirk was bringing him up.

"Yes," McCoy said cautiously.

"He's nothing like me. He's . . ." Kirk made a vague gesture, "cerebral. A scientist, like his mother. The only thing that makes me certain I'm his father is Carol's word, and we agreed that I would stay away . . . or at least she agreed." Kirk shook his head. "Years of gallivanting around the galaxy, Bones, and then you start to realize that when you're gone, you've left nothing of yourself behind you. Some impact on an individual, something . . . that you can help shape. David is his mother's son. I had thought of myself as mentor of sorts to Garrovick—bringing him along, and then being able to take personal pride in his achievements in a way that I never will be able to with my own son."

Kirk flexed his back muscles and winced. "I'm getting old, Bones. Maybe too old for this."

"And Garrovick was your way of continuing your 'adventures' vicariously through the galaxy."

Kirk actually permitted a small smile. "You make it sound ridiculous. I suppose it is."

"No such things as ridiculous dreams," said McCoy. "Just dreams we realize, and those we don't."

"He was a good officer," said Kirk. "One of the best I've seen. And it makes me realize how lucky I've been, to survive as long as I have. What makes me any more worthy to survive than Garrovick?"

"Jim . . ." McCoy put a hand on Kirk's shoulder. "You can sit here until doomsday, trying to make sense out of the incomprehensibility we call the universe. Deeper and more learned men have been trying for as long as man was able to think. And when all the shouting dies down and is just so much hot air, it leaves us with this: Nobody knows a damned thing."

Kirk glanced up at him. "I do. I know that my ship and my crew need me. And I'm damned well going to do something about it."

He got up and then turned to McCoy and said, "I suppose I should be grateful that David is with his mother. When all is said and done, Garrovick wasn't my son. He was a crewman. A valued crewman, whose loss was tragic, but a crewman. Not my son. My son is a scientist and, thank God, has no interest in Starfleet, and he'll probably outlive all of us."

Chapter Twenty-eight

Japan, 1600

ONEKO AND HER ESCORT left when the sky was still silver with fading night. There was no helping it if a spy were watching from the surrounding plain. Once on the road there would be no fluttering banners bearing Mototada's crest to betray their identity. Oneko was secured in a curtained palanquin, bumping along on the sturdy shoulders of her lord's soldiers. Sulu rode behind her, his bridle led by a soldier who set the slow pace along the road. What would have been a short trip without a pregnant woman, even by contemporary standards, was going to take the better part of a week.

Sulu went over the map of the route once again, as if he doubted his memory or feared he might somehow lose track of the clearly marked road. He thought back to his first cadet command, but somehow the thought was now as fragile and fleeting as the world around him had been at first, while his current surroundings were taking on a solidity that at once thrilled him and terrified him. A stab of guilt struck him as he thought that he should be doing something to get back to his ship, but he didn't have the faintest inkling as to what that might be.

If there was a simple solution to his situation, it had so far eluded him. And there was still that nagging hole in his memory. He *knew* something had happened, or someone . . . but, he shrugged to himself, it all really didn't matter now. All that mattered was escorting Oneko and, he told himself firmly, getting the hell out of there.

He tried to put Sadayo's comments from his mind. It was as if the old samurai knew what he was thinking. Yes, he had said he would be loyal to Mototada, but that was before he knew . . . what? That it was suicide? Would he abandon James Kirk if he knew the mission was certain death? Of course not. But this was entirely different in many ways—none of which were coming to Sulu at the moment.

At least he had managed to keep from acting like a complete fool around Lady Oneko, and he congratulated himself for that blessing, although he suspected it was merely the earliness of the hour and the rush to get started. And the tearful departure of the lady from her husband. Sulu had managed to repress a stab of guilt over his feelings for her when he bowed to Mototada before he left. *After all, I haven't misbehaved in the slightest,* he rationalized as he moved the party out onto the road. For most of the first day he kept his distance from her anyhow, not trusting himself, and hearing the warning of the sword master mocking him in his head.

The lady had taken a kitten with her to amuse and comfort her in the swaying silken prison of her palanquin. At first when Sulu heard the soft crying, he had taken it for the complaints of the confined pet, but with a shock he realized it was the lady.

"Halt," he ordered, and the jogging party of armed men and litter bearers came to a ragged stop. They lowered the palanquin, and Sulu drew back the curtain. Oneko's lady companion ran up to the litter.

"Lady, lady, are you ill?" the woman cried out. Sulu had been told the woman had been the lady's old nurse and now was her lady-in-waiting, probably a poor relative of her noble clan.

"Oh, Kiku, please," Oneko moaned, turning that peculiar shade of green that heralds seasickness.

Sulu discreetly got clear as the lovely woman, the wife of his lord, got sick all over the road.

"I cannot ride in that thing all the way to Edo," she said, gasping for breath.

"Well, you cannot walk all the way," the woman, who was some years her senior, said with prim authority.

"Kiku, I will loose the child if I sway all the way to Edo."

"Lady, ride awhile," Sulu offered, dismounting and lifting her to the saddle. Slowly they proceeded, but soon she became tired, and he lifted her back into the palanquin, where she blissfully fell asleep.

By evening they came to a large farmhouse. A worn, wrinkled man greeted the armed party, on his knees, with his family, their heads respectfully in the dirt.

"Please, accept the humble hospitality of my house," he pleaded hopefully. This current civil war was only the most recent of many which had erupted in the instability of the past century. If the man were lucky, he would only be eaten out of house and home, not burned out or killed.

Sulu dismounted and ordered his men to bivouac around the property, with what he considered a nice mixture of armed protection for the lady and a low enough profile to avoid attracting trouble. The farmer and his wife were busy moving personal articles into the kitchen while they abandoned the sleeping rooms to the lady and her samurai protector.

"We've brought rice enough for our men," Sulu

offered graciously. "Some early pumpkins and radishes would be welcome."

The farmer groveled in the dusty courtyard. He was lucky indeed. He called out orders as he scrambled to his feet, his sons and assorted relations hustling to drag baskets of vegetables to the troops. If there were daughters, they were not in evidence. There was, after all, no purpose in tempting fate.

The farm wife had busied herself with a country meal for her distinguished guests, her fear giving way to a kind of pride. She would have good things to tell her neighbors. Soon the salty aroma of a simple stew, rich with fish and soy and thick with root vegetables, wafted out of the kitchen and throughout the house and courtyard. Kiku stood watching the proceedings with distaste. Clearly, in her opinion, such country manners were not worthy of her mistress.

The farm wife scooped out rice and a bowl of the stew for Kiku to take to the lady, who was resting in her room. But as Kiku appropriated the tray from the peasant, Oneko appeared at the doorway, dressed in a peach kimono with an over robe of pale green, although of a much more practical cut than the flowing garments she wore at home, but so fine in these rude surroundings that she could have been the goddess Amaterasu come to earth.

"It is not necessary. I would rather eat with the family," the lady said, with a gracious smile at the farm wife.

The woman bowed low, but Oneko gestured her to sit with her.

"I am the Lady Oneko. Thank you for your hospitality."

"I am Yoshikete Hana," the woman stammered. "I am honored to be of service."

Oneko's politeness and courtesy put the woman and

her household at ease, and before long a large pair of wide eyes peered out from behind a barrel.

"Come out," Oneko urged, reaching out her hand.

"Oh, that is only my small, ugly daughter," the woman said with humble deprecation.

The child, beautiful and fine-featured, shyly came out. She was about seven. "Show some politeness to the lady," the mother chided harshly.

"Come, girl, sit by me," the lady said, and the child haltingly came forth, bowing with the help of her mother's firm shove.

"She is lovely," Oneko said, smiling at the appreciative mother, whose harshness did nothing to hide her real pride in the child. "I remember being so young," Oneko said wistfully. "How easy life was for me then."

Sulu entered, bowing to Lady Oneko.

"Come, sit and eat with me," Oneko said to Sulu. Kiku glowered but said nothing. "Let us pretend we are simple farmers, and all a family. Come, Hana-sama," she said, using the polite honorific which made the peasant feel more like a lady of the court than she ever thought possible, "tell your husband to sit with me, and we shall eat your good food, and gossip, and tell tales. For this evening, we shall pretend we are in celestial heaven and there is no trouble in the world."

Sulu watched Oneko shyly as she charmed the simple family into easy conversation. But the charm worked on him as well, and as the evening drew to a close, the web of warmth and trust that Oneko wove only served to strengthen the respect he felt for her.

Suddenly Oneko doubled up, crying out in pain.

Kiku was at her side. "This is no good for the lady. She shouldn't be on the road at all," she chided. "This is her first pregnancy, and she will miscarry if she is not allowed to rest." She hustled the lady off, reluctantly accepting the herbal teas which the farm wife offered.

"If I had known she was in that condition . . ." the woman stammered.

Oneko was still pale the next day. Sulu knelt protectively by her huddled form.

"Lady, I don't think you should travel for the next few days. You are safe here."

"No. It is my duty to go where I have been sent, and for you to bring back information about the western army's attack plans. I am well enough to travel," she insisted, rising up to her elbow, but the effort brought on more nausea, and she lay down again.

"Look at you!" Sulu exclaimed. "You risk your life and the child's."

"You don't understand." Her face was tortured, and tears began to run down her cheeks, ravaging the remnants of her makeup.

"Understand what?" Sulu said with exasperation. "I understand that you are to be hidden to protect Torii's blood line if all is lost in Tokugawa's campaign. And I understand that if you travel too hard, you are going to lose the child. And I understand that you are safe here, for now, and that staying here until you are well again is the best choice we have."

"You are right," she said with demure submission that made Sulu's heart melt. "Very well. For today only, then. But at least stay with me. I am very lonely. You never told me about yourself. What is your home? You come from the mountains, *ne?*"

"No, lady. I come from the land beyond the horizon," he said. Even if it was a half truth, it felt good to say it. "I didn't realize how . . ." he struggled for the word, "how hard it has been for me to pretend I belong here. I don't know how I got here, but when I woke up, I was far from home and from my world. I don't belong here, but yet I do. I think I wanted to be here. And now I can't go home."

He got up and paced, the rolling samurai gait becoming more familiar with each passing day. "I am forgetting, already, who I am, was." He dropped down cross-legged on the ground with the attitude of any other angry samurai.

"Tell me what you do remember," she urged quietly.

"Let's speak no more of it," he replied quietly, afraid of giving away too much.

She inclined her head slightly, honoring his request. "My Lord Torii thinks very highly of you," she said.

"I think highly of him," replied Sulu neutrally.

To his astonishment, she placed a hand on his. He felt his throat go dry. "And you honor him."

He looked into her eyes, and there was something there, something unspoken.

It was one of the most difficult things that he had ever done, but he removed her hand from his and said softly, "Yes. In all matters."

All things except being counted on to return and help him in his final battle. Can't forget that. Honor your promises, but only when convenient. It was a very sour thought that went through his mind.

Oneko smiled, and he wasn't sure whether it was approving or regretful . . . or some of both.

The next morning, they moved out, to the tearful farewells and repeated bows of the farm family. Oneko gifted the daughter with the kitten. Sulu rode next to Oneko's litter. She had left the curtain on his side open.

She smiled at him in that same maddening way that expressed both interest and lack of interest. He began to think that perhaps the word "inscrutable" had been coined expressly for her.

Sulu didn't remember much of the rest of the day. He rode near her, making polite small talk, pointing out a flower here, a cloud there. Yet, when they weren't talking, he found himself sneaking glances at her from time to time, feeling almost like an adolescent schoolboy. It was extremely annoying.

That afternoon a scout reported a rockslide blocking the road, which had turned into a narrow ribbon hugging the cliffs overlooking the pounding waves and jagged rocks. A deer trail, narrow but passable, was nearby. Oneko, who had been pressing to go on, now pleaded that they turn back, her eyes never still as she nervously searched the woods for brigands or goblins or some other terror.

They finally rejoined the road where it turned inland, and followed a narrow mountain pass. Sulu pointed to the dark spots of habitation that nestled in the seaside valley at the foot of the mountain road. "That's the home of Mochizuki, the inn Minaguchiya. That is where we will stop."

Before they moved on, they took a moment to treasure the breathtaking view, the purity of Mount Fuji rising majestically from the blue of Suruga Bay. The dark violet ribbon of the Okitsu River wound down to the sea. The mounted party rode down the mountain road, until they came to what was left of a bridge. The swollen river bubbled between them and the inn.

"It seems fordable," Sulu said, riding carefully out into the swirling water. "Whooaaa," he shouted suddenly as the horse slipped slightly, sending him faltering in the saddle as a fan of water splashed up his side.

Oneko giggled, and shouted, "Let me show you how." She stepped gingerly into the swirling foam.

"No!" Sulu shouted back. "Stay on shore. It is deep. We'll carry you in the litter. Or mount a horse and let me lead you."

"No, Heihachiro-domo. It would be even safer if you carried me," she said fetchingly. He leapt from his horse and ran up to her side, but she only giggled, saying, "Come here, my noble pony," and she ordered him to crouch down as she scrambled up on his back piggyback fashion.

"I don't know why," he said, sweating but straightening out under the fragile load, "you didn't let me lead you on the pony."

But she only giggled. He dutifully carried her across the river, keeping his precarious footing with each step, slick or squashy as he picked his way by feel over the rocks and mud of the shallow river bed.

"There, we are almost safe," she said triumphantly, tapping his shoulder in a mock imitation of a rider driving a horse.

She twisted around on his back, treating the entire business as a game. And then the sudden shift in her weight overbalanced Sulu. He shouted out a warning, cried out her name and then toppled over. There were shouts of alarm from shore as Sulu and Lady Oneko were swept away by the power of the river.

Chapter Twenty-nine

Scotland, 1746

"COME OUT! In the name of the Duke of Cumberland, surrender!"

Scotty looked around the cabin desperately. "Is there another way out of here?"

Megan shook her head numbly. She looked as if she'd just been given a death sentence, which indeed she had.

Seamus reflexively put his arm around her shoulders. It was a charming gesture, and in a more cheerful time, it might actually have indicated the possibility of something more.

"Don't worry, lass. We'll be fine."

"We will?"

"Absolutely. You see, Mr. Scott here—he's a miracle worker."

Scotty glared at him, but Seamus seemed absolutely sincere. "Usually," he said dryly, "I have a bit more to work with."

But he was looking out desperately, trying to figure out something. At least the windows were firmly shuttered. They couldn't fire in through there . . .

Fire.

He looked at the fire in the hearth. He looked at the

twine that had wrapped the swords, and the rags scattered around.

He went to the wood that was standing over in the corner, and gripping the twine firmly, flexed it. He looked up at Seamus. "Get some rags. And take that longer piece of wood—the one that's a rod . . . and start breaking it into sections about a foot and a half long."

"Why?" said Seamus in confusion.

"*Do it!*" ordered Scotty.

The officers looked at each other, the snow coming down around them not leaving them in the best of moods. The sun was already coming up on the far horizon, and it wasn't too soon for them.

"This is ridiculous," said one of them, who was named Halsey. "There are nine of us. There're two of them . . ."

"Plus whoever's in the cabin," said another officer.

"There's no one else in there," said Halsey with confidence, and then grinned, "except for perhaps the body of that slip of a girl we had fun with. Remember?"

"Was this the cabin? God, you're right."

"I've had quite enough of this," said Halsey firmly.

He leaped atop his horse and, with a yell, charged forward. As he pounded toward the cabin, he pulled out his saber, holding it above his head. "Surrender!" he shouted.

The door of the cabin was thrown open.

Seamus was standing there, holding firmly in one hand the long piece of wood. Twine had been affixed to either end, and he was pulling it firmly back with the other hand. Nocked in it was a makeshift arrow, and on the end of it, a rag that was furiously burning.

Seamus let fly with a *twang*.

The arrow shot through the air, its path uneven but

true, and slammed into Halsey. It knocked him clean off his horse, and his splendid coat and shirt immediately went up in flames. He writhed on the ground, screaming and rolling.

Other British soldiers were charging forward now, to the aid of their fallen fellow. By this time Seamus had nocked another arrow, and again he fired. This time he missed, the arrow just grazing the flank of the horse. It was enough, though, to cause the horse to rear back in pain and shock, and it threw its rider.

"Those bastards!" shouted Halsey, the only comprehensible words in his continued scream as he tried to extinguish himself.

Seamus slammed the door shut and shoved his back against it. "It worked!" he said gleefully.

There was the sound of a musket report, and a huge piece of the door disappeared just over Seamus's head. He hurled himself to the ground and rolled toward Scotty, who was standing next to a far wall.

"Looks like we'll need another miracle," Scotty sighed.

For some reason the words "Beam me up" floated into his head. They had some sort of meaning, but damn if he knew what it was.

Then, from outside, there was the sound of more gunfire, a virtual volley, and the three trapped people hit the dirt floor.

Several more musket shots hit the door. Megan screamed, and Scotty gritted his teeth as wood splintered over his head. He heard more shouting, and the sounds of panicked horses, of thundering hooves and pounding feet.

And then . . . after an eternity . . .

Nothing.

Seamus and Scotty, lying on the floor, looked at each other. Megan's face was still buried in the dirt. Slowly, she raised her face—covered with filth.

The door of the cabin slowly creaked open.

A man was standing there, backlit by the rising sun.

He was well-dressed, his kilt of brightly dyed wool and his jacket of a continental cut. The heather on his bonnet, along with a brace of feathers, was fresh and crisp. On his arm he wore a round shield, covered with leather but bossed in brass. He was holding a fine sword that was, at the moment, covered with blood.

"Problem here?" he asked, sounding somewhat amused.

Seamus, amazed, jumped to his feet. *"Duncan!"* he cried out, and running forward, threw his arms around the older man. Scotty could now see just beyond the door, the unmoving bodies of the British soldiers. Followers of the duke who would follow him no further.

"Duncan, Duncan," Seamus kept saying over and over.

Others, dressed similarly to the one called Duncan, were now visible behind him. "I wondered," said Duncan, "if you hadn't of got yourself hanged or shot."

"Ach, it was a close thing, but this fine man here saved me." He waved toward Scott. Then his eyes went wide. "He knew you'd save us, Duncan. He knew! He has The Sight!"

Scotty shrugged modestly.

Duncan looked at him appraisingly. "The Sight. Excellent. We're on our way to Inverness, and I have a strong feeling that the prince would be quite pleased to spend some time with a man who knows what is to come."

Not when he finds out just what that is, thought Scotty.

Chapter Thirty

KRAL HAD NOT SAID ANYTHING to Vladra for some time. She sat across the room from him, and finally, exasperated by the silence, he said, "You have co-operated with the Starfleet men."

She looked straight ahead. "To where are my loyalties supposed to be, my lord? To the Klingon empire which thought nothing of dispatching me into space? To the former commander who berates me and hushes me? Or to the Federation men who rescued me and asked nothing in return? Whom do I owe my loyalty to, Kral? Whom do you owe yours to?"

His lips thinned. "We are Klingons. Nothing can change that."

"Nothing will change that. But what does that mean, to be a Klingon?"

He stared at her in confusion. "It means to be strong. To be one with one purpose. To disdain weakness, and know that the greatest death is death in combat, with honor."

"And what honor is there in the way we were treated? What honor is there in backstabbing, Commander?" she said with desperate urgency. "What honor, what sense is there, in adhering to principles and beliefs when all it will result in is dishonorable death and pointless hatred."

"No hatred is pointless," said Kral.

"This one is. For God's sake, open your eyes, Kral. Earlier you spoke words of love, when you thought you were to die. Speak words of cooperation now, and think of living."

He stared at her for a long moment. "What would you have me do?"

"Whatever it takes, my lord. Whatever it takes."

The doors hissed open and two security guards stood outside. "The captain wants to see you," one of them said.

Minutes later Kral and Vladra were ushered into a conference room. Their eyes opened wide as they saw the array of Klingon food put out for them.

Kirk and Spock were standing there waiting for them, their hands folded behind their backs in unison, like bookends. Kirk slightly inclined his head, and the security guards who had accompanied Kral stepped back out of the room.

"You trust me in a room with you?" said Kral.

"Mr. Spock, this is Commander Kral and . . . I'm sorry, I don't know your rank," he said to Vladra.

"Your equivalent would be 'lieutenant,'" she said simply.

"Commander, Lieutenant . . . my first officer, Mr. Spock."

"A Vulcan," said Kral with curiosity. "I have never actually seen a Vulcan before."

Kirk was inwardly amused at the mild sense of wonder Kral exhibited, a sign of his relative youth. "Shall we be seated?"

They sat opposite each other, and an ensign seemed to materialize from nowhere to serve the steaming food. Kirk studied Spock's impassiveness and did his best to emulate it. It wasn't easy. The food looked absolutely stomach churning.

When the food was served out, Kral eyed it suspiciously.

Kirk knew immediately what the problem was. "I assure you, I would do nothing so crude as to poison you," Kirk said with an amused tone. He ate first. "Delicious, truly delicious," he lied graciously.

The Klingon shoveled some food onto his plate, eating it greedily. And then he repeated the operation until he had demolished most of what was on the table. Vladra followed suit.

The moment the food was gone, Kirk said, "We're running out of time, Kral. My ship, your ship, and my missing crewmen are all running out of time. There's only one thing that's going to get us out of this. A treaty between the two of us."

Kral sent his plate spinning across the cabin, whizzing past Kirk's ear, slamming off a wall and clattering to the deck. "Damn you all to Durgath's Hell. You're at me, and my woman's at me, and what I want most is to have my hands around Kbrex's neck and squeeze and squeeze until his eyes pop out." His fist pounded down onto the table, sending the remaining dishes dancing. Then he looked up at Kirk. "Am I supposed to like this situation? Am I supposed to embrace you and call you brother?"

"Likes and dislikes are irrelevant, sir," said Spock. "What matters are questions of honor."

"There is no honor among Federation men," said Kral.

"And none among Klingons, is that it?" said Kirk tightly. "Is that what's supposed to happen? We sit here and shout at each other while our ships spiral into the atmosphere and three of my men face God-knows-what? I refuse to accept it. You have no idea how difficult this is for me. You were responsible for the death of one of my men."

"Kbrex was," said Kral. "He threw that grenade."

"Kbrex," Kirk said slowly. "The one who ousted you."

"Yes. So tell me this, Captain," said Kral. "If it meant having to ally yourself with Kbrex in order to save your crew, would you do it?"

"To save my men, I'd ally myself with your Emperor."

Kral regarded him thoughtfully. "Kbrex would never ally with you."

"That," said Vladra, "is because he lacks your insight and wisdom, my lord."

"Yes, he lacks that, but he has my ship." He turned to look at Kirk. "If I do this thing—if I agree to help you, for what that is worth—will you help me regain my ship?"

"I could easily promise you that, Commander," said Kirk. "I could promise you many things. But that would be lying, and I don't want to do that. The bottom line is, I don't know if I can help you. I don't even know if I'm going to be able to get us down to the planet surface to face our captor. I believe this Weyland has his own game plan, and all we can do is guess at what the rules are. I don't like this business any better than you, Kral. But I have a gut feeling that if we don't agree to this . . . we go down in flames. It's up to you. I suggest you decide now."

Chapter Thirty-one

Stalingrad, 1942

"GERMAN AIRCRAFT Ju-52 to ground," Chekov repeated over and over again, through gritted teeth. "Don't shoot. We are Russians. We are coming in to land at the People's Hero airstrip. German aircraft Ju-52 to ground . . ."

Ivan was now standing next to Chekov, and his eyes widened. "You're hit," he told Chekov.

Chekov glanced down at the ugly splotch on his arm. He was feeling a bit giddy. "My mother told me . . . never to scratch insect bites. See what happens?"

"Hey, Ivan," Kirk said. "What's so all-fired interesting about this transport, that you risked your fool neck to get it?"

"Bigwig who needs a lift to Moscow," Ivan said. "We got it for him."

"How big is his wig?" asked Kirk.

Ivan grimaced. "We're talking Khrushchev big," he said.

Chekov's eyes opened wide. "Premier Khrushchev?"

Ivan laughed. "You think as big as he does. Comrade Commissar Khrushchev is more than enough for him."

Chekov nodded and winced, and scolded himself once more. Of course, of course. Khrushchev would not reach that level of power for years yet.

He shook his head. Every minute that he spent in this place—in the motherland—was another minute he risked screwing things up. He had blurted out his foreknowledge about Khrushchev totally by accident. What else might he accidentally say or do? He was a walking bomb, threatening to go off at any moment and disturb time. A time bomb, he thought, smiling weakly.

Ivan rested a hand on Chekov's left shoulder. "I just want you to know, I appreciate what you did for me back there. You saved my life."

Chekov glanced up and gave a brief smile. But inwardly he was in turmoil. Here was another thing. Ivan was right. He had indeed saved the man's life. And what did that mean? Was Ivan supposed to have died? What if Ivan, now unexpectedly alive, sired someone who turned out to be a mass murderer, a killer of dozens, hundreds, thousands? Or what if Ivan now, in the course of war, killed someone who was not supposed to have died?

Considering all the possibilities was giving Chekov a headache.

He looked back at the instruments and tried not to pass out. He kept repeating his message, hoping that the right people would hear and react in the right way.

Kirk was continuing to whistle that maddening tune, and Chekov was momentarily tempted to belt him.

"All right," said Kirk. "I see the strip below. Ivan, get to the back and get ready." Ivan nodded briefly and did as he was instructed.

Kirk leaned forward and tapped on the fuel gauge.

The needle was perilously close to the empty mark, yet Kirk simply shrugged as if it were a minor inconvenience. "Could be a little rough," he said.

"How little?" asked Chekov.

He shrugged again. "Any landing you walk away from is a good one."

"Here's hoping for a good landing," said Chekov.

The plane came in at dizzying speed, the strip stretched out before them. Chekov squinted in the darkness of the night, manning the controls that were simplistic next to the far more complex workings of a starship. He could barely make out their target, but Kirk operated with a smoothness and sureness that indicated either he knew exactly what he was doing or he was one of the world's greatest bluffers.

The transport came down, faster and faster, and Chekov could see soldiers scattered about the field, as small as ants and scurrying around. For a moment he entertained the notion that Germans had taken over the strip and, as soon as the plane landed, everyone on board would be shot. Well, that would certainly solve all of his problems, wouldn't it? Chekov mused.

"By the way, Chekov," Kirk said, "what was that all about, that thing about my having brothers?"

"Er, well," Chekov stalled, thinking furiously for another lie. "I was thinking of, er, your mother, and if you were the only son how sad it would be . . ." he rattled on lamely.

"A man has to take risks for what he believes in," John Kirk said. "What are you going to do after the war, Chekov?"

"I don't know. I guess I'd better survive the war first. You?" He fought to keep his mind on the topic.

"Stay in the Army Air Corps, if they'll have me. Go back to school and be an engineer if not. Get married, have kids."

"That sounds nice." Even the small talk was making Chekov's stomach knot. He almost felt guilty about getting to know his captain's ancestor, sort of like peeking in a private window. And the prospect that this Kirk was all the link he would ever have with his captain was making him feel shaky.

The world began to slip out of focus around him, Kirk's brisk chatter blending together into a constant, faint buzzing. Oddly, he started thinking about his childhood, and enrolling in the Academy, and the first girl he had kissed, under the shadow of the great statue commemorating *glasnost* that was located in Red Square.

He heard his name shouted once, twice, and a pleasant warmth that had been building within him finally became overwhelming. And it was calling to him. He nodded and smiled and surrendered himself to it.

He felt a screaming of air, and suddenly the world was jolted around him. He noticed the jolt as if from a distance, a shaking and pounding and trembling, the screeching of metal and the stench of burned rubber and fear. Everyone was shouting, and the world was nothing but roaring and burning.

And then there was nothing. Nothing at all.

Chapter Thirty-two

"SIR, WE STILL CAN'T get the shuttle bay doors to open."

Kirk was seated at the controls of the shuttlecraft *Columbus*, receiving word over the craft's communicator that was less than heartening. "Keep working on it, Mr. Two Feathers," he said briskly.

At the controls next to him was his copilot, Commander Kral, formerly of the *Ghargh*. It was an odd sensation for Kirk. He couldn't recall having been next to a Klingon for such an extended period of time in such close quarters.

"Now what?" said Kral brusquely. "We stood on the transporter waiting for it to be activated, because you believed that this alliance is what that cretinous Weyland wanted. We stood there and nothing happened. Your communications to him went unanswered. So if you are so good at second guessing him, what does he expect now?"

Kirk stared at the great closed doors of the bay. "Maybe he wants to see just how much we want this alliance."

"Meaning what?"

Kirk looked at him. "Meaning, just how far do you trust me?"

Kral stared back. "I have no choice. I gave my word of honor. I will not renege on that. Whatever happens, happens. We see this business through together."

"Fine. Hold on."

The Klingon blinked in surprise as the shuttlecraft lifted off abruptly. Over the comm unit came the alarmed voice of Two Feathers, saying, "Captain! We still haven't got the doors functioning!"

Kirk ignored it, guiding the shuttle through the air toward the farthest end of the bay. He brought it around and hovered there for a moment. He glanced at Kral. "Still trust me?"

"Have I a choice?"

"None."

Kral shrugged. "Today is a good day to die."

Kirk gunned the shuttlecraft toward the closed bay door.

"*Captain!*" came Two Feathers's alarmed shout.

Kirk ignored it, speeding up. The doors remained serenely shut.

"Let's see how much honor you've got, Weyland," muttered Kirk, passing the point of no return. Kral closed his eyes and muttered the name of one of his gods.

The bay doors leaped open, as if jet propelled, and the shuttlecraft sprang into space.

Kral turned and looked behind them in surprise at the starship. "Those doors are massive," said Kral. "I'd never have thought they could open so quickly."

"They can't," replied Kirk.

Kral nodded slowly. "It seems the game has rules after all."

"Yes. But there's nothing to say they can't change at any time."

Chapter Thirty-three

Japan, 1600

SULU BROKE SURFACE, coughing up water through his nose and mouth. The water roared around him, and at first he wasn't certain why he wasn't being carried along. Then he realized that he was clutching onto a boulder jutting up out of the river. He looked around madly, trying to catch sight of Oneko.

He saw her just off to the left, a few yards away, the weight of her robes dragging her down. She was fighting furiously against the current, not crying out, but instead swimming with all her strength. It simply wasn't enough.

He launched toward her, shoving forward with the full strength of his powerful legs. He flailed outward with one hand blindly, praying, and snagged her by the wrist.

His legs churned, trying to fight against the water. But the current was too strong.

He heard voices crying out from the shore, receding quickly. He had no idea what was ahead of them, but he didn't want to stay in the water to find out.

She tried to cry out his name but swallowed water instead. Her robes billowed around her, her hair sopping.

Off to their right, several small trees clung to the shore. Sulu searched desperately to spot a branch or root protruding into the water, but none was evident.

They were approaching rapidly, and Sulu felt his strength waning.

He had one chance, an incredible long shot that was worth taking because it seemed to beat the hell out of drowning.

He grasped at the hilt of his shortsword and withdrew it, holding it with one hand while grasping Oneko with the other. The trees were coming up fast, and for one brief moment Sulu's feet hit an uprise on the river bed. He knew that the current would pull him forward in an instant, but for the seconds that he had purchase, he acted.

He drew his arm above water and let fly, desperately, praying to whatever gods would hear him.

The blade flashed through the air like a propeller and whirled into the lowest hanging branches. It hacked partway through one and then fell to the ground, useless.

And then the branch sagged forward, partially severed from the tree, and began drooping toward the river.

Sulu reached upward, grasping, approaching at full speed while the branch moved with maddening slowness, drooping lower.

As they passed under it, the branch dropped low enough for Sulu to ensnare it with his fingers.

"Hold on!" he gasped, and shifted Oneko around so that both her arms were encircling his chest. He pulled himself forward, slowly and agonizingly, and just as they reached the shore, the branch snapped off with a loud crack. Sulu lunged forward and pulled them to safety as the branch quickly floated downriver.

He turned himself around to look at Oneko, gasping.

She tried to get words out, and then crawled forward and kissed him firmly on the mouth. He felt the heat of her breath in him and it blew the chill out of him.

They separated and she gasped out, "Thank you."

He tried to find the words to express everything that was tumbling through his mind—the confusion, his word of honor, his feelings for her. All of it.

"Don't mention it," he said. And he added silently, *To anyone.*

They reached the inn with no further mishaps. Sulu was relieved about this—any more incidents like the scene at the river and he would have been a basket case.

A small gaggle of bowing servants had already descended upon them from the inn, wrapping the gentlefolk in dry quilts and leading them up the path to the large house. A gentleman sat sunning himself in the courtyard.

Mochizuki had been a samurai until his master had lost his lands and life in one of the endless wars. Although the old man had been forced to put aside his swords and turn his house into an inn, he was not without honor in the little fishing village.

"Mochizuki-sama," Sulu began with careful courtesy, "if it would not be too much trouble, if out of your generosity you could lodge this noble lady for this night, and perhaps a few days . . ."

The old man nodded, touched by the deference the young samurai showed him, despite his fallen estate. "It would be my honor to offer my unworthy house to so fine a lady and her escort," he said, his voice slurred slightly by age and missing teeth. "If you would take the rooms of myself and my wife, and my worthless son," he offered, although the family had long given up their own rooms to the endless number of lodgers who had made this place a stop on the way down the mountain. "And you must take the time to go down to the ocean shore to Miho beach. There lies the finest view of the sacred Mount Fuji to be seen in all the land," the man said proudly.

Again the senior travelers were lodged indoors while the soldiers and carriers were bivouacked on the surrounding land. But unlike the intimacy of the farmhouse, this place was as formal and public as any daimyo's court, and the ladies took their carefully prepared meals in their rooms.

But Sulu took the opportunity to take his meal in the common room at the invitation of the ancient innkeeper.

It gave him time to ponder what had happened, and reflect on his situation.

The thoughts that he was having about Oneko—he could never act on them. Would never act on them, because they were *dishonorable*.

Yet he was not intending to return to the castle and fight beside Mototada. That too was dishonorable.

How was one more acceptable than the other? In this land that was governed by honor, how could a hypocrite be abided?

How could he?

The next day Oneko pleaded illness until midmorning, and then called for Sulu.

"Lady," he said, bowing as he entered her rooms.

"I would feel so much better if I could make a pilgrimage to the Seikenji monastery nearby. My lord's daimyo, the great Tokugawa, studied there as a boy with Abbot Sessai. It is very famous."

Her tone was about one part request and nine parts demand. Sulu gave a brief thought to protesting, on the grounds that, first of all, this was not a sightseeing tour, and secondly, she had been complaining of pains, and any extra effort was putting more danger on her pregnancy. But he merely bowed in acquiescence and set out to make arrangements to suit her will.

She presented herself for the trip dressed elegantly but simply, with a string of prayer beads wound around her hands, the very image of piety. Sulu followed her, a second shadow, as she made the slow walk up the mountain to the main temple building. While she prayed, he made his own private devotions, facing for a quiet moment his torturous longing to understand why he was here at all, and how he could make this displaced life meaningful.

The surrounding gardens were complex in their simplicity, seemingly natural but actually the result of art and artifice.

Upon her return, she seemed to have come to a decision. "Heihachiro-domo, I would speak with you plainly," she finally said. "I—" She faltered. "You are in great danger. I do not wish to see you die."

Sulu reached out to her, taking her hands in his. She pulled them back to her side, but he insisted, and when he took her tiny, soft hands in his this time, she did not protest.

I'm going to be safe. I'm going to run away, he told himself. *Say to her what will sound noble. But only you will know the truth.*

"I am samurai. I do not fear honorable death," he said with quiet strength, but as much to assure her as himself. "I know that when I return to Fushimi, the chances that any of us will survive the battle are small. But that is my duty. Oneko-sama, I . . . feel strongly for you," he said carefully. "But I have a duty to our lord. I would give anything to live with you in peace like that farm family back there. But I can't. It is my duty to deliver you to the lord's family in Edo, and then I must return to Fushimi Castle. If I am to die there, as I most surely am, then I must accept that as the will of the gods. Let us enjoy each moment of this journey."

Her eyes misted over, and she pulled her hand free, dabbing at her tears with her silken sleeve.

He realized and understood the truth of what he was saying, and heard the conviction in his own voice. *My God, I'm really starting to believe,* he thought.

"Perhaps the Buddhist monks are right," she sighed, looking deeply into his eyes. "Perhaps it is all illusion, and the only peace for man is to withdraw from the world and seek Nirvana. If I live long enough, perhaps I will seek the serene life of a nun in such a place as this, and pray for the pain in the world; for mine and for yours."

He drew her to him, holding her tightly, but they both pulled back in embarrassment. Sulu was almost shaking with repressed emotion. He stared at the gravel path that strayed through the carefully planted mossy garden. An ornamental stone caught his eye. It was about knee high, flat on one side, with a natural knob on the top. It looked like a memorial stone in a graveyard. He rolled it over, exposing the damp earth, sending a family of bugs scurrying for the dark damp earth. He drew his short sword, the *wakizashi*. With swift sure strokes he scratched the character for her name, and next to it his. Then he rolled it back over to hide their secret.

"There is our ancestor stone," he said solemnly.

She lowered her eyes. "But the monks will find it and remove it."

"Perhaps not," he said hopefully, smoothing the moss blanket around the base.

She pressed her hands together in prayer before the silent sentinel of their secret. He took her hands and pressed them to his lips. But they lapsed into the distant courtesy expected of them long before they risked being seen by curious eyes.

Chapter Thirty-four

KBREX HOWLED in fury at what he saw.

A shuttlecraft had emerged from the back of the cursed starship and was plummeting toward the planet below with the speed of a plunging falcon. Kbrex pounded on the arm of the command chair and shouted, "Where are they going? Who's on that cursed shuttle?"

One of the few things that was functioning on the *Ghargh* was the sensors, and Kevlar ran a quick sweep. He was extremely unhappy with what he discovered, and suspected he was taking his life in his hands in informing the new commander of his discovery. "Picking up two life readings, sir. One human, one . . . Klingon."

"Klingon!" howled Kbrex.

"I believe it's Kral," Kevlar added.

"How dare he," whispered Kbrex, and then louder, "How *dare* he? Has he totally forgotten who he is?"

"A deposed and dead commander?" suggested Kevlar.

Kbrex turned, leveled his blaster at Kevlar and fired. Kevlar threw up his arms and screamed, except the scream wasn't heard. He vanished before it took form.

Kbrex turned a slow and furious gaze on the remaining members of the bridge crew. "Does anyone else wish to make an insulting remark?"

The bridge crew sensed, correctly, that it was a rhetorical question.

"Raise that bitch on the *Enterprise.*"

The communications officer dutifully followed the order, but he prayed that anyone would respond on the *Enterprise* other than that infuriating woman.

"Enterprise here," came the silky, all-too-familiar voice.

Kbrex sighed loudly. There was no point in venting his frustration and anger at this woman. He already had a mental image of her—about four feet tall, weighing 400 pounds, with a skin full of boils and pustules, and hair like dead wheat. A woman totally unappetizing to any man, and who delighted only in torturing dedicated Klingon soldiers who were trying to go about their business. "I wish to speak to Captain Kirk."

"That's not possible right now."

"It's quite possible. Raise the shuttlecraft that he and Commander Kral are on."

She was dead silent. A hesitation.

It was all he needed. "They are on that shuttle, aren't they."

"What shuttle?" she asked.

"You need say nothing else," said Kbrex. "By not speaking, you've told me all I need to know. *Ghargh* out."

Uhura removed the comm piece from her ear and stared at the communications panel in irritation.

"Damn," she said softly. "I hate him."

Spock stepped close to her and said calmly, "It is not relevant, Commander Uhura. The Klingon ship is helpless to impede the shuttle's progress."

"Yes, but I hate to have tipped him off to anything." She sighed. "I'm afraid we can't all be as perfect in our conduct as Vulcans, Mr. Spock."

He nodded slowly. "True."

"They've disappeared from our sensors, Commander," said Maltz, who had taken over the sensor station. He was not thrilled that his first report had to be one of failure. "I do not understand why."

"I think I have a clue. Communications—beam the following message to the planet, broad band: 'Attention great and immortal Weyland. We have reason to believe that our former commander—who had been disciplined for his poor handling of your concerns—is mounting an attempt against your people. We would be pleased to thwart his heinous plan as a way of showing respect for you. Please reply.'"

The communications officer said, "Should I repeat that message if we get no response?"

"Yes. Continuous repeat. But I think," and his eyes narrowed, "that we may indeed get some response. Perhaps more than our late commander—and the soon-to-be-late Captain Kirk—bargained for."

Chapter Thirty-five

Japan, 1600

NIGHT.

Sulu woke up, struggling with sleep and a hangover, trying to make out the source of the muffled sounds around him. A shadow of black in the black room dropped with noiseless efficiency on the floor, its presence revealed only by a slight *humph* of breath as it landed with a soft thud. Sulu rolled off the pile of quilts on the floor which comprised his bed, feeling for his swords on the floor.

He felt the cool *whoosh* of a blade slash by his hand, and he pulled it back quickly. By sheer luck—certainly no skill—his fingers brushed the lacquered sheath of one of the two swords. His hand closed on it. It was the short sword, the *wakizashi*. He drew the blade, still holding the scabbard in his other hand.

He felt more than saw the other man close in. A stray beam of light from the passageway sparked a muted glint on the steel in the assailant's hand. Sulu ducked as the deadly *shuriken,* the star of death, spun by, ripping into the wooden post in the corner. Sulu closed fast, tucking and rolling half the way, blocking the man's dagger with his sword sheath and slamming

the hilt of his sword into the man's head. The assassin
fell without a sound.

Sulu was panting hard. He groped through the
tangle of bedding for his long sword, the *katana*. In
the tight confines of the room the shorter weapon had
given him an advantage, but he knew this assassin was
not alone, and to fight more than one, he needed the
range and power of the long sword. He ran down the
corridor to Oneko's room, shouting for help as he
went. But the house was empty.

He skidded to a halt at the ripped paper screen door
that led into the lady's room. He winced and drew
back, guarding against the cut that did not come from
a ghostly opponent who was not there. Drawing and
cutting the air in a whirlwind of steel, he leapt in,
tripping on a still warm body. The faithful Kiku.
Dead.

Sulu's back crawled as he felt the stirring of a man
padding with catlike speed and silence.

"No," the soft whisper of a woman's voice, "not
him."

Then fingers came, as hard as bone, and unconsciousness which tasted of death.

When he came to, it was golden morning. Sulu lay
helpless, the sword heavy in his hand. But the sound
of a man running down the hall roused him, and he
pulled himself to his knees, crouching like a tiger to
spring at whoever came.

"No, no, lord," the old proprietor shrieked, leaping
back.

"What happened?" Sulu barked at him. "Where
were you?"

"I am so sorry," the old warrior sobbed as he
kneeled over the now stiff body of the dead guard.

His daughter-in-law ran up and knelt by him,

cradling the old man in her arms. She too was crying as she apologized.

"The ninja came and attacked, sir." She gasped out the story to Sulu. "Most of the servants ran away. Some died. The master and our family were huddled in the kitchen. They did not attack us. We could do nothing. Nothing."

Sulu strode out into the garden, the dew of the summer night still beading the leaves. He watched the servants carrying off the body of Kiku.

Was that all? Could he wash his hands of her now? Where did honor end? If it ended . . . was it honor?

What are you prepared to do now, Sulu? he asked himself.

He returned to his rooms only long enough to don his armor and to pack, and he mounted a small gray pony and rode out. Just outside the compound he saw farmers cultivating a small field, the men chopping at the soil with hoes in the mindless rhythm that brings tranquility. As he passed, one of the men turned his head slightly, watching him out of the corner of his eye.

A man with a scar down the side of his face. He looked maddeningly familiar.

Sulu went cold as he realized that he had seen the simple farmer before, somewhere. He rode on nonchalantly, but he shook with urgency as he remembered who the man was.

Then it hit him. That scar—he'd seen it on the gardener. It was the gardener, the old gardener from Torii's castle. What was the old man doing here?

He rode out of sight, then reigned the pony off the road and slipped off its back. As quickly and quietly as he could, he stripped down to a simple loincloth. What he had in mind would require speed and stealth. He shinnied up a small tree and waited. If the old man were following him, sooner or later he would pass beneath Sulu's ambush.

Shortly, the man almost slipped past him, moving with such unassuming and ordinary casualness that Sulu didn't pay attention at first. So this was a ninja secret—not stealth, but ordinariness. Sulu relaxed his grip on the tree, falling like a stone and collapsing the man into a grunting heap.

"No, lord, don't rob me. I have nothing," the old gardener/farmer simpered.

"Don't give me that," Sulu shouted at him, pinning his arms back to a point where he expected some serious protest.

But the man's arms just seemed to disjoint, and he was suddenly slipping from Sulu's grip like a ferret.

"No you don't," Sulu muttered, grabbing at him, but the man was loose and running with a speed Sulu didn't expect from someone so old. Sulu was after him like a shot.

"Got you," he shouted triumphantly, tackling the man to the ground. "What the hell?" he said as the man's eyes bulged and his color faded. Somehow he was choking himself to death. "No you don't," Sulu shouted, forcing open the man's mouth and pulling his tongue free from his throat. "You are involved in this up to your ears. Where is the woman, damn you?"

"I will never say," the old man said simply, suddenly calm.

This was getting Sulu nowhere. "Listen to me. If you know where she is and are her friend, tell her the Great One Cut Heihachiro pines for her. If she is held captive, help her to escape and she can find me here—no, let's say in the pine grove near the beach, the one that frames Mount Fuji. If you are her enemy, then come there with all your friends, and we will fight to your death or mine."

With that he released the old man and sank to the

ground in total exhaustion, not even watching the man, who quickly disappeared into the thin woods. Methodically he armed himself and rode the animal down to the beach. And he sat down to wait.

The irony of the situation was not lost on him. He was counting on the honor of others—kidnappers, perhaps murderers—while he, one of the "good guys," was questioning his own honor. Or lack of it.

The moonlight sparkled on the beach where the tide rushed up to pattern the sand and rolled back out to swell again. Even the shadows who approached Sulu had shadows, shadows cast by the ripe moon. He stood ready to draw.

The party stopped just out of range of the cutting death of his sword. The leader called out to him.

"You are the Great One Cut Heihachiro-sama?"

"Just simple Heihachiro, yes, I am he."

"Simple? You are modest as always." A voice shimmered like tinkling bells. Sulu started. At first he took it for the figure of a young man, not a woman. Not *that* woman. The slender body strode boldly with the other swordsmen, dressed in a *hakama* like any other soldier.

"Oneko?"

She stepped past the leader, approaching him alone. In the moonlight he could see her face, the moon making her skin as white as the rice-powder makeup had at Fushimi Castle.

"So it was your voice in the dark," he said with calm conviction.

"Are you so surprised? I, too, am a warrior," she explained with ultimate simplicity.

"Yes. I had forgotten . . . I saw you fight that first day, but . . . you look different."

"It is the woman who is the fighting demon who cuts down the mounted enemy at the castle gate. Sometimes you are such a country bumpkin," she chided. "From the beginning of time women have ridden to war in this land. And it is the task of a noblewoman to train her son in courage, and even skill at arms, before he is old enough to train with the men. You are troubled, Heihachiro-sama," she said finally, in a half question, half statement.

"I don't understand. You are riding with a band of, what, bandits? Or ninja?"

She laughed in the familiar coquettish way that left the sound of bells chiming in the air.

"I am of an ancient ninja family. I have been rescued." Sulu thought he heard a hint of irony in her voice. He stared at her, seeing the steel under the porcelain.

Again she spoke with the gentle coquetry that entrapped him in a web of magical glamour. "You wished to find me. You have. Come, we must leave this place." At a low whistle from the leader of the group, a small man appeared out of the shadows leading horses. It was the old gardener.

Sulu and Oneko rode side by side, but Sulu did nothing to encourage conversation, although the lady made a few desultory attempts. But Sulu's head ached. Rescued! Yes, he had been so worried he had changed history. Well, he had, twice—two incidents that canceled each other out. They had been trying to rescue her the first time he saw her, and they had finally succeeded.

By the time they arrived at a secluded farm, morning was just breaking. Oneko slipped easily from the saddle, striding into the courtyard with the leader of the group, who Sulu could now see was a wiry middle-aged man. Oneko had called him uncle on the road, and now, in the light of day, Sulu was pretty sure that was not just a country courtesy, but a kinship statement. But whereas her delicacy was beautiful, his made him look like a hawk hunting for lunch.

The uncle kneeled at the door to the house, calling out to his father, the family head, telling him that he had returned with a hostage.

Uncle and Oneko entered, but Sulu was bid to stay outdoors, under close guard. The walls were thin, and he couldn't help but hear the loud, angry argument concerning him. And the order for his execution. And Oneko's pleading for his life. And then he heard nothing that he could make out. A servant summoned him to enter.

"Come closer," the scrawny ancient patriarch ordered from his dais. The old man asked no questions. He just stared at Sulu for a while. Finally, he seemed satisfied and grunted his approval. That was all.

Sulu was led out, cleaned up and fed. He had just finished putting on the clean clothes provided when Oneko entered the room.

He was all business. The no-nonsense, Starfleet officer, determined to get to the bottom of a confusing situation.

"These people, they are your relatives?" he asked without preamble. "Why did they attack my party? Kill Kiku?"

"Kiku's death was an accident. It is regrettable. I will tell you our secret, but you must tell me yours. Please," she urged, leaning toward him and pleading with her eyes.

"No promises. Tell me." It was not a request.

"I am the granddaughter of the head of a clan of ninja warriors originally from the Koga province. Our clan opposes Tokugawa. He is so clever, he would have been a great ninja himself," she said bitterly. "His tricks to destroy his opponents are famous. It is an endless game of spy and counterspy. Kiku was my aunt. She had been placed in a noble house to spy. She was assigned to accompany a new concubine who was being sent to Mototada three years ago. The plan was for Kiku to spy in Mototada's house. The girl caught a chill on the road. That was the real Oneko. Kiku forced the soldiers to bring the sick girl to a farm which was nearby and which she knew was allied with a friendly clan of ninja. The farmer sent a messenger to grandfather, who hatched a plot. The soldiers and retainers who accompanied the young concubine were killed. The girl had already died of the lung illness. The soldiers were replaced by our men, and I took the girl's place.

"My perfumes, my gestures and voice . . . all carefully designed to bewitch any man. I'm well-trained. I was to observe Mototada, learn his weaknesses, find out what I could about the deployment of his troops . . . anything that would prove useful. I am surprised I was not ordered to kill him. I was being rescued when you arrived on the road. I had no choice but to be the faithful concubine and fight my attackers. You are a very fine swordsman. Grandfather had sent men to bring me home with what I had learned before the western army attacked. But I also think that grandfather could not bear to see me die."

"How can you?" Sulu blurted in shock. "You are carrying Torii's child—"

"Shhh . . ." She reached over before he had finished, placing her hand on his mouth and gesturing toward the thin wall. She shook her head, her eyes filled with such sadness that Sulu reached out and cradled her in his arms.

Nothing had gone right. Oneko was not what she was supposed to be, the lord of the land was untrustworthy, his own "lord" was duped by a slip of a ninja woman . . . and who was he to say that he was any better? How could he expect better of a land when he himself thought of honor as eminently disposable?

"Now you must tell me your secret. It is very important. I've convinced grandfather that you are a god, or at least a mountain goblin, a *tengu,* one of the magical warriors who are worshiped by our clan for their martial skill. I can see it in your eyes, in your soul. You are not of this place, of this world. Is it true?"

Sulu laughed hysterically. "No, no! I'm no god. I'm just a perfectly ordinary man." *A perfectly ordinary twenty-third century Starfleet helmsman,* he thought bitterly. Sulu felt the romance shatter. So much for his childhood dreams. He was stuck in a confused and complex world. He didn't belong and he couldn't leave.

"Please, say it is so," she begged with quiet fear, but Sulu was too caught up in his own disillusionment to notice.

"I am nothing special. In fact . . . I'm starting to realize just how common I am . . ."

"You have no skills, no magic? Please, say you do."

"Yes, say you do." The tall hawk-faced uncle strode into the room. "Oneko, out," he ordered.

"Please, please," the girl sobbed, throwing herself at her uncle's feet, clutching hopelessly at his legs. He kicked her away.

"I don't know what this foolishness is, but I am tired of it. You are Torii's man. That is all. Not a *tengu* or a god. Just an enemy. And you will confess it," the hawk-faced man shouted, calling in four armed men. "And tell us of the fortifications and troop strength in the castle. Tell us what Oneko can't, about the battle plans."

They grabbed for Sulu, but he sprang forward, kicking and punching, sending them sprawling. There was no handy weapon this time. He yanked up the quilt, throwing it at the two men who were up again and charging at him. Then he dove through the paper screen that separated him from the next room, only to be grabbed by two more men who were posted there.

He kicked one of his assailants in the stomach but was punched and beaten for his trouble.

"Talk or die!" was the scream. A knife was at his throat.

He could talk. He should talk. What was it to him? The castle was doomed anyway, whether he spoke or not. What was the point in keeping the knowledge to himself?

"Talk, or on my honor, I will gut you, now," came the warning.

Honor.

Sulu looked up at him and smiled wanly.

"You are cordially invited to disembowel yourself," Sulu informed him.

A sword was drawn back, and he started to struggle, knowing he wouldn't make it. He heard a voice cry out.

And then all hell broke loose.

Chapter Thirty-six

Scotland, 1746

"So . . . I AM to be defeated, eh?"

Scotty stared at the young, cloaked and hooded man who stood across from him with a rakish grin and a confident air.

Scotty didn't know what he was feeling, but he was certain that, to a large degree, it was awe. He was standing face to face with Bonny Prince Charles, Charles Edward Stuart. The young man who was the would-be heir to the throne of England, Scotland, and Wales.

I'm not supposed to be here, thought Scotty. He was sure of it. This was wrong, all of it wrong. It was more than that he was standing there, in Inverness, in the tent of Charles himself. It was a sense that not only could this not be, but this should not be. It should be impossible.

Why impossible? Because . . .

Stuart was dead. Generations dead. Centuries dead. *(Will be. Is. Will be.)*

"Are you quite all right?" asked Charles with genuine concern.

Charles's inner circle of command stood nearby. One of them was notable for a bedraggled wig, which he removed, displaying a shaved head. He beckoned to an aide, who produced a wool stocking cap that gave him the comical appearance of a disreputable Father Christmas.

"Yes, that's better," the man said. "I am General John Murray, sir, son of the Duke of Atholl, and I'll tell you frankly that I have not much use for soothsayers on the prince's war council."

"Yes, but perhaps I have," Charles said sternly. Murray fell immediately silent. Charles turned back to Scotty and said, "Well . . . if I am to be defeated, then am I to be executed?"

"No," sighed Scotty. "You will live in exile all your days. For what it's worth, in the future your portrait will grace a million Scots' homes, and many more millions of Scottish whiskey bottles, biscuit tins, and china plates."

Charles stared at him for a long moment, and then tilted back his head and laughed delightedly. "So I'll not be a ruler, but an icon, is it? Sir," he said, "you may have The Sight. You may not. But I'll warrant you have a splendid sense of humor. Come, sup with us."

The table was a glitter of candlelight, dancing in merry reflection from the generous quantity of silverplate. Scotty's mouth was watering at the rich gravy smell of a lamb roast which wafted in from the kitchen.

The simple country dinner consisted of a thick creamed leek soup, roasted capons, the lamb, a variety of breads and condiments, and a good supply of French wine. The prince was quite right. Scotty had not eaten this well for a long time, and he was positively groaning after the pudding, a rich mold of candied fruits and suet steamed to savory perfection, then laced with brandy and ignited at the table. A spectacular end to an excellent meal.

But after the pangs of hunger had been satisfied,

Scott took to looking at his dinner companions, especially the prince. He was a handsome young man, with excellent manners and a far less haughty disposition than his counterpart and cousin, the Duke of Cumberland. He certainly seemed sincere enough, exchanging bits of information and advice with his nearest councillors, a pair of doughty old Irishmen and a French cavalier, who seemed his favorites. But the eyes of another man, Alexander Keppoch, kept straying toward the prince as well. Whatever was going on, Scotty could smell the rancor of political unrest a mile off.

"Well, then, Mr. Scott," Murray broke in, "what does your second sight say of our campaign? Is there anything that we can do to forestall the doom you preach?"

"Well . . ." He thought about what he knew (would know, did know) of the British armament. "What I do know is that the British Train of Artillery is going to shoot your private parts off if you don't have some cannon of your own."

"Alas, we captured the magazine at Falkirk, but some fool blew it up. But no matter," one of the Irish contingent offered, adding, "for I feel that the highland man is fiercer with his trusty sword than a musket, and more reliable it is, too."

The prince nodded in agreement, Keppoch and Murray scowled, and the three favorites grinned. So that is how it was. The prince was a romantic, and the battlefield was certainly no place for airy-fairy notions. That at least ended the talk, much to Scott's relief, and after supper they retired to a sitting room, where the prince himself took his place at the delicate harpsichord and played a few short pieces in the crisp, almost mathematical style of the period.

Discussion turned eventually to domestic matters and the difficulty in keeping the men united. Scotty was appalled to hear of how internecine squabbling had already prompted the Glengarry men and the Clanranald men to desert in protest.

"My God," Scott said. "How can we hope to win this thing when cadet branches of the same clan can't make peace among themselves?" No one contested the comment.

Later in the evening Scott thanked his hosts and prepared to leave. Murray caught up with him at the door.

"I would speak with you concerning the artillery train. If you would allow my man to take you to my quarters and wait for me there, perhaps we might discuss this matter."

"Aye, sir. If I can be of any help, it would be my honor, sir."

The general's quarters were in a home on the same street, and Scott was soon settled in a well-appointed sitting room. He napped awhile in a great wing chair, his feet propped warmly on the grate, waiting for Murray to get loose of the party with the prince.

When Murray arrived, he had Keppoch with him. The clan chief made himself at home with Murray's supply of port, pouring three glasses of the rich red cordial. It was Murray who got down to business.

"Tell me of the artillery train," he ordered.

"I think it would be more useful to tell you some past history," Scott began in his best lecture tone. "Queen Boadecia of the ancient Celts, with her clans, numbering some 200,000 warriors, attacked a legion of the Roman army, perhaps five hundred or a thousand men in all. Do you know what happened? The Romans, vastly outnumbered, slaughtered the Celts. The Celtic strategy was to run into battle, screaming, their swords swinging wildly. The Roman strategy was to hold their line. The Romans hacked the Celtic clans to death, one man at a time. To quote, 'Those who do not learn from history are condemned to repeat it.' What I see here is a disaster in the making. From what I see, those two Irish captains, whom the prince holds so dear, are saying that loyalty and courage are enough. But you, my lords, although great traditional chieftains, seem to be wise enough to understand the value of the modern cannon. I think perhaps I have spoken too boldly, gentlemen," he ended.

Murray interrupted, "I would pray to convince the young Stuart to modernize his army, and quickly. Alas, though, what you heard of the problem between the Clanranald and Glengarry, both of Clan Donald, is but the twig of a problem whose roots lie buried in time. Between the lack of support among the small householders, and the endless feuding amongst the clans, it will be a miracle if we can field an army."

"But where can we get cannon? It is a dream, sir, a dream," Keppoch said with passion.

"What about Fort Augustus?" Murray suggested. "We've taken the forts on the Great Glen before, but not held them. Perhaps what we needs must do is take them, strip them and burn them. Thus we shall have our guns, and the English will not be able to recapture them. They lie on your lands, my lord, do they not?"

"That they do, and a blight I would be glad rid of. Fort William and Fort Augustus are indeed the two best prizes. Mr. Scott, if we can capture cannon, can you engineer a way to mount them on wagons and port them to Inverness, and if so, can you also train gunners to prime and fire them?"

"*Aye*," Scott said, standing up again, his chest swelling with pride. "That I can do!"

The suggestion of an attack down the Great Glen was soon presented to the Council of Chiefs, where it was hailed as a brilliant stroke of military tactics.

"By God, gentlemen," the prince enthusiastically

proclaimed, slapping his hand sonorously on the table, "it will indeed serve to secure our western flank. Keppoch and Lochiel, you shall bring your forces to bear."

And so the next morning, Scotty marched out to war under the banner of Alexander, Seventeenth of Keppoch, laird of the Clanranald branch of the Donalds. The pipes screamed defiance to any and all who would oppose these proud men.

There was something in the back of his mind that told him he shouldn't be doing this. But it was now but a dim, fluttering memory, and he brushed it away as he would a gnat.

Chapter Thirty-seven

Moscow, 1942

CHEKOV FELT a soft hand touching his face. Slowly his eyes fluttered open.

He had that brief disorientation that always hits when one awakens in an unfamiliar place. How much stronger was that disorientation when one awakens in an unfamiliar time.

The woman who stared down at him wore an odd costume, and he wondered why in the world she was dressed like a twentieth-century nurse in a Soviet army hospital. Blond hair framed her face.

He frowned.

"Nurse . . . Chapel?" he asked.

Her eyes widened and she dropped her voice. "If you wish to pray, comrade, you have picked the wrong place to do it. There are no chapels here."

He tried to shake off the confusion, and then the reality of where he was started to come back to him. His vision cleared up and he could now clearly make out the woman standing over him.

The error had been entirely his. The woman was obviously not Christine Chapel . . . didn't even look like her, really, except that she was a nurse with blond hair. What disturbed him was the fear in her eyes when his incomprehensible (to her) first words seemed a plea for a place of worship.

Of course. One didn't do that in the Soviet Union of 1942. He had always known that intellectually. Yet now, seeing her reaction, the full meaning of that concept was brought home to him for the first time. What a hideous situation to be in. What a way to live.

How to tell the people of this time that better times were to come? There was no way, really. It was not his place to do so, and besides, even if he tried, they wouldn't believe him.

He felt a bleak depression over their situation, and then came to the even bleaker realization that their situation was his own.

"Of . . . course, comrade," he said. "I was delirious."

"Of course," she replied neutrally. Able to so easily dismiss his first words, she now smiled. "It is good to see you have come around, Mr. Chekov. You've floated in and out of consciousness for close to a week now."

He glanced around and saw the beds nearby, packed much too close together, filled with wounded men. "Stalingrad is still standing, it seems."

"Standing it may be," she said, smoothing her skirt as she rose, "but you couldn't tell from here."

He looked at her in confusion. "What?"

"This is Moscow."

"Oohhhhh," he said slowly. "Might I ask how I got here, or would that be treading on state secrets?"

The coldness in her eyes informed him that she clearly did not approve of jokes at the expense of the state. For a moment Chekov wondered if perhaps she wasn't a part of the secret police. *Now I'm getting paranoid,* he realized bleakly.

"You were brought here on a transport . . . the one that brought the commissar here."

Chekov nodded. Obviously John Kirk had executed the landing safely. Well, what else did one expect of a Kirk, after all. And they had also obviously managed to fix the fuel line.

Chekov tried to sit up and felt a sharp pain shoot through his arm. He winced and sagged back on the bed.

"Be careful," she said.

"A little late," he muttered.

"You lost a lot of blood. Also you should be careful or otherwise you might open up the stitches."

"I'll be careful," he assured her.

She stood. "There's someone who demanded to be informed the moment you awoke."

She walked away briskly, leaving Chekov alone with his thoughts. Who might the someone be? John Kirk? Probably. Hanging around, making sure that he was going to be okay before he went on with his life. The life that Chekov had managed to save.

Hadn't he? Actually, Kirk seemed to be pretty much in control of most of the situations they had gotten themselves into. It was quite possible that the streams of time were more than capable of flowing in their proper channels without the aid of . . .

"Chuikov?"

He looked up in confusion. The man standing there was clearly a general in the Russian army. Next to that man was another man, dressed in civilian clothes and wearing a long coat that seemed to swallow him. He had his hat pulled low, which was curious considering they were indoors.

The general was an avuncular-looking man, and yet there was a clear canniness and thought going on behind those narrowed eyes. It had been the general who, in that gruff voice, had spoken a name that was only a slight mispronunciation of Chekov's own.

"Yes?" said Chekov slowly, carefully.

"Full name?"

"Pavel Andreievich Chekov," he told him.

The general's eyes widened. "Do you know who I am?" he asked.

"A general?" was Chekov's cautious reply.

"I am General Vassili Chuikov. You are the son of my late brother Andrew?"

Chekov's mouth moved for a moment. His mind raced and he said, "I . . . am not sure. Forgive me, General, but . . . after the revolution . . . the streets . . ."

"You lived on the streets," said Chuikov. "You are not the only one, my boy."

And the man in the coat said silkily, "Where did a boy on the streets learn how to fly a plane? And how to infiltrate behind German lines?"

Chuikov turned and looked piercingly at the other man. "You live for your suspicions, Paulvitch. You know that?" He turned back to Chekov and inclined his head slightly in the man's direction. "You have to ignore Paulvitch. It is his job to be suspicious of everything."

Chekov felt a chill through him. This man was KGB. There was no question in his mind.

"I learn very quickly," said Chekov. "I always have. And I became friends with a pilot. He showed me a great deal. Everything, in fact." He was talking quickly, because he was not the world's greatest liar and had a tendency to speak fast, as if trying to get past the lie with all due speed.

"I have no doubt," said Chuikov. He sat next to Chekov on the bed and studied his face carefully. "You certainly have a lot of Alexander in you. Especially around the eyes."

Chekov nodded and forced a smile. He wondered if this man was an ancestor. If so, it would explain the resemblance that Chuikov saw. On the other hand, he might also simply be a lonely man who was hoping to find some hint of his family still in existence, to give him comfort in his old age. Whatever the reason, Chekov was hardly in a position to disenchant him.

Chuikov stood. "I am convinced. So tell me, my nephew . . . how would you—who acted in so daring and brave a manner while on his own—like to be in the army, eh?"

Chekov looked from Chuikov to Paulvitch. Paulvitch looked as if he would like nothing better than to blow Chekov's brains out.

The *army!* He wasn't a soldier, for pity's sake. He was an officer in Starfleet. He was . . .

He saw the way Paulvitch was looking at him. Paulvitch's coat was hanging open, and he saw the butt of a gun protruding slightly from under the KGB man's jacket.

He was in trouble, is what he was.

"Sounds great," said Chekov with forced enthusiasm. "Excuse me, but the American . . . Kirk . . ."

"He is on his way to London," said Chuikov. "Everyone from that brave mission is safe and sound. And now, you get your rest . . . Lieutenant."

Fear of religion and KGB men . . . and now he had been conscripted into the army. Somehow the future seemed a lot further away than ever.

Chapter Thirty-eight

THE HOURS it was taking to traverse the distance from the shuttle's landing point to the castle was maddeningly long. Kirk imagined the *Enterprise* up there, her orbit decaying, and inwardly he cursed the amount of time everything was taking. There was not going to be much margin for error to . . .

To what? He wasn't even sure what he was going to do once he got there.

Neither was Kral, although he wouldn't admit it. He walked with a swagger and certainty that only youth could bring.

Kirk slowed for a moment, leaning against a large boulder.

Kral regarded him with ill-concealed amusement. "Getting tired?"

Why deny the obvious? "Yes," Kirk admitted. "And when you get older, you'll get tired, too, doing the same things that never fazed you when you were younger."

"There are no such things as old Klingons," said Kral with a touch of pride.

Kirk studied him with curiosity. "You consider that a good thing?"

"The old must contribute to society, or they have no use."

"Everything is so black and white with you, Kral." He shook his head. "The universe isn't like that. It's not you versus them. There's just 'us.' Not realizing that is limiting and shortsighted . . . I'm saying open your eyes," continued Kirk. And he pointed. "And look up there. It's the castle."

Kral turned to see where Kirk was indicating. There, several hundred yards away, its spires visible above the tops of trees, was indeed the castle. "You're right." He paused. "So . . . how do you propose we do it?"

"Do it?" said Kirk.

"Which one of us will attempt to kill him?"

Kirk's eyes widened in amusement. "How do you suggest we do that?"

"You have your phaser. And I must reiterate my anger over not being allowed to carry a phaser or blaster of my own."

"What, this?" Kirk held up his phaser. "Just out of curiosity," and he pointed and aimed the weapon. He squeezed the trigger.

Nothing happened.

"Oh, splendid," said Kral.

"He didn't interfere with our weapons capabilities last time we were here, and one of his people died," observed Kirk. "Obviously he wasn't going to allow the same thing to occur."

"Which means he knows we're here," said Kral with surprising softness.

"Yes," said Kirk. "And the question is, what's he going to do about it?"

There was a soft *thwop* sound at their feet.

They looked down.

A grenade was lying less than three feet from Kirk.

"Move!" shouted Kirk, even as he leaped backward to get away.

Kral hurtled through the air and slammed into him and the two of them tumbled backward into the shelter of the brush just as the grenade went off.

They broke out of the other side and started to roll down a short embankment. Around them flares of plasma fell and set small fires that quickly extinguished themselves.

Kirk and Kral tumbled, arms and legs flailing, and when they reached the bottom they scrambled to their feet as quickly as they could. Kral was limping slightly, clutching his leg, and Kirk refrained from tossing off a remark about the weaker of the species.

Just ahead of them was a run-down hut, and Kirk hesitated to make for it, not wanting to endanger the occupants. But then the ground to his left exploded in a hail of blaster fire, and the decision was made for him. Besides, Kral was already ahead of him, leaping forward and smashing in the door with his shoulder. Kirk saw no choice but to follow him.

He leaped into the darkness after Kral.

Chapter Thirty-nine

Scotland, 1746

EVEN SCOTTY, used to the stark expanses of space, was moved to sighs by the pristine beauty of the rolling fields, still white with snow, and here and there by the thunder of a waterfall, its sparkling cascade dancing with a raw power that this simple world could not create nor control.

Marching next to Scotty was Seamus, grinning broadly, thrilled to be a part of it all. Truth to tell, so was Scott.

They marched southwest, down past Loch Ness, her black, still water shadowed by even starker ragged mountains which cheered the highlanders twice over, once for the reflection of their hardy souls, and once for the knowledge that Cumberland's men would find no succor here, so harsh a land it was.

And so down the Great Glen they marched and through the narrow Glen of Birds, its air chill in the perpetual shadow of the gorge. The blare of the pipes uplifted their spirits.

Fort Augustus stood gray, her stony foundation arising from a stony field, hard by the stony shore of the loch. Above the walls stood wooden pickets, adding both height and invulnerability to the structure. The army camped silently, not lighting fires which would give the enemy their position and number.

The command staff stood on a hill overlooking their goal.

"Well, Lochiel, any suggestions?" Keppoch asked.

"We'll rush at it, and they will quiver with fear, and let us in," he proclaimed.

"It is suicide, sir," Scott burst in, shaking his head, "and I would advise against it."

Keppoch shook his head. "We cannot afford a long siege. If we were pinned here, sooner or later a messenger would escape and reinforcements from Fort William to the south would crush us as a smith flattens a piece of iron between his hammer and his anvil. But have you a plan, sir?"

"We could mine the wall with a few barrels of gunpowder," Scott suggested. "At least we'd have a breach to rush."

"There is little cover," a captain pointed out. "We'd lose anybody who tried to plant it."

"You know," Keppoch said thoughtfully, "in the old days we would be building a siege tower."

"In the old days there were old trees," Lochiel pointed out. "Can't build one out of saplings."

"Could we get someone in? Then he could sap the wall from the inside, or open the gate for us," another captain suggested.

This brought jeers of derision until Scotty said, "Wait now. That just might do the trick. There is gunpowder aplenty inside, and if one or two men were to get in, they could set a charge from there. But it would be a suicide mission."

"Do you think you could do it, Mr. Scott?" Keppoch asked.

Scotty groaned. Rule number one in anybody's

army is Never Volunteer. "I think so, my lord," he said with resignation.

Just after sunup Scott and Seamus snaked their way across the field, seeking what little cover there was behind rocks and shrubs and pitiful little clumps of dried grass.

"How are we going to get through the gate?" Seamus asked.

"I'm not sure yet, lad. But something is bound to turn up," Scotty said, adding to himself, "My lips to God's ear."

The sound of marching men and creaking wagons drifted on the breeze. Soon the two men could see the patrol and a couple of wagons shambling up the road.

"There, lad, I told you," Scott said, adding a thanks to whatever deity had provided their good luck. They scrambled close to the road, and as the first wagon rolled by, they rolled out into the road, missing the great wheels by inches. The shaggy hooves of the horses drawing the next wagon were kicking dust into the men's faces as they scrambled to their feet, crouching. Scuttling clear of the horses, they rolled under the hitching tongue. Scotty grabbed onto it, and Seamus grabbed onto Scotty. They dragged along, Scott grateful that the wagon was moving at a slow walk. Finally Scott hauled himself up into the understructure of the wagon. Seamus did the same as they halted at the great gate.

They both hung on, straining every muscle as the wagon launched ahead and into the fort.

Seamus hit the ground with a thud.

"Something fall?" a man asked in English.

"Not here, Henry," another answered.

Seamus rolled into a pile of hay. Scotty let himself down from the belly of the cart rather gingerly. When he joined Seamus, he allowed himself a painful groan as he rubbed his stiff joints.

"Now what?" Seamus whispered.

"We wait."

While they sat huddled and silent, Scott tried to keep track of the passage of the occasional soldier on guard duty. The day dragged by endlessly. By night, when the yard was deserted, Scotty had the guard drill figured out.

Clump! Clump! Clump! Scotty waited for the guard to march by, then hissed "Now!" and he and Seamus broke loose of the straw bed and ran for the big building in the center of the compound. It had to be the magazine.

"It's locked," Seamus whispered.

"Here, let me," Scott said, pulling a slender blade from his boot, working the lock with a skill that clearly impressed his young companion. The big lock dropped open. "In. Quick," he said, pushing Seamus ahead of him.

Clump! Clump! Clump!

"That was close," Scott muttered, wiping his brow and trying to still his thumping chest. What he would give right about now for a light. It took a while for his eyes to adjust to the tiny glow of moonlight that filtered in through the few windows. There were crates and barrels . . . and the smell of gunpowder.

They rolled one of the powder barrels to the door, and Scott wrestled it over the doorsill as Seamus went back for another.

"Halt!" A musket was thrust up to Scotty's face. He slowly, very slowly, stood up with his hands in the air.

Chapter Forty

Moscow, 1942

SHORTLY AFTER being "recruited," even though there was still an occasional twinge in his arm, Chekov was hustled off to a secret training school about five miles from the main airport. He found a small airstrip and a few low buildings that housed the primitive facilities of the Red Guard squadron. Chekov felt resplendent in his new uniform. He also felt nervous as hell. Although Chuikov, who had since returned to Stalingrad, had accepted his flimsy background story almost without question—motivated by his own desires, Chekov suspected, both for family and for more soldiers—Paulvitch had kept looking at him with great suspicion. Paulvitch had been even less enthusiastic when the general had rather forcefully insisted that Chekov be placed in the elite Red Guard flying squadron. He had also ordered that identity papers be cut for Chekov immediately.

Chekov was somewhat old for a cadet and was looked on with some amusement . . . at first. But he made quite a splash among his fellow cadets on his first flight. He had been taken up in a lend-lease P-39. Chekov quickly mastered the feel of the vehicle, impressed his flight instructor with his skill and astonished the other cadets with his aerial acrobatics, pushing the propeller-driven pursuit vehicle to its limit. They were finally convinced he was some sort of saint when he was ordered to report to the Kremlin.

The order did not thrill Chekov, however, for he had his own game plan.

He was determined to get out of Russia.

At first he had felt a patriotic devotion to the people and place that he had grown up in. But he was rapidly beginning to realize that his vision of the past was heavily romanticized. The Russia of this time was completely alien to him. The general air of fear and oppression that hung over the country like a gray sheet was suffocating.

The problem was, he wasn't sure how to get out. Borders were carefully watched, and for that matter, so was he.

The usually silent, almost spectral Paulvitch had, it seemed, made Chekov his special case. He had hand delivered Chekov's new papers to him and said nothing, but merely regarded him with those ghostly, glowing eyes. He didn't have to say anything to Chekov, really. His thoughts were clear. Paulvitch did not trust him, not for a moment.

It seemed to Chekov that, whenever he turned around, Paulvitch was somewhere in the background. Paulvitch, or one of his cronies.

It wasn't paranoia, Chekov told himself, if they really were out to get you. And what he had was a serious situation on his hands.

As the old saying went, he knew too much. Too much about Russia, about what would happen. Nowhere in the world was more dangerous for Chekov than the Soviet Union, and yet here was the place he was stuck.

He had to get out, and the only way to do that was in the air.

So his intentions were hardly honorable, and the constant paranoia from the oppressive KGB made his people seem more like the Klingons than the enlightened society he remembered.

Informed by his commanding officer that his presence was required at the Kremlin, Chekov blanched inwardly. Insane as it sounded, he was sure that somehow the KGB knew that he was from the future. He envisioned another small room with shining lights, Paulvitch leering down at him.

"Why me?" he asked, a question directed both to his C.O. and to the heavens above.

"Why, to meet Stalin, of course!" said the C.O. incredulously. "It will be a great honor to meet Stalin, no?" Chekov's commander said, shaking his new cadet's hand and sending him off to the waiting car.

The sound of the tires bouncing over the cobblestones of Red Square was a drumroll of fear and thrill to Chekov as he sat stiffly in the backseat of the car, his stomach doing flip-flops. The splendor of old Saint Basil's, with its fairy-tale onion domes, soared toward the gray sky, a surrealistic blend of color and fantasy set in a wasteland of somber government buildings.

And then he was in the Kremlin. After miles of corridors, and dozens of identity checks, Chekov was finally deposited outside the doors of an office, on a graceful chair whose tattered brocade seat and carved woodwork bespoke a more gentle time. He was fetched by a staff aide who outranked him by a decade or two of well-earned promotions.

One figure loomed in the center of a group of officers who were discussing some papers spread on a large map table. Even with his back turned, Chekov knew who it was. It was almost as if an electric field emanated from the man. If he ever doubted what charisma really was, now he knew.

The man turned, the Georgian peasant who had

risen to be the new czar of the People's Republic. Chekov snapped to attention. Stalin was younger than Chekov had remembered. Remembered from what? The pictures in school? He pushed away the dangerous thoughts the excitement of the moment had unleashed. He saluted, drinking in every feature of the man, his hard paternalistic manner, made more so by the old-fashioned moustache, the sheer physical strength, and the eyes. Those piercing eyes, which were both kind and cold. But Chekov's stomach remembered that this man had "purged" countless millions of peasants during the terrible years of collectivization, and things more terrible than that to come.

And then he saw, lurking in the corner, Paulvitch. He was glowering at Chekov in that unmistakable way, as if waiting for Chekov to suddenly lunge forward at his leader.

"So you are the candidate for the medal, are you? Do you think you deserve to be a Hero of the Soviet Union?"

"Comrade Premier," Chekov said shakily, "no more nor less than every man and woman who fought in Stalingrad with me." Stalin's eyes softened a bit, and Chekov stumbled on, "There are thousands, and all are heros." Then he stilled himself, before the skilled strategist drew any more from him.

Stalin reached out a hand, and an officer obediently handed him a small box, his face impassive in the presence of this powerful dictator. Then Joseph Stalin pinned a gold star hanging from a red ribbon on Chekov's chest. Chekov stood at attention. He saluted, his mind a torrent of mixed emotions, and waited for the signal to withdraw.

But Stalin looked him in the eye, this time with the frost of winter. "And who do you admire the most among my staff?" he asked.

Chekov's eyes flicked uncontrollably to the men in

the room. There was Marshal Zhukov. That was the man, without any doubt! But Zhukov's eyes held a warning. To acknowledge the fact that he was a brilliant and beloved war leader could be his death warrant at the hands of this dictator.

Chekov looked back into Stalin's eyes, allowing himself to be drawn into the charismatic power of the man. Then, with what he hoped would pass for perfect sincerity, he said, "If Lenin was our grandfather, then you are our father. All the other officers are our uncles and brothers. We each do our best for the state, and some do better than others, as is their talent, but it is you, sir, who is the greatest People's Hero."

Stalin looked at him and raised his eyebrows. "You have political sense, lad, but I want a name. Someone I can reward, perhaps."

"Then I name General Chuikov." Chekov could feel the relief in the room. That certainly was the only answer that would have no political repercussions. Stalin seemed satisfied and dismissed Chekov, who managed to march out without tripping on the rug, walking into the doorway, or otherwise making a fool of himself, despite the fact that he was shaking like a leaf.

The driver was long gone, and with the shiny new medal on his chest, and feeling obvious and embarrassed, he set out to hitchhike back to the base. This time he got to experience the enormity of Red Square, stone by stone. A troop carrier going in his general direction rumbled by, and he waved it down, running and shouting until the bored driver rolled to a stop.

"Where you headed?" the driver asked, eyeing the medal.

"Er," Chekov began, knowing that his destination was classified, "sort of northeast a few miles."

"Oh, the secret Red Guard training base. Sure," the man said cheerfully.

215

They both grinned. And then a hand fell upon Chekov's shoulder.

He turned to see Paulvitch glaring at him.

"I know you are not what you seem," said Paulvitch. "And somehow, soon . . . I will find a way to prove that."

He turned and stalked away, and Chekov felt a chill come over him.

He had a distinct feeling that the sooner he got out of there, the better.

Chapter Forty-one

Japan, 1600

THE SOUNDS OF metal on metal told Sulu that the camp was under attack.

His captors momentarily distracted, Sulu moved quickly. His left foot lashed back, slipping around and behind the man who was holding him. He yanked fast and the two of them went down in a tangle of arms and legs.

Sulu rolled away quickly and kicked the man in the face. Then he leaped to his feet, ready to take on another opponent.

The hall was empty.

Sulu blinked in surprise. Maybe there was something to that ninja magic after all.

Suddenly he was smashed on the back of the head, and cursed himself for forgetting about the man he'd just flattened. He rolled forward, coming to his feet, and the ninja leaped at him, a sword already drawn. There was a knife on the floor, just out of Sulu's reach. He tried to get to it, and the ninja blocked his path. Sulu braced himself, arms up, ready to try and ward off an attack even though he knew he didn't have a prayer.

And suddenly a man on horseback smashed through the paper-thin walls. Sulu looked up in amazement. So did the ninja, which was the last thing he had the chance to do, for he went down under the pounding of the horse's hooves.

The horseman had cloth wrapped around his face for protection. He gestured briskly, and Sulu, not one to pass up an offer, leaped onto the back of the mount. They turned and hightailed it out of the compound.

There were other men in the compound, also in simple peasant clothes of dark blue indigo, their faces covered with cloths. But the swords they were using with deadly efficiency were not simple peasant farm tools. Sulu's savior threw a supporting arm under Sulu's armpit, and tossed what turned out to be a smoke bomb.

The other men also threw out smoke devices, some also tossing out small dark objects, handfuls of hard, sharp plant seeds which bit into the feet of the pursuers as viciously as any metal caltrop.

Sulu and his rescuer sped away into the dusk.

Each galloping stride jolted Sulu on his precarious perch, his ribs screaming with bruised pain. He set his jaw, enduring the pain, and wondered obliquely if perhaps this was some other trick, some attempt to make him grateful to another group of devious strangers, some other way to obtain his nonexistent magical secrets.

When the man finally reined in the frothing, exhausted horse, Sulu slipped off the saddle and landed on the ground in a pained and unceremonious heap.

His rescuer leaped smartly off the saddle, giving orders to his men to cover their tracks. He had to help Sulu to his feet.

"Well, so you are not a Koga spy?" The man unwound the dark cloth that had masked his face.

"Watanenabe Sadayo?" Sulu shouted upon seeing Mototada's gray-haired, samurai sword master. "How did you find me?"

"I have ways," he said, a reassuring smile spreading over his face. "We knew there was a spy, but we didn't know who. When you showed up, we were sure you were a plant. Seeing you about to have your head at your feet disabused me of that."

"I saw an old gardener from the castle. He must be the one," Sulu blurted. But he couldn't tell about Oneko. Something in him was screaming to expose her part in this, but something else remembered her sad eyes. And he couldn't betray her.

The sword master shouted to his men. "Come, we can camp here. You there," he shouted at an underling. "Bring the samurai water. Now come, sit. The men will boil rice for us. Tell me. What happened? Do they hold Oneko-domo for ransom? We followed you to the inn, but we were too far behind to help when the Koga bandits attacked. Why were you not killed if you are not one of theirs? I can understand why they wanted the girl alive."

"Why did they let me live?" *Because the woman you would rescue saved me,* he thought. But he answered in truth, "Luck, I guess. They wanted my secrets. Military secrets. I really don't have any. I told them nothing. They didn't have me that long."

"Will they ask ransom for the girl?"

"I don't think so," Sulu answered neutrally.

"We must rescue her. She cannot be left in their hands. Is she still with child?"

Sulu choked. "Yes, I guess so."

Sadayo saw the brief tremor and said brusquely, and incorrectly, "You tremble in self-mortification. Do not. You have not dishonored yourself. Indeed, I see my first instinct was incorrect. You are indeed a man of highest honor."

219

No, your first instinct was dead on, thought Sulu glumly.

The next day, after an impromptu bath in a cold stream, Sulu was again dressed as befit the station of a hundred koku man in the service of Torii Mototada. He mounted, and gave the two swords at his belt a sharp tug, adjusting them more firmly.

When he arrived at the clearing, Sadayo was grimly outlining strategy.

"The Koga clan would not expect another attack so soon, and so it is our chance to eliminate them once and for all, and find Lady Oneko," the samurai sword master ordered, "when we get close to the Koga stronghold, you will go directly to rescue the Lady Oneko. We will attack the ninjas."

"Hai," Sulu acknowledged. He was going to have to get to her fast. Sadayo was no fool, and Oneko wasn't going to last long if she was wandering around the compound like the family member she really was.

The trip back seemed a lot shorter than the trip out, bouncing over Sadayo's saddle. They assembled in a thin woods some few yards from the gate. A servant opened the gate, and two women left carrying vegetables for sale at the nearest town. "Now," Sadayo shouted, and kicked his horse into a charge. The servant tried to slam the gate, but Sadayo's horse ran him down. Mototada's men slashed down the ninjas as they ran into the yard. Soon the air was thick from the ninja smoke bombs, their tactical effectiveness lost as both sides choked and wept from their noxious fumes. This time the foot soldiers threw the caltrops, avoiding them by gliding along the ground, while the horses were getting the worst of it as the hard nutlike kernels of the seeds bruised their hooves. Sulu saw Sadayo pitched from the saddle into the cloud of dust and smoke.

Sulu searched the chaos for Oneko, wheeling his snorting, screaming mount back and forth across the bloody, screaming battle. A lanky figure emerged from the blinding dust, a long *naginata* slashing at Sulu's horse. Sulu countercharged, drawing his sword and striking the weapon aside. He rode past, leaving the frustrated man known as uncle screaming invective, until he was lanced by another samurai. So much for uncle.

In the shouts and chaos Sulu heard her voice. Turning the horse this way and that, squinting through the dusty cloud of weapons and limbs, he saw her running toward him. He spurred the horse and rode to meet her, reaching down and scooping her up to the saddle. And he rode, rode for both their lives, while the battle raged on behind him.

Chapter Forty-two

Scotland, 1746

SCOTTY RAN HIS HANDS OVER the walls of his cell, feeling the bars on the windows, praying for a loose one, but the cell was as tight as a drum. And that made him think of drums and hangings, so he felt the walls again, desperately seeking hope.

He sagged to the ground, determined not to let depression overwhelm him.

"I'm a Miracle Worker," he whispered.

"Mr. Scott," a familiar voice hissed. "Stay clear of the door."

Scotty's eyes widened. He was starting to believe it himself.

He had just about enough time to tuck and roll across the small room before the shock of the powder charge hit him. He ignored the rear end full of splinters from the shattered door.

"Quick, run," the boy ordered. It seemed like a good idea.

They scurried like rabbits, darting around the dozens of men who spilled out into the yard. Seamus had the lead. He was headed for what seemed like a dead-end against a back wall behind a barracks.

Then all hell broke loose. The fort went up like a

bomb of the sort that would not see the light of day for two hundred years.

Scotty was thrown a dozen feet, landing painfully on a pile of rocks and a heap of Seamus.

"I set a fuse in the magazine. All the ammunition went up. Isn't it glorious?" he panted, grinning in the glow of the terrible fire that consumed the fort. "Now," he said gleefully, staggering up, and the two men ran for what was left of a wall. By then the Keppoch and Lochiel forces were in the fort, screaming their various clan battle cries and cutting down anything that moved.

The rest was easy. The English broke ranks, looking like bobbing lobsters in their red coats as they ran, seeking refuge in the dawn of the cold foreign hills.

"It's a shame about your cannon, Mr. Scott," Seamus said sadly, kicking aside a piece of slag that had once been the pride of the English army.

Scotty had been melancholy since he first inspected the carnage. "Well, it couldn'a been helped," he said wistfully. "I do thank you for saving me."

"Now I suppose we are even, sir," the boy said awkwardly.

"Aye, ye might say that, lad."

"I owe you that, er, and more, sir." He was silent, looking down at his feet for a bit, then he blurted, "Oh, Mr. Scott, I must confess. You have been a father to me and Meg, and I have this terrible burden on my soul. When I brought you the clothes at The Hanged Woman, and you asked why . . . ?"

"Aye, an' ye said ye had your reasons . . ."

"Well, my reasons were . . . oh, Mr. Scott, the English knew there was a spy, and I had hoped to shoot the duke and then leave the weapon with you, so that they'd arrest you and I could continue as a spy uninterrupted. And I . . . ." His face went red with mortification and shame. "I . . . I wouldn't blame you if you'd never forgive me. I thought you were just someone I could use. I never . . . I dinna . . ." He hung his head, barely able to blink back the tears.

"Son," Scott said, taking the lad in his arms. "Of course I forgive you. Such things happen in war. They always do."

The two men pulled away from each other with the embarrassment this society put on that sort of display.

"What will you do now?" Seamus asked.

"I will go back to Inverness and report my failure to General Murray. And you?"

"I must go with the Keppoch. I still have my duty. I am to send reports back to the prince's staff. Mr. Scott, when you get back to Inverness . . . take care of my Megan for me until I return," he begged shyly.

"Of course I will, son, and I'll dance at your wedding."

Before Scott left for the lonely journey back to Inverness, Alexander Keppoch sent for him.

"Mr. Scott, what can you tell me of Fort William?"

Scotty deliberated for a moment. "Sir, I fear that you will not find Fort William the plum for the picking that Fort Augustus was. Without cannon, you may find yourself mounting a long siege."

"Aye, and the army is not up to strength. The Campbells, those damn traitors to the prince's cause, have been sent to ravage our farms, and many men have deserted the cause to protect their family, and who can blame them for that?"

"God give you the victory, my lord," Scott offered.

"And give you peace," Keppoch said, looking into Scotty's haunted eyes.

Shouldering his small pack, Scott strode back up the road to Inverness, his kilt swinging with a jaunty rhythm that Scotty certainly didn't feel.

Chapter Forty-three

Moscow, 1942

CHEKOV'S RETURN to his new squadron again brought the blessed oblivion of hard work. He was soon assigned to train some of his comrades on the problems of the P-39. He had picked up the new material easily. After all, he had been a trained officer, and most of these new friends were farm boys who had never seen anything more complicated than a tractor or a vacuum tube radio.

And so the days were filled with droning lectures which began, "This is the AirCobra. You will note that the engine is amidships, behind the pilot. The drive shaft runs forward below the cockpit. A thirty-millimeter cannon is mounted on the front propeller hub . . ." And then on the deadly business of the plane's tendency to go into a flat spin during a dive. Except for the jargon, which he had once thought so romantic and was now so routine, it was just like any other flight training, except that at the Academy they trained for science and exploration first, and then battle as a final contingency. Here the deadly business was the only business.

The afternoons were filled with flying, and that was good, and the evenings with new friends, brave young pilots filled with that ineffable Russian exuberance, and that was even better.

But the frequent and oppressive mandatory meeting with the Political Officer, receiving the catechism of Marx, was not just boring, but terrifying to someone brought up in a free society. Again the doubts clamored to be heard. And what made it all the more terrible was that there was no one Chekov could talk to. It was a society built on mistrust.

He was relieved when Paulvitch seemed to vanish into thin air. If Chekov never saw the KGB man again, it would be far, far too soon.

Soon the time came for Chekov to earn his keep, and his wing was assigned to a mission. A bunch of the new YAKs had been shipped in. They were trim little planes, and the best Soviet-made vehicle in the air force. The men had a scant four days to qualify on the new planes before they were shipped out. Chekov was assigned as wing commander. He didn't feel ready for command, but then again, he hadn't been asked. With a fleeting thought, he remembered Starfleet and the years it took in peacetime to grow into command. In war there was no such luxury. Survival was the test of promotion.

Chekov was a nervous wreck. Flying into a combat situation was unthinkable. The Prime Directive was clear. The time paradox possibilities were catastrophic. His could not be the hand that ended other human lives of the twentieth century. It was impossible. Officers of Starfleet had pledged that their lives would be forfeit before doing something like that.

And then salvation came to him in one word.

Sweden.

It was brought up during an evening's discussion. Sweden was neutral. Since they did not participate in the war, nothing Chekov could do there would possibly affect the war.

The thought of leaving Russia forever saddened him, but then again, it was not really his Russia. And it would not be the Russia he remembered for generations yet. Not only that, but the longer he remained in Russia, the greater the possibility that he might do something to prevent that future from ever happening.

And he had to get there quickly. Paulvitch had decided to leave him alone, but who knew how long that would last? And if he were sent into a combat situation, well . . .

Of course, getting shot down would certainly solve all his problems. And Chekov hadn't ruled that out. But all things being equal, he would prefer—not unreasonably—if matters didn't come to that.

That night, he lay in the barracks and waited until he heard only the sleeping sounds of the others. Then, slowly, he slid out of bed. He dressed quickly and pulled out his gear, which he had already packed up during the day. He glanced around right and left, making sure he wasn't observed, and then slid out the back door, a specter.

Watching carefully, and masterfully avoiding the sentries, Chekov made his way across the camp to the hangared planes. He pulled open the hangar door, and there, gleaming before him, was his plane.

He wasn't sure if there was enough fuel in it to get him all the way to Sweden, but it didn't matter. He knew of several refueling stops from his classes. And even if he decided not to risk stopping, in the event that word was out about him, he would come down somewhere and make it from there. Anyplace was better than this darkened, paranoid version of what his beloved Russia was like.

There was the soft click of a hammer being drawn behind his back. Chekov froze, clutching his duffel bag.

"You won't get away. Don't move please. Turn around."

"Which is it?" asked Chekov reasonably. "Don't move or turn around?"

"Turn around. Very slowly."

Chekov did so, knowing what he would see.

There, in the dim light of the hangar, was Paulvitch, whose gun was pointed unwaveringly at him.

"I have run a complete history on you," said Paulvitch. "It has taken a great deal of time. As you say, records can be hazy, and I wished to be thorough. Do you know what I have found?"

"That I'm an exemplary citizen and role model for children everywhere?"

Paulvitch smiled thinly. The smile didn't make his face look any better.

"You have no history. No one knows you . . . not in the streets, not in the neighborhoods. No one. Nowhere. Your fingerprints have no trace. You are a nonperson."

"Then I suppose I couldn't have done anything," said Chekov, trying to sound casual.

Paulvitch took a step closer. "You, Pavel Chekov, will be taken for interrogation. We of the KGB have perfected methods that the Nazis are only just beginning to test. Their methods stress torture and cruelty. We stress efficiency. We have drugs that will make you tell us everything you are, everything you know. Within seventy-two hours not a single thing in your mind will be secret from us."

Chekov's face was set.

"You see," said Paulvitch, "I knew that if I gave you enough rope, you would hang. You are sloppy, Chekov. And you should have watched your back."

"So should you," said Chekov, and eyes wide, he shouted, *"Get him!"*

Paulvitch half turned, reflexively.

Chekov moved like lightning, swinging the duffel around. It slammed into Paulvitch, sending the gun clattering into the darkness.

Paulvitch scrambled to his feet just as Chekov charged forward and smashed a booted foot into his face. Paulvitch fell back, blood pouring from his nose.

He didn't go down easily. He staggered forward and swung a roundhouse punch. Chekov blocked it easily with an upswept arm and kneed Paulvitch fiercely. Now there was no longer paranoia and fear. Here was the enemy incarnate, the symbol of all that was wrong with Russia made solid. Chekov took out his anger on him, hurling Paulvitch against the side of the hangar. Paulvitch slammed up against it with a crunch and then slid down, consciousness fleeing him.

Chekov grabbed Paulvitch under the arms and dragged him to a far corner of the hangar. There he used some rope to tie the KGB man thoroughly, and stuffed cloth into his mouth to muffle him. With any luck, Paulvitch wouldn't awake for hours—hours Chekov was certain he would need.

He threw newspapers and rags over the KGB man to thoroughly obscure him from view. Then he walked out of the shadows of the far end of the hangar.

Standing at the opening was General Chuikov.

"I am amazed," said the general, his fingers straying near his holstered gun.

Chapter Forty-four

KIRK LOOKED AROUND slowly and saw the family huddled against the far wall—a man and woman, and a small girl clinging to the woman's leg. Some farm implements sat next to them, leaning against the thin wall.

"We're sorry," said Kirk immediately. "We didn't mean to involve you." He turned quickly to Kral. "We've got to get out of here. If any more of Weyland's people are injured . . ."

Kral made a disdainful noise. "If they die in combat, what of it? They die with honor. Honor is everything."

And to Kirk's astonishment, the woman kicked Kral, who had been crouching, in the face.

The astonished Klingon fell onto his back, clutching at the bruise on his cheek.

"My son is dead!" shrieked the woman. "He didn't die with honor! He died with the skin burned from his bones!"

"That little boy . . . your son?" said Kirk slowly.

The woman said nothing, but instead turned to her husband and began to sob against his chest. Piteous, wracking sobs, and Kirk watched the Klingon carefully for some reaction.

"It was an accident," Kral said.

"That doesn't make much difference now, does it?" Kirk pointed out.

"Oh, that's right, Kirk," said Kral, bristling. "Lay the blame entirely at the door of the Klingons. It takes two to make a war, you know."

"Yes. And two to end it."

Kral stared at him.

Then, from outside, came a shouted voice that both Kirk and Kral recognized. "Kirk! Give Kral up! This is not your affair. It's between him and me. If you give him up, I will allow you to live."

They looked at each other. "What are the chances of that?" said Kirk dryly.

"Good, I think. This is between Kbrex and me, just as it always has been. Since we were young."

"You're old friends?" said Kirk in surprise. "An old friend would still oust you violently from your command?"

"No. We're not old friends." Kral paused and said ruefully, "Kbrex is my brother."

Kbrex crouched outside the cabin, hiding among the bushes, and shook his head. He couldn't believe the situation he'd gotten himself into.

He had been ecstatic when Weyland had responded to his message. The formidable being had kept a carefully neutral expression when Kbrex informed him of the unquestionable attack by Kirk and Kral. Kbrex was certain this indicated that the immortal Weyland was not quite as all-powerful as he claimed.

Weyland had agreed to permit Kbrex to transport down to the planet's surface. He had even agreed to allow Kbrex's weapons to function, a courtesy he said he would not allow Kirk and Kral.

But Kbrex initially balked when Weyland informed him that he could only beam down alone.

"You, with weapons, against a Klingon you defeated and a weak Federation man," observed Weyland. "Do not tell me you're afraid."

"I'm afraid of nothing," replied Kbrex.

"Be afraid of this: be afraid of what will happen if, in your pursuit of the invaders, you should happen to injure any of my people."

Kbrex opened his mouth a moment, and then closed it. Something warned him not to challenge Weyland on this matter.

So Kbrex now found himself on the surface of Cragon, with those he was pursuing pinned down in a hovel. He couldn't just open fire on them, since he was nervous about what Weyland would do if the peasants were harmed. But Kral and Kirk didn't know about that:

"This is your last chance! Kirk . . . this isn't your fight! This is between Kral and me. Give him up. You don't owe him anything. He'd kill you as soon as look at you."

Kbrex was silent for a moment. Certainly Kirk had to realize the wisdom of his words. Of course, he was lying. He intended to obliterate Kirk at the first opportunity. But he wanted to make absolutely sure of Kral's demise first.

He heard a chopping noise and frowned. He didn't know what the source was, but he wasn't sure he liked it.

"Kirk!" he shouted. "Last chance! I mean it!"

Again that chopping. Where the devil was it coming from?

Then a crunching sound, like . . .

A wall collapsing.

He craned his bull neck and bellowed his fury. There were Kirk and Kral, on the far side of the house, dashing into the woods. He didn't have a clear shot at them, and then they were gone.

But he knew where they were going, and all he had to do was circle around and cut them off. Then he would have them.

Kirk and Kral bolted through the woods, tossing all but the barest of caution to the wind.

Every crack of branch sounded like a rifle shot, and every dancing shadow contained a hundred enemies. Kirk wasn't even sure if there was any point to their rushing, for he had no idea what sort of reception awaited them.

There was the whine of a blaster, and it chewed off a branch to Kirk's right. He veered off and suddenly realized he'd become separated from Kral.

Kral glanced over his shoulder and saw that Kirk was no longer around. Well, that was to be expected. At last the cowardly Federation man had shown his true colors.

Oh sure, Kirk had not come out at Kbrex's behest, but that was undoubtedly because Kirk knew that Kbrex's offer was merely nonsense.

There was a flicker of disappointment in Kral's mind. For all of Kirk's posturing, it would almost have been refreshing if Kirk had actually been sincere. Ally. Treaty. Cooperation and talk of honor and loyalty. What rubbish.

That was the moment that Kral's foot hit a hole.

He tripped, cursing himself for his clumsiness, and went down at a bad angle. He felt and heard a snap, and realized with sinking horror that it was his ankle.

He grunted, blocking out the pain, and started to crawl forward, seeking the welcoming cover of the brush. And that was when he heard a low, mocking laugh behind him.

He turned, propping himself up on one elbow.

There was Kbrex, shaking his head slowly, his blaster aimed at Kral's head.

"Finally," he said.

"Finally," agreed Kral. "Finally, brother, you will have the opportunity to indulge your pathological hatred of me."

"There was nothing pathological about it," replied Kbrex. "It is a good, clean hatred."

"It's wrong."

"There's no such thing as a bad hatred," Kbrex told him.

"Yes . . . so I've said myself," Kral admitted.

Kbrex's blaster did not waver. "You have no idea of the humiliation and lack of honor I felt when my younger brother was promoted over me. The honor of command was given to you. To me was given the ignominy of serving under him who is as a child to me."

"I asked for you to serve on my ship because I could think of no one I'd rather have at my side," said Kral.

"To make me face your superiority every day."

"No," said Kral, shaking his head sadly. "I realized that was what you thought . . . but by then it was too late. By then you were already plotting my overthrow. My one oversight, Kbrex."

"Don't ascribe to yourself such noble motives, Kral. Realize instead the baseness of your intentions . . ." His finger started to tighten on the trigger. "And the ignominy of your defeat . . ."

Kral braced himself for the impact and wondered if he would feel it.

That was when the rock smashed the blaster from Kbrex's hand.

The Klingon howled, clutching at the injured hand as the blaster sailed away into the bush. He spun and looked for where the crude missile had originated.

Twenty feet away stood Kirk, another rock at the ready.

"You have superb aim," said Kbrex.

"Not really. I was aiming for your head."

Kbrex reached down and pulled a knife from his boot. "I use this only, Kirk, because merely snapping your neck would take too long."

He charged toward Kirk, who stood there, eyes blazing, arm drawn back and ready to hurl the other rock. Inwardly Kbrex was laughing. As if such a pathetic attempt would even slow him down. He never took his eyes off Kirk, waiting for the pathetic human to make some sort of motion.

Kirk didn't. He stood there, poised, gaze locked with the Klingon's, as if trying to bore his way into the Klingon's soul, or perhaps scare him off with the evil eye.

Fool.

Kbrex drew back his arm, ready to hurl the knife, and still Kirk had made no move.

"See you in hell, Kirk!" he snarled.

His ankle hit something.

What had he hit? His mind digested it. Something thin and taut.

A wire.

A trip wire.

His mind screamed a warning as a board with three carefully arranged knives sprang up from its hiding place in the bush. It slammed into Kbrex with a sickening, triple *spluch* sound that mingled with the high-pitched cry ripped from the throat of the Klingon.

Kbrex fell back, arms vaguely trying to pull at the board, and his eyes caught the Klingon alphabet letters carved on the tree . . . letters that had been carved there by his own hand. Letters that served as a warning to those paying attention, a warning of a trap he himself had set.

He thudded to the ground, arms outstretched, life flowing out with his blood. The world was hazing around him, and then he caught a glimpse of Kirk.

And again, except this time in a voice thick with death, he said, "Kirk . . . I'll see you . . . in hell."

Kirk looked down at the dead Klingon. "Feel free to start without me," he said.

He went quickly to Kral, who said, "Is he dead?"

Slowly Kirk nodded.

"I want to see him."

Kirk helped him up, and with Kral leaning on him, brought him over to stand next to the body of Kbrex. Kral prodded the fallen Klingon with his toe.

"You think he was the only one down here?" asked Kral.

Kirk nodded. "Otherwise we'd be dead by now. Kral . . ." His voice trailed off. He wasn't sure whether to offer congratulations or condolences.

Kral tilted his head back and screamed.

It was deafening, and Kirk winced against the power of it. When Kral had exhausted the shout, Kirk said, "What the devil was that about?"

"The Klingon death scream. He died with honor."

Kirk looked at him in amazement. "He died trying to kill you."

"Of course," said Kral reasonably. "A Klingon could do no less."

Chapter Forty-five

Japan, 1600

SULU LAY in the warm sand, listening to the rush of the waves. Oneko stirred slightly as he shifted to a more comfortable position. His arm had gone numb hours ago, but he hadn't the heart to disturb her, curled in his arms with the trust of a child. He tried to let the endless rhythm of the waves crashing on the rocks below remind him of things more universal and timeless than the fate of a man.

"Heihachiro-sama," she muttered, waking.

"Shhh, sleep. It's still night," he comforted her.

They both slept, lulled by the sea, until morning light.

"Where to?" he asked her.

"Perhaps it would be better to leap off the cliff to our deaths," she said wearily. "Where is there to go?"

He looked at her in amazement. "No, you carry Torii's child. You cannot even think about it."

She burst out sobbing, mopping away at her tears with her sleeve. Finally she became calm. "We could go into the mountains and hide. We could become farmers," she said hopefully. "Heihachiro-sama, come with me. Let us live together." She held him yearningly. He hugged her savagely. Wasn't that what he had wanted since he had first seen her? What did he owe Torii? A hundred koku stipend couldn't be spent by a dead man, and death was all that awaited him at Fushimi Castle.

And what of Oneko? He would gladly raise her child, together with ones of theirs that would surely follow.

Even if it meant breaking his word, depriving the child of his birthright? Had the ethics of his own era made him unwilling to accept this? Or the ethics of this proud clan-oriented culture, which was beginning to rule his heart and mind? Or was it the old Sulu himself, who never could make a commitment to love?

"Please," she pleaded, again using that silver voice.

"Stop it," he shouted, his usual reserve and courtesy shattered by his own internal struggle to keep his will and soul, not to mention common sense, from being seduced by her again. "I don't understand my feelings for you, Oneko. I think I love you," he explained. "But I can't trust my feelings. After all, am I only another stone in an endless game of *go*, a game piece to be used up, or thrown away?"

"That is the way life is," she said, her voice steady, her eyes lowered. "I believe you when you say you have no magic. But for me you do. There is something . . . Your love for me, it was so . . . young, fresh. You are the opposite of me," she said, looking in his eyes. "I am all artifice. You are all honesty. My only regret is that Torii is also all honesty. I was raised to believe that it was a weakness to be exploited by the crafty and sly. But I watched Torii, and he is greater than his master. Perhaps his master will be remembered, perhaps his trickery will unite Japan under one rule. Perhaps that peace will benefit rather than suffocate. I do not know. But in the eyes of heaven, the gods and the buddha, Torii is the righteous one. I wish I had been what he believed me to be."

The nagging voice inside Sulu whispered—history must be fulfilled. You have a duty to this honest Torii, because you gave your word, and what kind of man will you be if you base a life on a broken oath and a stolen wife? And for good or ill, the Tokugawa shogunate is the history of Japan.

"I will take you to Edo as planned. Your part in this was not known. Believe me. And I doubt that any of your family survived back there to reveal otherwise."

She settled into his arms, a trusting child with an older brother. He felt her tears soak into his sleeve. The night sang with the chirping of crickets, the rustle of leaves, as though the brief time left to him made every second alive and precious.

They didn't talk much on the road that next day, each cherishing the moments together, neither daring to face the time of their parting. They held each other with chaste loving the following night, taking the joy of a lifetime of companionship in their few hours remaining.

They went directly to Torii Mototada's house in Edo. They both thanked a lot of gods when they were told that the uncle who was supposed to lodge her had already been sent to Sekigahara, and Oneko was admitted to the Mototada mansion without problem or question. And in this world, it was likely that she would never be allowed out to visit her "relative" for the rest of her life. She was safe. He was sure of that.

But the gates of the Mototada mansion loomed dark as the gates to hell for the young couple. Oneko had assumed the trained, unreadable and restrained face of a noble lady. Sulu straightened his back and strode with the pride of a samurai in the employ of so noble a lord as Torii Mototada. Oneko was whisked away, but Sulu was announced and shown to the audience hall even before he had a chance to bathe away the dust of the road. Sulu bowed low and sat as indicated.

"I see you survived. Well done," a familiar voice said to his left.

"Watanenabe Sadayo, you too survived," Sulu shouted in delight, bowing to the handsome gray-haired sword master.

"Yes, well done, Heihachiro-domo," the eldest son of his daimyo, Torii Mototada, praised him. Sulu saw the father in the son. For this generation at least the Torii family would be safe. "The escape with the concubine Oneko was brave, and well-executed. Sadayo-domo killed all the ninja responsible."

"Thank you for your kind words, lord," Sulu said briskly, bowing. *Kinder than you know,* he thought. With all the ninja dead, Oneko's identity as a Koga *kunoichi,* a female agent, was safe.

"You must take letters showing the deployment of Ishida's forces around Fushimi. You must ride like the demons of hell to bring these letters to Mototada-tono, my father."

"Hai," was the simple reply.

While Oneko was brought in, distant and lovely in her silk cocoon, Sulu was again thanked, and he acknowledged the honor, but he could hardly answer when Oneko herself thanked him, her bell-like voice controlled and distant. The older men chuckled at the young samurai's embarrassment, thinking it only his modesty and the natural confusion young men had around women. The couple's eyes barely met as he bowed his way out, the important documents tucked securely in his kimono. There would be time for sorrow on the road.

Sulu was dismissed and left the audience chamber to take up the offer of a hot meal while his horse was packed for the trip. He was on his way back to Fushimi Castle within the hour.

Sulu tried not to think about the battle he was riding toward. It was all he could do to keep his resolve. Part of him was bone-tired of this rigid world, so full of death. Why couldn't he just ride off as a masterless samurai? What good were the letters in his pouch to the upcoming battle? The outcome was pretty clear.

He came to a crossroad and reined in his mount.

He thought about the world that he was in. He thought about the world he had left behind.

He thought of what James T. Kirk expected of him. He thought of what Mototada expected of him. In every respect, the expectations were identical.

So the question became: What did *he* expect of him?

One road led to the castle. To death. To honor.

The other led to far lands. To life. To no honor.

Life without honor. Death with honor.

Simple enough.

He suddenly felt very tired.

Chapter Forty-six

Scotland, 1746

THE MINDLESS MARCH and the bracing cold were the only things keeping Scotty sane. He felt almost light-headed as he shut out the crushing depression of his failure. "The guns, the guns," he moaned once or twice. His only chance to make a difference in this war had gone up in smoke back at the rubble that had been Fort Augustus. And now? What was left but to play out the tragedy? The clammy sweat of a fever broke out on his brow. He wished for the presence of a doctor, and a strange device that pressed against his shoulder and made an odd hissing sound. Mac . . . Mac something. A Scotsman he knew in a past life? Or a future life?

He almost passed by the small cottage unheeding. He certainly no longer noticed the breathtaking beauty of the harsh, pristine land. But the sound of the quiet chanting managed to penetrate the fever. He staggered up a mound by the side of the road to better see the source of the repetitive song. The cottage itself was a broken-down thing of wattle and daub walls and thatch roof. A small wattle fence, its woven branches more tangled than neatly twisted around posts, enclosed a small yard. In it a man sat on his haunches, presiding over a firepit of glowing and smoking peat. He was toasting some sort of grain, carefully stirring and shaking it from time to time, and all the while chanting at it in a nasal singsong.

"Come down," the man ordered without looking up.

"I didn't mean to disturb you," Scott managed to get out, and he turned to leave. The world was spinning.

"I said come down," the man ordered, his creaky old voice cutting into Scott. Obediently, he turned and slid down the slope to the house, sending gravel and dirt cascading down in his footsteps.

Scott stood waiting, but the little man went back to his humming and stirring.

"Well, now, what are you standing about for?" the strange old fellow said suddenly, looking up at Scott. One of his eyes was bright as sun on a lake, while the other, although he had sight in it, was squinted down. "In the house with you."

Scotty did as he was bid. The house was a wonder of odd bits and pieces. A stuffed owl decorated a niche above the hearth, or at least Scott thought it was stuffed until it hooted and moved its head. But there were also bones, skulls of deer and cattle, and little bundles of herbs and feathers.

A large iron kettle hung from a hook by an open fire, and a savory smell wafted from it, but it was almost overpowered by the smoky smell of the warm, sprouted barley and the smell of fermenting mash. And through an open door Scott could see a vat on a tripod, and a tangle of odd equipment. The whole cottage reeked of a distillery—but what a smell! The heady bouquet bore as much resemblance to the common brew as a venison stew did to thin porridge.

"Sit down, Montgomery Scott," the old man ordered.

"How did you know my name?" Scott said in confusion.

The old man said nothing, but instead ladled a bowl of the stew out and handed it to Scotty along with a hunk of bread.

"Dare I eat of your food?" Scott asked warily. The almost forgotten memories of the tattered book of folklore his grandmother had read him suddenly felt very real and important. They all said that the fairy folk would offer food and drink, and if you ate, you'd never go back to the world of men.

The old man laughed and slapped his knee. "I didn'a think you knew such things. Good, good. Eat or not, as you will. It makes no matter." He turned away to ladle a bowl for himself.

Scott shrugged and took up the spoon and ate. It didn't matter. What more could happen to him? He was lost, and alone, and he had failed in his duty. What matter if he was snatched by the fairies?

He was polishing off his second bowl and feeling much better when the old man pulled out a bottle of whiskey.

"Now this is the nectar of the gods," he said proudly, holding the bottle aloft. "This batch was brewed almost a century ago. There are casks in these hills that are older than that. Here, drink. *Slainte mhor,*" he toasted, "To your health!"

The bouquet was only a faint promise of the liquid wonder. Scott rolled it around his mouth, luxuriating in its smoothness, and even more with the almost orgasmic shock of its burning force.

The old one poured Scott another, and another. Scotty's head was spinning and his ears burning, and he didn't care.

"So," said the old man. "You think you have The Sight."

Scotty stared at him through glazed eyes. "The future . . . is open to me. I'm a Miracle Worker."

The old man laughed coarsely. "Ran out of miracles in the war, I see."

"Ach, yes. I failed. I failed. I've never failed before." Something twinged in Scotty's conscience. But he went on. "I always managed to do it. No matter how dangerous the situation, no matter how tight the deadline, I always managed for . . ." His mind hazed out. "For . . ."

"Haaahaha," chortled the old man. "A little short-sighted when it comes to yourself, eh? And what makes you think you failed, eh?"

"I failed because I didn't succeed!"

"You succeeded, because you could only fail!"

Scotty glared at the old man, and then, with a furious lunge, leaped at him. Somehow the old man was out of his way and Scotty hit the floor, in a dead sleep.

He woke to the light of a full moon. The air was uncommonly warm. The strange old man was nowhere to be seen.

Then the moon was blotted out by a dark form that seemed to float across the horizon. He blinked as it passed, the renewed moonlight suddenly blindingly bright. He threw his hands to his face and rubbed his eyes. When he took them away, there stood before him the figure of a woman in a long, loose robe.

"Monty," she cooed.

"Mother?" He had not heard that voice for a long time.

"Monty, you did not fail. It was just not your task. You always were one to take on the world."

"But Mum!" he called out in frustrated anguish.

"It wasn't your task. The die is cast, my son. You cannot change it." She loomed up, filling the sky.

"You are not my mother. Who are you?" he asked in wonder.

"I am the land," she said, shimmering. "I am the land. You are all my children. What is to be is to be. I suffer with you, but it is the way it must be."

"I do not understand . . ." he groaned, reaching out for her with outstretched arms.

"Didn't he tell you . . . the brewer? My children are not spiritless slaves of the big gun. They are dreamers and warriors. For the land to live, they must be true to their spirit, whatever the cost. In the Dance of Time, their ways will change, but what happens here will strengthen their spirit to face their destiny. You have a great heart, Montgomery Scott. Listen to it!"

As she spoke she became more and more transparent, until she was but a thin film across the sky.

"Be at peace," she whispered, and faded from sight.

"Wake up, man, wake up."

Scott woke up. Someone was shaking him. He managed to open his eyes. A scrawny middle-aged man with thin gray hair sticking out from under a large black hat, and thick-lensed spectacles over his watery eyes, was vigorously shaking him back to consciousness.

"Thank you, dear Lord," the man prayed, addressing the blue sky above. "I am William Smythe, vicar of the parish over that hill." He gestured. "I was on my rounds when I espied you, lying for all the world a corpse. Ah, my good man, you are soaked with sweat." He pressed his hand to Scott's brow. "A fever, no doubt. But, thank God, it has passed. Have you been out here all night?"

Scott nodded. The minister shook his head. "Terrible things happen out here at night. They say the ancient ones and the fairy folk walk the moors at night."

"Now isn't that the silliest thing I've ever heard," said Scott.

Chapter Forty-seven

Moscow, 1942

CHEKOV WAS FROZEN as the general stood there in the doorway of the hangar.

"I am amazed," the general said again.

Chekov tried to think of something to say. Nothing came to mind. "General, what are you doing here?"

He scratched his hips just to the right of his holster. "Do I not have the right to go where I wish, nephew?"

"Yes. Yes, of course. General, I—"

Chuikov put up a hand. "I should not be surprised, of course. How did you know?"

Chekov frowned, uncertain. "How?"

"Yes. How?"

He didn't have the faintest idea what the general was talking about, but he realized that there was no need to make that obvious. Chekov drew himself up and, with a slight swagger, said confidently, "How could I not?"

Chuikov winced. "I suppose you are right. Our knack for secrets-keeping . . . it's a joke, is it not?"

Chekov laughed and blew air disdainfully through his lips. He was in a complete fog.

"Does everyone know?" asked the general.

"If they do, they haven't told me."

"At least *someone* can keep a secret. Well, they'll all know of the mission within the hour. I must admit, when I was coming across the base and I saw the lights glowing from here in the hangar, somehow"—he waved a scolding finger like an annoyed parent, although there was no annoyance in his eyes— "somehow I knew it would be you. I had to see for myself, though. So eager to get into the air that you had to start checking over your plane immediately, eh?"

Chekov laughed and patted the nose of the plane fondly. "Oh yes. You know me so well, General."

Chuikov shrugged. "It's a knack. I can tell things about people. So . . . come with me, nephew. By now the rest of your squadron has been roused. I regret the short notice, but you know how there can be miscommunications."

He didn't spot Chekov's duffel, which the Starfleet officer had fortunately tossed over to the side. Chekov walked toward him, and Chuikov put a firm and friendly arm around Chekov's shoulders. Together they walked toward the now-active barracks, leaving behind Chekov's duffel and an unconscious KGB man.

Chekov sat in the squad room, surrounded by the rest of the men, some of whom were still rubbing sleep from their eyes. The C.O. briskly laid out their mission.

It was a diplomatic one, but no less dangerous for it. The American statesman Averell Harriman had been in Moscow as President Roosevelt's personal representative, with the latest package of lend-lease aid from the Allies. He was flying back to London on a tight schedule, and that meant flying through a lot of enemy-held territory. The Red Guard squadron was to fly cover for the transport. With any luck, they wouldn't see action, but if luck didn't hold, it was their mission to protect the diplomat by whatever means necessary.

"The transport has a twelve hundred mile range, so he can fly to London without problem," said the C.O. "We fly west as far as Riga on the Latvian coast, where there is a secret refueling station. Then we turn back," the base commander droned on, "and the transport with Uncle Vanya—the code name for our diplomat —will pick up RAF squadrons flying from Sweden, to escort him the rest of the way."

Chekov's eyes went wide. This was perfect! Within the hour they would be airborne, and then he could break off at the earliest opportunity and hightail it for Sweden. He could report that he was having engine trouble and needed to set down. No one would doubt him.

Then he looked at General Chuikov, who was beaming at him from across the room. Regret flashed across his mind. How could a decorated Hero of the Soviet Union run away during the most terrible war in their history? And what about General Chuikov? Would not Chekov's defection certainly reflect on him and his own survival? But could Chekov live and survive the postwar Stalin era? Of course, it was all moot. The unconscious KGB man had settled it. There was no turning back.

It ached inside him to think that he would have to keep still for the rest of his life, ignoring the terrible injustices to human rights that would haunt this society for decades to come. It certainly was the darkest period of his people's history, or so it now seemed. And how well could he hide his knowledge and skill in engineering? Would he be the cause of World War III in a world where the delicate balance of power was suddenly upset by a future technology? At least in a place like Sweden he could be relatively safe.

But despite his clear knowledge that this was the only ethical course for him, the idea that he was going to leave his motherland forever, a traitor in the eyes of these new friends and companions, made him hurt in places he didn't know he had, and he cursed the unknown demon that had brought him here.

Chapter Forty-eight

Japan, 1600

IT WAS the eighteenth day of the seventh lunar month, the warm days of late summer, when the first wave of the enemy attacked Fushimi Castle and its fortified towers.

They rushed against the walls, shooting with the guns that both the Portuguese Catholics and the English and Dutch Protestants had supplied the Japanese to lure them into their religion and politics. But the Japanese had taken the guns from both and made promises to neither.

"Keep your heads down," Sulu shouted, running up and down the line, forcing the men on the wall to take cover against the wads and balls of the primitive muskets. Far in the distance he thought he could make out the split in the road where he had hesitated for so long. He could even see the curve of the road that went off in the other direction, to safety—the road not traveled.

No one noticed, of course, that Sulu wasn't hitting anyone. He still couldn't take the chance of killing someone and possibly wiping out not just one life, but the innocent lives that would be affected if he changed history. When he fired, it was always away from any target.

It was better this way. No more concerns with possibly violating the Prime Directive. No inner wrestling with honor. He could be accused of many things, ranging from being a fatalist to outright stupidity—but not being a man of honor would never be one of those things.

And it wasn't so bad a thing to be part of a legend. Even a small part.

Fiery arrows volleyed into the compound, their flaming heads seeking random death and mayhem.

"Damn, put those fires out," Motonaga shouted. Firemen in heavy woven garments soaked with what water could be spared rushed to beat out the flames in a world where paper was a principal building material.

"Look, look," a terrified man shouted, standing up and pointing. "The tower is on fire." It was his last service to his lord. He fell with an arrow in his back. But his warning sent men up the ladder toward the flames. One bold man plunged directly into the billows of black smoke that puffed out from the observer's platform, his hollow coughs audible above the shouts and screams of the wounded. Tongues of yellow flame shot out around him. Then there was more black smoke, but the fire was out. The body of the hero dropped back over the edge and down to the ground below—he hadn't survived the smoke and heat.

Two days later they were still on the wall, sending out volleys of arrows, putting out fires, and counting the dead. It was almost dark before any food arrived. Servants groaned under the weight of the barrels of cooked rice.

"Here, Great One Cut," Motonaga said, handing

Sulu a bowl of rice which sported some fish and vegetables. Sulu settled himself on the paved ground, his back against a box of arrows.

"Thanks," he grunted, and waited for the young man to collect his portion and settle down beside him.

"I really didn't expect to see you back, you know," the boy said thoughtlessly.

"I was ordered back," Sulu answered.

"So you were stuck. They ordered you back. But you did follow orders. Good for you," he said with a pompous and somewhat patronizing flourish of his eating sticks.

Sulu groaned quietly, but let the implied insult go. There was no point in flexing the muscles of his ego when he knew, as by now they must all know, that this was their burying place.

"Tell me, Heihachiro-domo," the boy continued, somewhat subdued. "Are you ever afraid?"

"Of course I am. I have no desire to die," he said simply.

"You don't ever seem afraid. You are a brave samurai. I am afraid, not of death, but of not being brave when I die."

Sulu's face softened into a gentle smile as he watched the boy straighten with pride at this. "There is no good way to die," he said. "Death is the enemy. The warrior doesn't seek death, by the hand of his adversary or by his own hand. When death is inevitable, he cheats death, his great enemy, by embracing death with the love of a man for his wife. He doesn't feed death with fear. And that is the bravest thing any man or woman can do. However it comes to us, if we face it with a pure heart, we have already paid death's dues. You will serve bravely to the end. I do not doubt it."

"Thank you, Heihachiro-domo," Naito Motonaga replied, bowing humbly. The two men sat together quietly for a while, savoring the simple fare, watching the small contained fire where men were heating sake or boiling tea.

After ten days of hell the forces in the cluster of fortresses that Mototada commanded were depleted by the random arrow or shot over the wall, the fires, and the desperate sallies from the gate. They could see the banners of General Ishida, who had come to encourage his troops, but that only encouraged Mototada's men. A ration of sake was issued to congratulate the defenders because they had forced the great general from his plans for the main attack at Sekigahara to try to break the bottleneck at Fushimi Castle. For a brief moment there was even hope that they might survive the siege.

But on the morning of the tenth day, the final assaults began and Sulu knew, witnessing the ferocity and desperation, that this was it. The castle had been held for as long as possible, and now the reaper of history was screaming for his final due. Sulu fancied he could hear the screeching of fate in his head, like nails on chalkboard.

Yet he heard it with only vague interest.

Again and again they rushed into the face of death, each time fewer and fewer coming back. And each time more of the enemy found a way to breach the sanctity of the castle, so that by the final charge there was no safety to retreat to. It was over, and Sulu knew it.

The last meeting Sulu had with Torii Mototada, his lord had looked wan but content. He had made Sulu his standard bearer and cheerfully added, with gallows humor, that the post carried a one thousand koku stipend. Sulu knew he wouldn't have to worry about where to spend it.

Death and hopeless combat faced him. So did honor.

And hell . . . anyone could fight a battle that could be won. The hopeless causes were the truly worthy ones.

He wondered where he had heard that before. Either from Mototada or from Kirk.

It occurred to Sulu, as the enemy faced him, that the two liege lords would probably have gotten on quite well.

Wheeling his mount around, he charged into the enemy. It was right and proper for Sulu to take his own life. That was the honorable way, a gift of dignity which a noble enemy offered a defeated foe. But the two worlds of Mister Sulu, lieutenant commander, Starfleet, and Okiri Heihachiro, banner man to Torii Mototada, crashed in on one another, and *seppeku* was not an option for this warrior. With serene calm he faced his fate.

"Captain, I apologize for not returning to duty," he shouted into the air, addressing both Kirk and Torii with a peculiar mixture of the two times and two commanders. "Farewell, Oneko; hello, honor!" he shouted as the enemy closed in on him.

Chapter Forty-nine

Scotland, 1746

INVERNESS WAS FROTHING with news of war. Murray paced back and forth, his shaved head glistening as he passed through a shaft of light from the leaded window in his study. He listened grimly as Scott detailed the action at the fort.

"You have done as much as any man could have under the circumstances," the general consoled him. "What galls me," he went on as he resumed his caged pacing, "is that now we have word that Cumberland did not split his men, but marches upon us in mass, so that we must recall Keppoch and Lochiel, with whatever of their men still remain. And it grows worse. The prince listens more and more to Mr. O'Sullivan and his ilk, and they council foolhardy ventures. I'm afeared that our Charlie was brought up on tales of glory but little practical training."

Scotty stayed with Murray, serving him as an aide and tactical advisor, but mostly as a bulwark of emotional support which the general badly needed in the endless war councils, which were battlefields in themselves. Several times he tried to fulfill his word to

Seamus and find Megan, but the city was a madhouse and finding one girl was well nigh impossible.

April 15 dawned, and the pipes screamed out their chant to arms, the men of the clans gathering.

"Mr. Scott," Murray shouted up the staircase. "To arms, man."

Scotty rushed to finish dressing and dashed down the stairs, his claymore and dirk already hanging from his belt. He ran out and, passing a small lake, suddenly stopped.

He saw his reflection. But he was wearing some other sort of uniform in it ... with an odd gold symbol above the chest.

And then the reflection was gone and he saw only himself. He moved onward to the site of the battle.

Scott scanned the horizon. The clansmen, those who were even there, were drawn up in a thin ragged line along the field. It was indeed a splendid field—splendid for Cumberland, the duke, unfortunately.

Scotty shook his head in disbelief. The flat, even ground was ideal for moving artillery, and for marching tight ranks of ordered soldiers. For the wild, untamed clansmen, whose only superiority was spirit and daring, it was a disaster.

"Oh, my God," Scotty groaned.

"Yes, Mr. Scott, may God have mercy, for surely Cumberland shall not." Murray wheeled his horse around and set out to seek the prince.

But all he found was O'Sullivan. His jaw set with rage, Murray put his pride aside and begged that the army be moved beyond the Nairn Waters, just a few hundred yards beyond to the soft, boggy, uneven ground that would give them a fighting chance. But his appeal fell on deaf ears.

Slowly Murray trotted back to his men, Scott at his side. And they waited.

About ten A.M. Scott, whose nerves were raw, asked, "Where are they?"

Murray shook his head. "We have a scouting report that the Duke is celebrating his birthday and his men are probably falling down drunk with toasting him. Meanwhile we wait, and wait."

"Why? Surely we could hit them when they are in their cups better than here," Scotty insisted.

"Man, you are right. That may be our salvation."

But again the chain of command was immovable, and the general of the army could not get a fair hearing from his royal commander. And so the men stood around, becoming dispirited and hungry.

Scott watched as the ranks of tired men thinned, many taking the hike back to the town for food and rest. And he wondered where Keppoch was. Were the scattered clans still raiding wild and free in the hills while Cumberland pursued his relentless and disciplined campaign to crush the Scottish prince and his ragtag army?

By midafternoon the prince rode to where Murray waited, his Irish favorites surrounding him like so many courtly sycophants.

"I think it is indeed a fine idea to attack the enemy in his camp. Would you be willing, sir, to undertake such an adventure?"

Murray bowed in acquiescence, not daring himself speech lest he call the prince a fool. Certainly, the time to begin that march had been hours ago. "At least," Murray whispered to Scotty as they rode behind the prince to make final plans, "it will force a retreat from this abysmal spot."

But the night march was more terrible than could be imagined, the few horses they had with them slipping and squealing in the more and more frequent patches of bog. The men did no better, slipping and tearing

259

skin from knees and legs, cursing the dark and each other.

At dawn they heard the drums of the general call in the English camp, and they were too far to strike the enemy a blow before the redcoats were up and assembled. And so they turned and ran away, having accomplished nothing. And still more men left the ranks, seeking a meal here, a rest there, many more discarding their muskets and even their round shields to lighten the burden of the march, heedless of the terrible consequences of this foolishness.

By this time Montgomery Scott knew it was doomed. He knew it was madness. He knew that they were all going to die . . .

And he looked out upon the tired, frustrated Scotsmen. He looked at their eyes, their weary faces, their haggard expressions.

He had The Sight. They didn't. And still . . .

They knew. They knew they were doomed as well.

And still they stayed.

Sometimes, he realized, having The Sight didn't make a damned bit of difference. It didn't change what you had to do.

The morning of April 16 found Montgomery Scott still there with his kinsmen. It also found the army of Charles Stuart on the same field as they had been the day before. But there were now fewer men, and those who were assembled were tired and hungry from the fruitless venture of yesterday. And the English army rolled into view, almost seven thousand strong, each battalion marching to the roll of drums and with the briskness of men sure of victory.

And still the Scots were not assembled. Insanely, the clansmen were still arguing over position. Scotty wanted to strangle them.

The rolling thunder of the artillery barrage started, and men fell to their screaming death, their fellows plowing the ground in impatience like tethered horses waiting for the command to charge.

"Please, my prince," someone begged, screaming at Charles as he rode by, "give the command to charge."

Murray echoed the plea, but in the confusion all that was clear was that the Scots were being shot to pieces as they stood.

From somewhere the cry of "Claymore" came, the pipes blaring in a cacophony as each clan filled the sky with their own battle hymn. But the command was slow to make its way down the field, and the clans broke into the charge piecemeal, presenting no front to the enemy, but rather rushing to certain death by little bits.

Scott was thrown in the air as a ball struck the horse on which he sat, killing the beast. Stunned, Scotty crawled to his feet. The men around him were charging into the enemy rank. He drew his claymore and ran seeking the enemy line, but in the press there was no room to swing a broadsword, and at the front the English, in tight ranks, bayonets fixed, were stabbing their way through the crazed clansmen, incurring few losses themselves.

Spun around and around by half-crazed clansmen who rushed past him with passion but no plan, Scott grabbed vainly at men's shoulders, trying to stop the hopeless charge, to organize even a small unit. And a voice within him screamed, *It's hopeless! You'll fail!* And a voice responded, *I don't care! I do what I must, and I don't care!*

He put his back into his work with renewed zeal, trying to stem the aimless charge. Maybe even a few men could take the cannon, to stop the slaughter. But no one would stop, no one would hear him. Finally he was thrown to the ground, where he groveled in the mud, trying to avoid the trampling tide of men who threatened to crush the life from him.

And as certainly as the line had broken and surged toward the enemy, it turned to flee the relentless army of death.

When he was finally free of the sweating mass of men, he ran with all the rest of them, ran from the battlefield, for it was clear there was nothing left to do. He didn't notice the warm sticky wetness that soaked down his side.

He finally fell, his breath screaming from his lungs like sulfur.

"Mr. Scott! Mr. Scott!"

"Megan, oh, Megan. What are you doin' here, lass?" he gasped as her face focused through the red haze. He looked about. He had run from the battlefield to well past Culloden House before he fell. The firing was over but for random shots. Men and women from the town had come to seek their dead and aid their living. Or strip the bodies of their little wealth.

"Oh, Mr. Scott, ye are hurt. Ye must move. Come, man. Quickly. The Sassenach dogs have already begun the slaughter of the survivors." She dragged him to his feet, and they staggered off together.

"Here," she said, dragging him to a small cave, more a crevice in the rocks. There was already a body huddling in the dank mud.

"Seamus, you survived!" Scotty cried out, reaching for the lad, until his own wound drove him to the ground.

The boy had a bloody bandage on his head, torn from his lady's shift. And his eyes were not focused.

"Ah, he has a concussion," Scott said, his voice milky and thick with pain. "Don't let him fall asleep. Keep him up, lass. Do you hear me?"

"Aye, Mr. Scott. I shall. Come, let me bind your wound as well."

They lay huddled and still for two days, praying in

fear each time they heard the sound of men, Englishmen bent on murder of the remaining rebels.

"Dare we go back to Inverness?" Megan had whispered at one point.

"Perhaps there is a general pardon," Seamus had offered hopefully, his recovery the miracle of youth.

"I dunna know," Scott groaned. "But I do know that we need food and water or we will die here."

At nightfall Megan sneaked out for water. Scott felt the hand of death on him as he lay in the dark, waiting for her to return.

"Seamus, are you there?"

"Aye, Mr. Scott. That I am," he answered. He was speaking clearly now, and Scotty was filled with hope that he would mend.

"You must return to your apprenticeship. Make a life for yourself, lad, and for Megan, too. Promise me."

"I promise, but do not take on so, man. You'll come, too, and be there to stand godfather to our children." The boy crawled over to him.

"Ah, lad," he said, holding Seamus's hand, "I doubt it. Remember that the spirit of the rebellion is more precious than its success or failure. The Scots may lack the English wealth and ambition, but the spirit of this land will be evermore the heart and courage of a Britain united." A fit of coughing silenced the engineer. Neither man acknowledged that Scotty was coughing blood.

Megan returned with water, and after a while they all slept. Late in the night Scotty awoke in pain. He had no doubts about his condition. In the cold of the night he felt a shimmering, and he knew it was over. He rose and dragged himself out of the cave and onto the moors. To see the stars one last time.

The stars . . .

And a voice, a gentle voice, said, "The stars. You know them, don't you?"

"Home. My . . . home," he whispered. "Blessed lady . . . my home . . ."

She floated before him, as ethereal as before. "You remember."

"Yes." It was an exhausted sigh. "Yes. I remember."

"Why didn't you remember before?"

"Because . . ." He sighed. "Because if I'd remembered . . . I couldn't have helped. I didn't want to remember, because I wanted to . . . to do something . . ."

She smiled. "You did."

"It was hopeless. I accomplished nothing. I fought in a hopeless cause."

"That was your accomplishment," she said, and reached down to cool his brow.

And the stars shone through her . . .

Chapter Fifty

The Sky, 1942

THE G-FORCES PUSHED AGAINST Chekov as his plane hurtled higher and higher into the air. It was an exhilarating feeling, even though it was an infinitesimal fraction of the power that was possessed by the *Enterprise*. This was truly flying.

He glanced at his wingmen, taking pride in the way they kept in formation. Then Chekov sighed inwardly. He could not recall a time when he had such regrets.

His squad made its rendezvous with the transport, a Consolidated B-24. They were maintaining a sort of radio silence, breaking it for orders and instructions, but keeping the sky free of the kind of chatter that was typical of bombing runs. There was no point tempting fate.

Chekov was praying there would be no combat. Please. It was all he asked. Because if there were combat, he could not possibly try to shoot others out of the sky. It meant that he could not participate in defending the B-24. It meant . . . he did not want to think about what it meant.

And then he heard a voice that chilled him, crackling over his radio.

"Uncle Vanya to Cherry Orchard," the transmission from the transport crackled in badly accented Russian, "we have contact."

"Oh my God," said Chekov.

"Pavel?" another voice broke in.

"Kirk?" Chekov answered. His heart sank. Of all people. Of all times. When the time came to break off from the squadron . . . well, Chekov was just going to have to hope that the others would protect Kirk in the event of problems.

"Good to hear from you, Pavel! So this is where they scurried you off to!" John Kirk sounded nauseatingly jovial.

"Don't worry, John. We'll take good care of you," said Chekov weakly. His heart pounded. Again his path crossed with John C. Kirk's.

Soon they had crossed the front and were droning over enemy territory. The air had been getting more turbulent all the time, and now they flew blind in thick clouds.

Chekov looked at his instruments. This was it. This was the perfect time to break off. Sweden was accessible. The RAF would be there within minutes. If he peeled off now, the rest of the squad would be compelled to continue without him. If he waited until the rendezvous, the others would very likely want to follow him down.

He bid a silent farewell to all that he was leaving behind. "Uncle Vanya—" he started to say, in preparation for telling them about his nonexistent engine problems.

But Kirk's voice came back quickly, "Yeah, I see them."

Chekov blinked and then his eyes widened in alarm.

German. Fockewulfe Fu-190s. The swift, maneuverable fighter was the finest in the air. But it hadn't been tested against the YAK. Chekov watched the compact little German birds swoop in, and he wasn't sure at all that his wing was their match.

"Enemy at three o'clock," Chekov's wingman yelled, his voice high and tinny through the tiny speaker. But already Chekov had his hand pressed to his throat mike . . .

And he froze.

His mind screamed at him to peel off. To get the hell out of there. It wasn't his fight. It couldn't be his fight.

And if he peeled off, he might even escape alive . . .

And John Kirk might not. Probably would not.

Two potentially divergent timelines. The no-win situation that he'd been dreading had finally caught up with him.

One choice was no choice.

"Cherry One and Three, peel off high and right. Lead them away from Uncle. The rest, follow me," he said, rolling left and diving low, coming up behind a pair of German planes.

He fired short precise bursts, aiming purely for the wings.

The skies were alive with planes, intensive firing from all over. His squad was outnumbered, and Chekov fought down mounting panic.

The sky flipped around him, and he kept looking at the transport plane. So far it was flying unscathed . . .

And then a German plane swooped down from nowhere and opened fire on it.

Chekov cried out in alarm as he saw the bullets strafe the sides of Kirk's ship. He broke formation and power-dived toward the German plane, firing from the rear. He blew the German's tail off and the plane spiraled downward. Chekov prayed that the pilot was able to eject.

"John," Chekov shouted, "get out of here. Go high. You have the ceiling," he yelled in English.

"I've got the guns, too," Kirk answered with a determination so familiar that Chekov's heart hurt.

"No, Keptin," he yelled back, "get out of here. You have to save yourself."

"No, Pavel!"

"You have your mission, damn it," Chekov argued again. "Harriman must get to London," he reasoned. "Please."

"Damn you, Pavel," Kirk answered with frustration. "You're right! And I'm not a captain yet!"

"Go!" Chekov shouted as he banked upward to intercept another German plane.

He rolled to the right, pirouetting gracefully out of the way of a German plane, and one of Chekov's men blew the plane out of the sky.

What a waste, thought Chekov, *what a waste. Using technology for war and destruction instead of the good of humanity. What a goddamned waste.*

There were more coming in. He allowed himself a second to watch John Kirk's big transport bank up, putting on the "juice" for a run across the border to Sweden.

His men were taking out the Fockewulfes like flies, the new YAK-1 showing its stuff and the Red Guard proving itself equal to any unit in the air.

Then the big long-range bomber was diving out of the sky, her guns blazing, and the Fu-190s were scattering like hens in a farmyard with a fox after them. But one pass was all Kirk could afford with so high level an ambassador on board, and with a dip of his wings to Chekov, he soared off to freedom.

"We did it!" Chekov cried out.

And then his left wing was blown off.

Chekov turned in alarm to see the smoking stub that was all that was left of his wing.

The plane spiraled downward. Chekov fought furiously, but he was utterly helpless. Every warning signal on his control board was going berserk.

"Oh hell," he muttered. This was in no way going to get him to Sweden.

The clouds around him had turned fierce, buffeting him. Thunder rumbled around him, and he heard Kirk's voice over the radio shout, "Chekov! Your men say you were hit! I'll come get you!"

"Nonsense!" replied Chekov. "Just a little turbulence. You come back here, Kirk, I'll flatten you."

"If you're sure . . ."

"I'm sure."

He waited for five seconds, then opened the cockpit and ejected.

He was barely clear of the damaged plane and pulled the cord. He felt the jerk as the parachute shroud deployed. He wondered how long he would survive in the freezing water. The blood was still oozing and he felt weak. He looked up at the black blot of the silk canopy above him. The rain had stopped, and through a break in the clouds Chekov could see the stars.

Then he saw nothing.

Chapter Fifty-one

WEYLAND SAT on his throne and studied the two men who stood before him. The Klingon was being supported by Kirk, and they both looked as if they'd been through hell. Their clothes were somewhat tattered, their skin dirty and abraded. Throughout the great hall natives of Cragon were peering at the two outworlders with unconcealed interest.

"You've been through a bit, haven't you?"

Kral stabbed a finger at him. "Because of you! Anything we've been through, it's because of you."

"Really," said Weyland calmly. "I didn't force you to come to my planet. I didn't create the Klingon and Federation enmity. I didn't cause people to die."

"You will shortly," said Kirk. "My ship can't stay in orbit much longer."

"Is that a fact?" said Weyland.

He said it in such a way that Kirk, never taking his eye off him, removed his communicator. "Kirk to *Enterprise.*"

"*Enterprise,* Spock here."

"Status, Mr. Spock?"

"Navigation and helm have just come back on line, Captain. Standard orbit is reestablished. And . . ."

"Yes?"

He heard a burst of confused exclamation, as if everyone in the background had started talking at once. Only the unflappable Spock sounded routine as he said, "Mr. Scott, Mr. Sulu, and Mr. Chekov have just appeared on the bridge."

"Their condition?"

"Bedraggled would adequately describe it, I think. Specifics will be forthcoming."

"What about the Klingon ship?"

Kral seemed to be holding his breath until Spock came back on and said, "Their orbit is continuing to decay."

Kral looked up angrily at Weyland. "What about my ship?" he demanded.

"Their orbit will continue to decay . . ."

Kral started to bristle. "You—"

". . . until such time that their rightful commander —yourself—returns to the bridge, whereupon all will be rectified."

"Oh," said Kral softly.

"Enterprise, stand by." Kirk flipped the communicator closed and eyed Weyland. "So that's it?" he said. "You put us through all this, and then we're supposed to go on our way, as if nothing happened?"

Weyland raised an eyebrow in a manner that seemed reminiscent of Spock. "Hopefully not as if nothing happened. Hopefully you will remember. And your men will remember, for they likewise acted most honorably. I admit, Captain . . . I did not credit you or your men with the ability to act as well as you did."

"So all this was a test," said Kirk. "You expected us to learn honor?"

"Oh, no. I expected you all to die. Don't make more of it than it was, Captain. This was not a test. This was an elaborate execution. Somehow, crushing you now after you've survived all this—and after you've swallowed your pride and created this charming, if only temporary alliance—it wouldn't seem fair somehow. It would not seem honorable. And I am, above all, a being of honor."

Kral opened his mouth.

"Shut up," said Kirk to the Klingon.

Kral shut his mouth.

Kirk had prepared an entire lengthy speech he had intended to give Weyland, about nobility and honor and courage of the human heart. He discarded it for the better part of valor.

He flipped open his communicator and said, *"Enterprise,* two to beam up. Quickly."

The air crackled around him, and the last thing he heard before the comforting walls of the *Enterprise* surrounded him once more was the low, mocking laugh of Weyland.

Chapter Fifty-two

As THE *ENTERPRISE* shot through space, en route to Starbase 42, Kirk studied the medical report on his three returned officers. Sulu was suffering from a sword cut to his neck and another to his belly. Mr. Scott had a wound from a musket ball on his right side. He also was suffering from lead poisoning as a result of his wound and various bacterial infections from a lack of septic dressing. And Mr. Chekov had water in his lungs, indicating imminent drowning.

And even though McCoy had healed the physical wounds, emotionally they were still at loose ends. Well, they were solid, experienced officers. Certainly the leaves of absence that he had granted them to return home to Earth—an odd enough request, but all things considered, not outrageous—would help them reestablish their equilibrium. Hell, Scotty was on his way to recovery already—he had declined the prospect of returning to Earth, instead electing to remain with his beloved *Enterprise*. And when Chekov and Sulu returned, and they and Scotty had been given enough time, then they would be back to their old form.

He hoped.

He went to his computer and began a lengthy report that would explain why Starfleet should be sure, henceforth, to give a wide berth to Cragon V. He suspected the Klingons would do the same.

He hoped.

On the *Ghargh,* Kral sat staring at a holograph of two young Klingons. One of them was now dead.

"Damn," he said softly.

The door hissed open and Vladra was standing there. She saw what he was holding, knowing that once upon a time he would have hurriedly stashed it away rather than give the slightest hint of displaying any sort of regret or weaker emotions.

"We are on route to Outpost 27, where the Klingon high command awaits your report," she said. She paused. "What are you going to say?"

"That we should stay the hell away from Cragon V."

She nodded.

He sat back and eyed her speculatively. Then he reached down under his desk and pulled out something that had belonged to his father, and his father's father. A book.

"I thought," he said with significance, "you might like to hear some . . . poetry."

Her breath caught and she nodded slowly. As he started to read, his voice husky, her hands strayed toward a heavy medal of honor that rested on a shelf. She knew right where she was going to throw it.

Scott sat in his room. Open journals lay scattered around, but he hadn't been able to finish a single article.

"Damn it, man," he chided himself, "you've got to face it." He stalked over to the computer console. "Computer, I want some genealogical information, if there is any. For a Seamus MacIntyre, shipbuilder, Scotland, Earth, circa 1750."

"Working. There is a death certificate for a Seamus MacIntyre, and a corresponding newspaper article in 1803. Working. He left two sons and three daughters by his wife, Megan."

Scott didn't hear anything else. He was fighting back tears, mourning a man centuries gone. The account droned on, becoming more detailed as record keeping had gotten better. ". . . a daughter, Jennifer Anne MacIntyre married George William Jeffries in 2137. Their only child, Benjamin McDonald-Jeffries was an engineer with New Bell Laboratories in the Centauri system. He married Isobelle Krautman, and they had one son, Frederick William Jeffries, designer of the Jeffries tube . . ."

That caught Scotty's attention, and he looked up at the screen. So the boy whose life he had touched all those centuries ago had reached across time and space to touch his. The image of the dream woman on the heath filled his mind. He heard the sound of pipes, and thrilled in the freedom by which those hopelessly romantic and impractical people had lived and died.

Pavel sat in an outdoor café, watching the daily traffic in the main square of New Stalingrad. But for a few plaques, and a monument or two, nothing remained of that terrible time. Chekov closed his eyes, listening, but all he could hear were birds, or the lazy footsteps of folks enjoying the spring warmth. He had begun to wonder if he had dreamed it.

"Would you care for another coffee, or perhaps a pastry?" the waitress dressed in a silly version of a regional costume asked. It was a tourist stop, and they used real people to serve, and even real chefs to cook.

"No, thank you. But I would like to visit the Data Library. I'm doing some research."

"It's two blocks that way," she gestured, "and turn right. You can't miss it."

He meticulously drained his cup, and walked the short distance, noting trees, buildings, and people with painstaking detail. Twice he stopped, and once turned away from his goal. *If I am not listed, it doesn't mean anything,* he argued with himself. *After all, a lot of records were destroyed in the war and in the political upheavals that followed. It doesn't mean anything.* But his palms were still wet when he logged in on a small terminal in the huge marble neorevolutionary-heroic hall.

"Pavel Alexandrovitch Chekov, or Chuikov. Lieutenant." He answered the few questions that followed and waited. It seemed like an insufferably long turnaround time.

"Pavel Alexandrovitch Chuikov, lieutenant. Lost over the Baltic Sea in battle, November 15, 1942. Awarded: Hero of the Soviet Union, third class, October 1942. Awarded: Hero of the Soviet Union, first class, posthumously, December 1942."

Chekov sat a long time staring at the screen. Then he requested a history for an American family named Kirk.

Sulu had spent weeks following the path of his memory. He had crammed a course in Japanese which he had learned with amazing ease. And to the delight of the scholars whom he had visited, and with whom he had pored over documents, his knowledge of classical speech and writing was top notch and way beyond the scope of his cram course. But, to his sorrow, in this land where literacy had been a legacy for millennia, there was not a word about Oneko.

The inn was still there, still as pristine as he had remembered it. Despite the ravages on the natural beauty of this land which economic wealth and modernization had brought, there were still pockets of traditional Japan. Above the inn the temple still clung to the mountain, and the bell was still rung each morning and night. He managed to persuade the current innkeeper to find him a place, although he had not reserved a room the requisite six months in advance.

The next morning he walked up the hill to the abbey. There was still a community of Zen monks in residence, but most of the grounds had been turned over to the curiosity of visitors. The day he arrived, the gates were closed, and a small sign announced that a group of archeologists were doing a dig on some older portions of the grounds.

Sulu turned to leave when he ran into a young woman, literally, sending her armful of tools and bags scattering down the hill.

"Oh, I'm so sorry," he said, helping her gather the load.

"Oh, no, it was my fault. I wasn't looking," she politely protested, the objects falling again out of her arms as quickly as he piled them on.

"Please, let me help," he insisted. He took most of the materials and followed her through the gate.

"I am Dr. Yae Takenada. I am assistant to Dr. Abe, director of the project," she said formally, although she was still panting and dropping things, "and I am late . . ."

"I am Lieutenant Commander Sulu, of the USS *Enterprise.*"

"Oh," she said, stopping and staring at him with awe. "What an exciting life! A starship. Good lord, Sulu, why root around on dusty old Earth if you can be dancing in the stars?"

"Oh . . . the ground has its allure," he said.

And before much longer he had ditched his jacket,

rolled up his sleeves, and was in tow as Yae's aide. Not that he was protesting a lot.

He spent the next few days digging, and the evenings with his newfound friends, especially Yae. A couple of times he wanted to tell her about his strange trip, but even though he felt that she was as close as a sister, he couldn't do it, yet.

Too soon he was notified that he was to report to his ship. It was the last afternoon he could spend at the satisfying work of digging trenches in the old garden.

Yae had trenched about two feet deep and uncovered a group of stones that had been used to support a wall. "Look at these. I'll bet they were once part of the garden arrangement. Look at the shapes."

Sulu shook his head noncommittally. He knew she was right, but how could he explain how he knew? He crouched down by her find, brushing away the dirt with the archeologist's friend, a small brush. Yes, the scratches were there. He wanted to put it back, to hide it, but she leaned over his shoulder.

"Oh, good. Look at that. Someone scratched something. Let me see." She appropriated the stone, and brushed, and spat until she had uncovered the characters.

"Well, let's see. It could mean . . ." she muttered, trying out the variants that each symbol could sound like. "Well, I'll be damned," she said staring at Sulu. "It could mean Sulu! How strange. And the other. It is a cat, *neko*, no . . . 'honorable cat' Oneko. It might be names. Two names. How touching," she said softly. "Two lovers, perhaps destined to part, who left their mark in the temple garden. Sulu, are you all right?"

"Oh . . . fine." Sulu smiled. "I just had the strangest feeling of déjà vu."